Kissing Hannah was

Dax should have quit while he was ahead. Hell, he would have been better off if he'd quit while he was behind.

He almost had. He'd asked her out, she'd said no, and he'd started to walk away. Then he had caught sight of his son, Will, looking their way and pretending not to.

He hadn't taught Will to give up easily, not with a horse or a math problem or fixing an engine. Females were no different. One try didn't cut it.

So he hadn't given up. And it hadn't been going too badly. Until that kiss. Until the heat roared through his blood and shimmered in his muscles.

He'd thought he could handle it. Thought he could stay in control. But kissing Hannah had definitely been a mistake.

He wondered if he'd have the chance to make that mistake again.

Dear Reader,

Spring is in the air! It's the perfect time to pick wildflowers, frolic outdoors...and fall in love. And this March, Special Edition has an array of love stories that set the stage for romance!

Bestselling author Victoria Pade delivers an extra-special THAT SPECIAL WOMAN! title. The latest installment in her popular A RANCHING FAMILY series, *Cowboy's Love* is about a heroine who passionately reunites with the rugged rancher she left behind. Don't miss this warm and wonderful tale about love lost—and found again.

Romantic adventure is back in full force this month when the MONTANA MAVERICKS: RETURN TO WHITEHORN series continues with *Wife Most Wanted* by Joan Elliott Pickart—a spirited saga about a wanted woman who unwittingly falls for the town's sexiest lawman! And don't miss *Marriage by Necessity,* the second book in Christine Rimmer's engaging CONVENIENTLY YOURS miniseries.

Helen R. Myers brings us *Beloved Mercenary,* a poignant story about a gruff, brooding hero who finds new purpose when a precious little girl—and her beautiful mother—transform his life. And a jaded businessman gets much more than he bargained for when he conveniently marries his devoted assistant in *Texan's Bride* by Gail Link. Finally this month, to set an example for his shy teenage son, a confirmed loner enters into a "safe" relationship with a pretty stranger in *The Rancher Meets His Match* by Patricia McLinn.

I hope you enjoy this book, and each and every story to come!

Sincerely,

Tara Gavin
Senior Editor and Editorial Coordinator

Please address questions and book requests to:
Silhouette Reader Service
U.S.: 3010 Walden Ave., P.O. Box 1325, Buffalo, NY 14269
Canadian: P.O. Box 609, Fort Erie, Ont. L2A 5X3

PATRICIA McLINN

THE RANCHER MEETS HIS MATCH

SPECIAL EDITION®

Published by Silhouette Books
America's Publisher of Contemporary Romance

If you purchased this book without a cover you should be aware
that this book is stolen property. It was reported as "unsold and
destroyed" to the publisher, and neither the author nor the
publisher has received any payment for this "stripped book."

This book is dedicated to wonderful neighbors. On
ranches or farms, in small towns or cities, good
neighbors help make a place a home. I've been blessed
with the best of neighbors all my life, so this book is
for my friends and neighbors from Halsted Road,
Fox Hollow Drive, Dickerson Street and—where I first
learned about good neighbors—Craig Place.

 SILHOUETTE BOOKS

ISBN 0-373-24164-X

THE RANCHER MEETS HIS MATCH

Copyright © 1998 by Patricia McLaughlin

All rights reserved. Except for use in any review, the reproduction
or utilization of this work in whole or in part in any form by any
electronic, mechanical or other means, now known or hereafter
invented, including xerography, photocopying and recording, or in
any information storage or retrieval system, is forbidden without
the written permission of the editorial office, Silhouette Books,
300 East 42nd Street, New York, NY 10017 U.S.A.

All characters in this book have no existence outside the imagination of
the author and have no relation whatsoever to anyone bearing the same
name or names. They are not even distantly inspired by any individual
known or unknown to the author, and all incidents are pure invention.

This edition published by arrangement with Harlequin Books S.A.

® and TM are trademarks of Harlequin Books S.A., used under license.
Trademarks indicated with ® are registered in the United States Patent
and Trademark Office, the Canadian Trade Marks Office and in other
countries.

Printed in U.S.A.

Books by Patricia McLinn

Silhouette Special Edition

Hoops #587
A New World #641
*Prelude to A Wedding #712
*Wedding Party #718
*Grady's Wedding #813
Not a Family Man #864
Rodeo Nights #904
A Stranger in the Family #959
A Stranger to Love #1098
The Rancher Meets His Match #1164

*Wedding Series

PATRICIA McLINN

says she has been spinning stories in her head since childhood, when her mother insisted she stop reading at the dinner table. As the time came for her to earn a living, Patricia shifted her stories from fiction to fact—she became a sports writer and editor for newspapers in Illinois, North Carolina and the District of Columbia. Now living outside Washington, D.C., she enjoys traveling, history and sports but is happiest indulging her passion for storytelling.

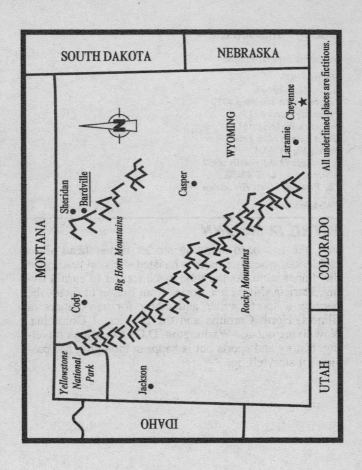

All underlined places are fictitious.

Chapter One

"A man's got needs. Physical needs."

Dax Randall heard the words coming from his mouth and fought back a groan. Sweat dotted his forehead and slithered down his back. And it wasn't adjusting this forty-foot irrigation pipe that was making him sweat. He'd probably toted this hunk of aluminum the equivalent of around the world, sixty feet at a time. He didn't need help. But asking Will to balance the other end while he lined up the lightweight pipe had been the best way he could think of to corral his son for this talk.

It was the talk that made Dax feel like a plague of grasshoppers had landed in his gut.

How in tarnation had he gotten into this?

He glanced over his shoulder to his fifteen-year-old son. Will rolled his eyes.

"Geez, Dad, you gave me this talk about a million years ago. And I already knew it all then. I've lived on a ranch all my life, you know," he added with exaggerated patience.

Wishing it was just *the* talk he faced with his son—he'd much rather talk about the mechanics—Dax cleared his throat as he straightened, and pushed on. "I know. But it's more complicated with a man and a woman than with a stallion and a mare. It's not just physical needs. There's more involved."

Will frowned. "Like what?"

"Like companionship and liking and respect." He thought a moment, then added, "And trust. That's what a woman needs from a man. And vice versa."

Hell, yes, he'd rather talk about the mechanics.

Will ducked his head. "It doesn't matter."

"What do you mean, it doesn't matter?"

"I don't need to know all that stuff as long as I stay away from females, and that's what I'm going to do."

Dax Randall looked at the tousled brown hair of his manchild and wished with all his heart that he could fold him into his arms and rock him the way he had when Will was a baby and had stumbled on to one of the million hurts the world had stored up for him. But even if this boy weaving between childhood and adulthood would let him, it would solve nothing.

Dax waited for his son to lower the far end of the pipe, then put his in place. With the couplings complete, he and Will met at the back of the pickup, where two more mended sections of pipe awaited their attention.

"All your friends are taking to girls, Will," he said softly.

And that meant they were leaving Will behind. Dax had seen it happening more and more. The picnics, the dances, the pool parties, the mixed groups going to movies or on trail rides. Will got invited, but never went. Since this past summer started, his son's isolation from his friends and his loneliness had become almost palpable. He'd seen no improvement since school had started late last month.

"They're all butt-heads."

"Pete Weston, too?" Dax asked. Will idolized their neighbors' son, who was three years older, an accomplished baseball player and had been dating a local girl the past year.

Will said nothing, but the stubborn angle of his jaw didn't budge as he started to haul the next length of pipe out of the truck bed.

"Look, Will, I know your growing up's been some different from your friends', with just you and me out here. Not having a woman around might've made you wonder 'bout some things—"

"We do okay, the two of us."

"Yeah, we do. Still, it's natural, come a certain age, for boys to start looking at girls, and enjoying their company. To seek out being with girls, maybe one girl in particular."

Will raised his head then and looked his father right in the eyes. "You don't."

Sweat collected on Dax's forehead again, as he mentally swore a blue streak.

Hell and damnation, June's right.

And he had to do something about it.

"Of course I'm right," his older sister, June, said with no surprise that afternoon. "All Will's friends have opened their eyes and noticed there's another creature on this earth besides horses, cows and dogs, and he's being left behind. That's what's wrong with the boy."

June plunked another jar of strawberry preserves on the top shelf. Dax and Will mostly did their own cooking, cleaning and laundry, but June came out now and then with homemade treats, and she gave the house a thorough going over a few times a year. In return, Dax kept up repairs on the house June shared with their mother, now that they were both widows.

"Don't look at me like that, Dax. You might like to

pretend women don't exist—except for your trips to Billings and Casper—''

"June," he warned.

She wasn't deterred. "But the female of the species isn't going away. No matter if you told Will to steer clear of girls from—''

"I never told Will that."

June snorted.

"You *live* it! And that boy's starting to live it, too. He's followed your footsteps close enough to be a shadow since the day he was born, and if you don't do something, he'll turn into the same sort of lonely, closed-off hermit his father is—only he'll do it before he's given love any chance at all!"

Angry words bubbled behind his tight-pressed lips, then sank back into his gut.

He'd learned long ago that love wasn't for him, and if it could protect Will from the painful lessons he'd had, he'd roll in prickly pear all day, every day, for the rest of his life. But Dax had eyes, and he saw love worked for some. He wouldn't deny his son a chance at that kind of life.

"Nothing to say?" Hands on her hips, June glared at him.

"You're a pain in the butt."

"Especially when I'm right. You've got to show Will it's natural and normal for a man to be around a woman—for more than a tussle between the sheets."

He glowered at her. An angular, raw-boned woman, she glowered right back. Twelve when he came along, June had been as much a mother to him as their mother had been. Probably more. She'd cut him no slack, ever. But she was one woman who had always stood by him.

"I'll talk to him."

June threw up her hands, the dish towel she held nearly catching Dax across the nose. "Talk? You could talk yourself blue in the face, but he's as stubborn as you are, and won't listen any more than you ever have. What you've gotta do is *show* him. And you know it," she added shrewdly, "or you would've done the talking to him instead of telling me about it."

"I'm not sitting still for any of your meddling matchmaking, June. I'm not getting tied up with anyone, and that's final."

"Heaven forbid, you fall in love and get married like a normal human being." June's sarcasm didn't fool Dax. "All I'm saying is ask a woman out. Go to a few movies. Have dinner. Hold her hand. Maybe give her a good-night kiss. I wouldn't expect more of you than most fifteen-year-olds can manage—only enough to show Will how it's done and, more important, that it's okay that Will Randall does those things."

"And afterward?"

June's act of utter innocence sat incongruously on her strong features. "What do you mean, afterward?"

"You're thinking if I get a taste of hand-holding and movie-going that more would come of it. Any woman 'round here I asked out would think the same." He leaned forward, almost nose to nose with his sister. "That won't happen, June. And I'm not going to lead a woman on. Not even for Will. It's not right."

"A few casual dates wouldn't mean—"

"Like hell it wouldn't." He leaned back and crossed his arms over his chest. "It would mean plenty in Bardville, and you damn well know it."

June drew the dish towel through her hands, over and over, while she stared dreamily at the calendar from the propane dealer on the refrigerator door. "So, what you need is a stranger."

"Not a lot of strangers in Bardville."

His sister didn't heed his mutter. "Someone decent and nice, like the girls Will would meet. Someone for you to flirt with and show Will it's okay to be interested in females, but who won't get any ideas about long-term commitment."

"None of that kind in Bardville."

"I know just the person."

A tickle of something like dread jittered along Dax's backbone. "What?"

"Not what. Who. Flew in this morning. I rented her a car."

June ran the sole car rental concession at tiny Bardville Municipal Airport. She lived so close she could be at the rental counter in five minutes, so she worked only when flights came in. The job added income to the benefits from Henry's modest life insurance, and it kept her abreast of the area's comings and goings.

"Who?"

"Hannah Chalmers. She's staying at the Westons' bed-and-breakfast." June tipped her head to the northeast. "She works for Boone's company in North Carolina—runs the advertising department—and she's here for a two-week working vacation."

Since Cambria Weston and Boone Dorsey Smith's wedding last summer, they had split time between his log-home designing business in North Carolina and the home they were building here on land bought from his in-laws. Several of his employees had flown to Bardville in the past two summers for combination business and pleasure.

"Two weeks," June repeated. "So there's no worry about leading her on or having her think you'd break down and make a commitment. You won't ever see her after the two weeks are up."

"But—"

"She's very nice. Attractive. Thirty-one. Unattached. Cambria says Hannah divorced a few years back and hasn't been involved since. She's been raising a younger brother and sister since their parents got killed. Twins. Off to college now. Lost their parents in a small-plane crash. Terrible hard it was on all of 'em. But now—"

"Did you get her social security number and blood type while you were at it?" Dax asked, half-amused and wholly alarmed by his sister's knack for discovering details of people's lives.

"I thought you should know a little about her before you meet. You can start tonight—at the Westons' cookout for their B-and-B guests. Irene Weston's always telling me how she wished you and Will would come. I'll introduce you to Hannah, then you take it from there."

Dax's jaw tightened and he wished he could refuse. The memory of two words stopped him.

You don't.

That's what his son had said. Behind those words came a whole train of other thoughts.

You don't, so I won't.

You don't, so I shouldn't.

You don't, so I couldn't.

From the moment of Will's birth—hell, even before—Dax had struggled to make himself an example for his child. Not a pattern for Will to repeat but a foundation he could rise above, so he ended up with a better life than Dax had.

Being lonely and isolated from his friends sure wasn't what Dax wanted for his son. He wanted better for Will.

Dax's life hadn't included much real love—only June and Will. He wanted better for Will there, too.

Flirting with some perfect stranger was a small price to pay.

"This is my brother, Dax Randall," said the friendly woman from the airport's car rental. "Dax, this is Hannah Chalmers, visiting from North Carolina."

Hannah turned from June Reamer to the man beside her. He stood maybe three or four inches taller than Hannah's five-seven, with broad shoulders and chest above narrow waist and hips. He wore a white Western shirt, jeans, boots and requisite cowboy hat, as well as a tight-lipped expression.

"Hello, Dax. How do you do?" She held out her hand.

"Pleasure, ma'am."

As a large, work-roughened but scrupulously clean hand surrounded hers, Hannah peered up through the shadows cast by twilight and his hat, and into grim brown eyes. If this was his idea of pleasure, she'd hate to see him displeased.

But she didn't look away. And he didn't release her hand.

Her hand felt odd. Tingly, as if the nerves had fallen asleep and now were waking up. Must be from all the hand-shaking she'd done since arriving at the Westons' ranch and meeting Cambria and Boone's friends and family.

The sensation spread to between her shoulder blades, and that got her moving.

"Uh, excuse me." She started to ease her hand from his grip. He let go with a jerk.

She started to say something more to June, but the woman had disappeared. Turning back to Dax, she encountered a man with his hands jammed in his front jeans pockets, his mouth pressed tight and his eyes not quite meeting hers.

Silence ticked away between them like a bomb waiting to explode.

She cleared her throat. "Your sister was wonderful this morning when I rented the car. A personal tour guide and chamber of commerce all rolled into one. I couldn't have asked for a warmer welcome."

His eyes came up, meeting hers for a second, intensifying the sensation between her shoulder blades. Behind the grimness she saw something else. A glint of affection for his sister? Yes. And amusement? Yes, that, too, though dry enough to qualify as the powdered form.

All he said, however, was, "Yeah, that's June's way."

But not his way, clearly.

Hannah glanced over her shoulder. Cambria and Boone stood by a camp fire encircled by stumps and smoothed boulders where several guests had taken seats. A quick "excuse me" to this taciturn man and she could return to people she knew.

For crying out loud, Hannah, it's about time you got back into the social whirl. When was the last time you flirted?

Hannah smiled at her sister's voice in her head. Not even Mandy, who at seventeen saw romantic possibilities in every meeting between the sexes, could construe this encounter as anything more than prosaic and awkward.

Though Mandy would be sure to notice Dax Randall's broad shoulders and muscled thighs. His jeans were as clean as his hands, but worn nearly white in spots, including the center front.

Hannah swallowed and redirected her gaze and thoughts.

Come to think of it, she dealt with prosaic and awkward encounters all the time in her work. As long as she kept this meeting in that category, it should be a snap. It was flirting and the social whirl that churned her stomach.

She pinned on the determined, professional smile she would have used on a layout man giving her trouble over the typeface on an ad readout, and tried again.

"Flying in today was amazing. To see all that expanse of land, miles and miles of that dusty gray-green with not even a road breaking it, and then the deeper green of the Big Horn Mountains—how spectacular. People kept talking about how much smaller the Big Horns are than the Rockies, but they were quite impressive from the air."

"From the ground, too."

His voice was low, gravelly. Maybe that was why she didn't catch the words immediately. Or it could have been being distracted by getting her first clear view of his face when he raised his head enough for the firelight to reach fully under the hat brim.

Oh, my.

He had a bone structure rough-cut from granite, then honed by tempests. A face suited to a Louis L'Amour hero come to life.

High, sharp cheekbones. A blade nose—sharp, thin and faintly curved. Deep lines curved from each corner of his nose to below the corners of his mouth.

Any advertising person with an ounce of instinct would use that face to stand for integrity, pride, stubbornness, independence. And there wasn't a soul who wouldn't believe it.

And most women would want to trace the stark lines with their fingertips and hope their touch would ease the tightness there.

Hannah swallowed again. It didn't help. She felt as if a blender had clicked on in her stomach. "What?"

"From the ground. The mountains are impressive from the ground, too. You ought to see 'em while you're here."

The blender kicked up from low to medium. "I'd like to."

Would he volunteer to guide her? Oh, Lord, it had been too long. She was too old. Too unaccustomed to this gut-level turmoil. Too—

"Yeah, well, you should. Nobody knows 'em better than Cambria."

The blender eased back to neutral, with relief and yes, an ounce of disappointment sloshing around in its wake.

"I, uh, I hope she'll take me, then."

Dax Randall's gaze dropped to his boots, came back to her, then darted off to the left. He cleared his throat.

"So, you're visiting from North Carolina."

"Yes." June had covered this, but as the only conversational lifeline he'd offered, it sure beat drowning in silence. Hannah grabbed hold. "I had some things to go over with Boone about next year's advertising. I work for Boone's company."

Her voice rose at the end of the sentence in a hint of a question. He made a brief sound that confirmed he knew that. He said nothing, his interest apparently snagged by something over her shoulder.

"I told him we could have handled this over the phone

and by fax, but he and Cambria insisted I come for a full two weeks.'' She twisted her neck to look behind her. She saw a casually dressed group of friendly people, the locals standing out from the B-and-B guests mostly because their tans reached layers-deep from years of outdoor work. ''A few days more than two weeks, actually.''

''Uh-huh ''

''They said I should see Wyoming.'' He hadn't heard a word. ''In case I wanted to buy it. Or open a Buddhist monastery here.''

''Uh-huh.''

Hannah turned fully around this time, pushing her wind-whipped hair out of her face to track Dax Randall's intense stare to a teenager on the opposite side of the circle of seats around the fire. The boy stood alone, several yards from a half-dozen boys and girls about the same age who jostled and joked like young roosters and preening hens.

''Is something wrong, Dax?''

His eyes jerked to hers. A frown dropped his straight brows low. His eyes bored into hers as if she had some answer he wanted.

She looked away from that intense connection. The blender muttered at the pit of her stomach. If this was an example of the social whirl Mandy and others insisted she plunge back into, no thank you. Her stomach couldn't take it.

''That's my son.''

She glanced from Dax to the boy and back. She saw the resemblance in coloring and bearing. Something else, too .

A *separateness.* How sad, she thought. Then she determinedly shook off the reaction. She had probably read way too much into subtle signs from a pair of strangers.

''He looks like a nice boy ''

''He is.''

Dax studied her as if he could read some answer in her face. That tingling started up between her shoulder blades again.

He drew a deep breath. "Hannah—"

"Oh, there you are, Hannah!" Irene Weston bore down on them like a welcoming tornado. Cambria Weston Smith provided the business sense of the bed-and-breakfast operation that supplemented the Westons' ranching income, but her stepmother, Irene, provided its hospitable heart. "I hardly saw you standing off here in the shadows talking with— Why, Dax, how wonderful to see you."

Surprise and pleasure weighed evenly in Irene's voice. She stretched up to kiss Dax's cheek. Hannah could have sworn his lean, smooth-shaven jaw flushed red.

"Hope you don't mind my coming by and bringing Will."

"Mind? Of course not, Dax. You know you're welcome anytime. And I've been inviting you to our cookouts for a month of Sundays."

He muttered something about "busy."

"Of course you are. But even running a ranch, you can't keep so busy you don't eat, Dax. So you go right on over and help yourself to those burgers Ted's taking off the fire, while I make sure this young woman has a chance to meet all our guests. Especially old Zeke, who's visiting us from his granddaughter's in Miles City. Zeke worked for Ted's grandpa as a boy and remembers Arnold Weston's stories about bringing cattle up from Texas."

"It was nice to meet you, Dax," Hannah said as Irene led her away.

They'd gone maybe two yards, when a hoarse, "Stop," came from behind them.

As they both turned around, Hannah met Irene's eyes for an instant, and saw there a surprise equal to her own.

Dax stood where they'd left him. Now that he had their full attention, he didn't seem eager to use it.

"What is it, Dax?" Irene asked.

He muttered under his breath—from the tone, a curse. "Hannah, I wondered if you'd...if we could, uh, talk more. Later." He made the last word sound like a reprieve.

Hannah felt Irene's eyes on her, but she didn't return the look. She had a hard enough time trying to return words.

"Okay."

Uninspired, but at least it was intelligible.

He nodded once.

"Of course you two can talk later," Irene said. "Right after I get Hannah introduced around and you get some food, Dax. Get that boy of yours some, too. Get plenty of my special sauce, I know how you've always loved it."

Dax nodded again and headed in the direction of his son.

Irene reclaimed Hannah's elbow with an energy that belied the gray outnumbering the strands of red in her hair and started her off. "Well. Dax Randall." Irene hummed a bit under her breath. "That's surprising."

"I don't know why he wants to talk later, he hardly said two words together before." And Hannah didn't know why she felt she had to defend herself.

"He's not one to waste words. He's not one to socialize much, either. Especially with women."

Again, Hannah felt the older woman's speculative gaze on her.

"Don't get me wrong," Irene continued, "he's a good man. A good heart and dependable as they come. Out here, a good neighbor's the best security you got, and Dax Randall's the best. He's done a fine job of raising Will on his own, too." She smiled. "Oh, and he loves that boy of his something fierce. But he's been hurt by...by life. He's spent a long time with him and his boy alone at that ranch. A long time."

"His sister doesn't...?"

"No, June lives in town. She and Sally—that's Dax and June's mother—moved into town, oh, must be thirty years ago now, and left Dax and old William living on the ranch. After June got married, Sally had her own house. But since June's Henry passed on, and with Sally's health not real strong, she's moved into June's place. Works out well for them, but it leaves Dax and Will alone at the ranch, like it once was with old William and Dax.''

Hannah gave a noncommittal murmur as she tried to finger-comb her tousled hair. Expressing the flash of compassion she'd felt at the image of Dax Randall living so isolated a life, as boy and man, was out of the question. She didn't know him. She had no right trying to change his ways—even mentally.

"Well, enough of my gossiping tongue," Irene continued briskly. "What I want to know is how you're handling this empty-nest syndrome they talk about, what with Cambria telling me your younger brother and sister are gone to college now. I tell you, I'm not sure how I feel about it at all, with my Pete off to Arizona. You want them to grow up, but it surely is hard to watch those fledglings fly away from the nest."

Hannah wouldn't have labeled Irene's talk as gossip—it held too much honest concern—but she was grateful the conversation had turned away from Dax Randall.

"I don't think I'm a good one to talk to, Irene," she said with a small laugh. "Most times I feel more as if *I* were the one booted out of the nest. Mandy and Ethan were forever telling me to get out more, even before they left home."

"As well you should," added a new voice. Cambria frowned fiercely at Hannah at the same time she tucked her arm around Irene's waist.

From the way Cambria had spoken of her stepmother last winter, when she and Boone had lived in North Carolina, Hannah had suspected they were close. Now she plainly saw their great affection.

"You've spent the past four years being a mother to the twins," Cambria added, "now it's time to go out and have fun for yourself."

"I have had fun," Hannah protested.

"Being the youngest member of the PTA? Chaperoning dances for kids not much younger than yourself? Being

seated with the parents old enough to be *your* parents?''
Cambria clearly didn't buy that Hannah hadn't minded any
of those things. ''What you need is a little excitement in
your life. Romance. Sizzle.''

Torn between embarrassment and amusement, Hannah
laughed. ''Oh, Lord, you've been taking to Mandy, haven't
you?''

''We did have a conversation before Boone and I came
out to Wyoming in the spring,'' Cambria said with great
dignity, though devilment lurked in her eyes. ''She strikes
me as a very intelligent, perceptive girl.''

''She could have been the tour director for Noah's Ark,''
Hannah said. ''She sees everything as two-by-two.''

''That's not all bad,'' Cambria murmured, and Hannah
noted that she looked across to where Boone helped his
father-in-law, Ted Weston, cook hamburgers on the grill.
Cambria patted her eight months' pregnant stomach and
added, ''Of course, sometimes two-by-two turns into two-
by-three.''

''It'll be wonderful to have a grandchild,'' Irene said
with satisfaction.

''And then you'll have another fledgling in your nest,
won't you, Mama? At least for the summer months when
we're here in Wyoming. Did I tell you— '' Cambria turned
to Hannah. ''Irene's coming to North Carolina when we
have the baby, Dad, too.''

''That's great,'' Hannah said with a smile for both
women.

''Ted and I wouldn't miss it for anything in this world,''
Irene said.

''And Boone wouldn't let you miss it, bossy man that
he is. Maybe that's what you need in your life, Hannah,''
Cambria added.

''What? A bossy man? I already have one, thank you.
Remember? I work for your husband.''

They exchanged a grin, knowing how hard Boone Dorsey ''Bodie'' Smith had worked at curing his bossy ten-

dency and giving his employees more responsibility and authority at Bodie Smith Enterprises.

"I meant a baby," Cambria clarified.

Irene spared Hannah the necessity of trying to unlimber her frozen tongue. "She needs a husband first," she said as matter-of-factly as if discussing a recipe. "It makes things so much easier that way, because—"

"Irene! Where's the sauce?" Ted shouted from behind the grill.

"It's right there," Irene called back to her husband.

"Where?"

"I'll be right there, dear. I'm sorry, Hannah," she added. "I haven't been much of a hostess. Cambria, I've been promising to introduce Hannah around, especially to Zeke. Will you see to that?"

"Of course."

"And then, Dax Randall said he'd like to get to know Hannah better. So find them a good place to sit for the singing."

"Dax?"

Cambria didn't sound merely surprised, she sounded amazed. Cambria turned to Irene, but she'd already started toward the grill to solve the mystery of the missing sauce, so her questioning gaze shifted to Hannah.

"We were talking before and got, uh, interrupted," Hannah said. "I don't know why he'd…"

She let it die when she saw Cambria's gaze return to her husband, then slide to a nearby couple. Cully Grainger had come to Bardville to visit Boone, but was staying to run for sheriff because he'd fallen for Jessa Tarrant. The falling clearly was mutual.

Cambria was still looking in their direction when she murmured, "I suppose stranger things have happened."

Then Cambria's gaze shifted, and Hannah followed it to where Dax Randall stood at the fringe of the shadows beyond the firelight.

"But not much stranger," Cambria added.

Chapter Two

If Bardville, Wyoming, had enlisted her to mount an ad campaign to extol its virtues, Hannah would have chosen this night as its centerpiece.

The people—all ages, several races, many walks of life—encircled a camp fire, a vaulted night sky as star-speckled and huge as imagination over their heads. The soft guitar and the blending of disparate voices in songs reached back to childhood to resurrect "Oh, Susanna" and "My Darling Clementine." Their circle sat shoulder-to-shoulder tight as if to keep the night-cooled air at their backs from slipping in. The crackling fire toasted their faces and toes.

Firelight carved angles and shadows in the most ordinary faces. On Dax Randall's face it had the unsettling effect of seeming to add emotions. A flicker this way, and she thought she read pain. A shadow that way, and a glimpse of triumphant joy appeared. Another shifting, and determination and pride came to the fore. Then a subtle shading revealed tenderness. It was as if the fire burned the controls he kept on his expressions, showing what he could feel if he let himself.

A log shifted, setting off a flare of light and sparks, and Dax's face seemed to take on a cast of passion, like a man about to—

Hannah jerked her gaze away, aware of increased warmth in her face. She stared into the fire, dragging her thoughts back to the charms of the night and her hypothetical ad campaign.

Oh, yes, the people in the hurried, crowded cities back East would be pulled in by this place's magic in a moment. Even she, living in a far less hurried, more-a-town-than-a-city corner of the Blue Ridge Mountains, felt the tug. Maybe it had to do with the past being near enough to touch here. People alive now had known the first whites to settle this land, had known the last Native Americans to fight for it. People like Zeke, who'd told her some of the tales.

As he'd talked, she'd envisioned Dax Randall as the flinty trail boss, tough but fair. Sitting tall in the saddle no matter what adversities—

"Want to take a walk?"

"What?"

"Want to take a walk?"

She shivered at the sensation of Dax's repeated low-voiced question stirring the hair by her ear. "I..."

"You cold?"

"No." But she hugged her sweater tighter around her.

When she'd landed this afternoon, the bright sun had heated everything, including her. But as soon as it sank behind the line of the Big Horn Mountains in a showy splash of red, the coolness of the earth and the darkening sky had wrapped around her, so she welcomed the cozy wool of the tunic-length cardigan sweater she'd added to her blouse and slacks. But it wouldn't cure this shiver.

"Maybe a walk's not such a good idea."

"No, it's fine. Yes. Let's." *You're babbling, Hannah.* And the blender in her stomach had kicked on again. She half stood. He didn't move. She dropped back to her log seat more rapidly than she should have for the comfort of her bottom. She shifted to one side to ease one discomfort and closed her eyes hoping the other one would disappear.

"You want to, or not?"

She looked up to find Dax standing solidly before her with, from what she could see under the brim of his hat, a decidedly puzzled expression.

For whatever reason, her never infertile imagination had taken to imbuing this newly met man with romantic over-tones. Good heavens, she was ascribing emotions to him because of accidents of firelight, connecting him with the highly romanticized remembrances of an elderly man about a time long past, if indeed, it had ever existed. Hannah straightened her shoulders.

"Yes, I do. I think a walk will be just the thing."

Just the thing to wipe out these ridiculous notions, and replace them with the reality of this man. This, no doubt, extremely prosaic man.

She stood, and followed his lead in stepping over their seats to the outside of the circle. She didn't hesitate when he put out his hand to assist her. She put her hand in his. It felt warm and hard and faintly roughened, which no doubt caused the tingling in hers.

He released her hand immediately and tipped his head to indicate they would take a path that led off the opposite side of the circle. As they moved around the outside, many eyes followed their progress. Will Randall sat on the far side of old Zeke, several yards from his contemporaries, and his dark glower zeroed in on her and his apparently unheeding father.

The glow of the fire didn't reach far, but their eyes quickly adjusted to the gentler light of half-moon and stars. They walked side by side, the crunch of her shoes and his boots on the dirt path softened by a layer of fallen cotton-wood leaves.

"Nice night," she offered.

"Won't be many left until it gets cold."

"Winter comes early here?"

"Comes right on time for here."

She glanced up to see if she'd mistaken the hint of a grin she'd heard in his voice. That bit of inattention to her feet caught up with her immediately when she stepped on a branch and tripped into him. He caught her elbow, his hand extending along the underside of her forearm like an iron brace.

"Oh, I'm sorry. Thank you."

He released her, then stepped back, letting her precede him. "Path narrows."

What is your problem, Hannah? she fumed at herself. She'd successfully run the advertising department for Bodie Smith Enterprises for four years, pleasing a demanding boss and serving a booming business. And before that, she'd handled one of advertising's most difficult tasks—convincing people to give to charity. More important, she'd done a darned good job of raising Mandy and Ethan the past four years, if she said so herself.

She was a competent, intelligent, accomplished woman who had come on this walk to erase foolish notions, and that was what she was going to do.

They'd reached a wooden footbridge across a narrow stream. She stopped abruptly and turned to face Dax.

"Let's stop awhile and talk."

"'Bout what?"

There, she thought triumphantly. *Was that wary response the answer of a Louis L'Amour hero?*

Heartened, she searched for a topic. A flash of light caught her eye and she looked down at the stream. The moon and stars turned to narrow, glimmering ribbons in the water's reflection as it slipped almost silently around dry-topped rocks.

"How pretty."

Dax Randall moved next to her, his hands resting atop the railing as he looked down, too. He gave a rusty chuckle.

"What's funny?"

"I was thinking it's low, even for this time of year. Ranchers don't see things same way as city folks."

She pushed her hair to the side, but the breeze teased it right back. "I'm not a city person."

"Heard you used to work in New York City."

"I did, but I grew up in Boone, North Carolina—in the mountains. And that's where I live now."

His grunt of acknowledgment held a tinge of skepticism that challenged her.

"Have you always lived on a ranch, Dax?"

He shook his head. "Grew up here, but got away as soon as I could."

"Where to?"

"Some college. Then spent a couple years in cities, myself. Denver, mostly. Dallas some."

"What brought you back?"

"Will. I wanted him raised here."

Caught up in wondering at the contradiction that he'd wanted to raise his son in a life he'd been eager to leave, Hannah hardly noticed that he'd paused. But she certainly noticed his next words.

"I'd like to see you while you're here, Hannah."

Startled by the change of subject, she stared at him. Between his abrupt tone and a new grimness around his mouth, she doubted *like* was the appropriate word. But even if she'd misread him, it wasn't such a good idea. "That's very nice of you, Dax, but I'll have work to do and I'm not going to be here long."

"I know. That's why—"

He broke off and looked even grimmer than before.

"Ah." She nodded once, understanding dawning and with it a surprisingly sharp disappointment. "I'm not in the market for a vacation fling, Mr. Randall. Maybe you've found that some women who visit here are more interested in the bed than the breakfast, but I'm not one of them. Good ni—"

"No, wait." He stepped into her path, but didn't touch her. "I didn't mean it that way."

The wind caught the material of his shirt, rippling it slightly, as if reaching toward her. Hannah backed up half a step, crossing her arms in front of her.

"What way did you mean it?"

Dax considered the silvery thread of water below them as if it might offer help, but faced her when he spoke. "I'm not looking for something permanent, that's what I'm saying. Nothing serious. I don't want you thinking otherwise. But maybe we could, uh, go see a movie or something."

"But I thought—" She broke it off as she spotted the cliff her words threatened to plunge her over.

He didn't ask what she thought. He didn't raise a questioning brow or alter his expression. He simply waited. His dark eyes bored into hers from under slightly lowered lids, and he waited.

"I thought you didn't date." The words rushed out on one short breath.

"I don't. Not usually."

"Why?"

At first she thought he might not answer, or might try to evade the question. But when he spoke, his answer was plain. "If I saw anyone from 'round here, as soon as I stopped asking her out, word would be out I'd dumped her. And there'd be no avoiding each other. That's why it's good you won't be here long. No misunderstandings. See?"

She thought she did. And she respected his blunt honesty.

She even agreed with his position. She wasn't looking for anything permanent, either. Nothing serious. Not yet.

With the twins in college, maybe the time had come to listen to those around her urging that she pick up the emotional life she'd set aside four years ago along with her marriage to Richard. But she wasn't one to plunge in. She'd need to ease back into the emotional waters.

Maybe a little light flirtation to start. A few comfortable, undemanding outings with an uncomplicated man.

Dax Randall was not that man.

"I'm not looking for anything serious now, either, and—"

"That's fine. That's great."

He closed the gap between them, took her hand in both of his and smiled at her. A smile that carved grooves beside a mouth that suddenly appeared anything but grim and traced lines around a pair of brown eyes that lightened from within.

The blender in her stomach churned as if it could make butter.

"No, no. You misunderstand." She tugged to free her hand, which had started that strange tingling again. He didn't release it. "I don't— "

"You *are* looking for something serious." It was an accusation.

"No, I'm not. I'm looking for...for..."

She didn't know. Precisely. But she knew he wasn't what she had in mind. Good heavens, she'd always fallen for men who communicated with ease and wit. Dax's conversations wouldn't have strained a telegram.

On the other hand, his bluntness—tinged with a hint of awkwardness— was refreshing. She couldn't imagine any of the men she or her friends had dated laying it on the line that they were not in the market for a long-term commitment—at least not up front. They waited until the woman started thinking "forever" to reveal they only thought "for now."

His honesty suited her. So did his expectations. Her breakup and divorce from Richard had left her feeling for a long time that a relationship was the absolutely last endeavor she wanted to try. She couldn't pinpoint when that feeling had eased, but she realized now that it had. Only she'd become so out of practice with anything approaching romance that she felt like an awkward adolescent, as tongue-tied and klutzy as any teenager.

Teenagers.

Like Will Randall.

Who had most definitely not approved of his father's apparent interest in her. If looks could freeze, she'd have been a Popsicle.

"I want something easy. No stepping on anybody's toes."

"I told you—"

"You're not involved with anybody," she filled in. "But you are—your son. And I don't think he would like us going out—"

"Will." He released her hand.

"I also don't think you'd like to make him unhappy. And I *know* I don't need that kind of trouble. So, let's leave it at that, Dax. Maybe I'll see you again before I leave. Good night."

She didn't run. She didn't think she acted oddly when she returned to the camp fire. And she didn't wilt under the questioning gazes from Cambria and Irene.

Unfortunately, she did dream. Brown eyes. Gravelly voice. Harsh face. Muscular thighs. And tingling that wouldn't quit.

"You okay this morning, Hannah? Did you sleep all right? I hope the cabin's okay."

"Huh? Oh, yes, everything's fine." She forced herself to smile across the round table at Irene. Most of the bed-and-breakfast guests had already left for the day when she'd dragged herself into the Westons' kitchen in the futile hope that coffee would clear this haze. "It's a lovely cabin."

"You look tired." Cambria sounded more like a scientist observing a bug than a solicitous hostess.

"Maybe it's the time change."

Cambria shook her head decisively. "Shouldn't bother

you coming this way. I suspect it's the company you kept last night.''

Images of dreams, hot and restless, streaked across Hannah's mind. She shifted in her chair and felt the burn in her cheeks.

"Cambria," Irene scolded. She reached across the table and patted Hannah's hand. "Now, don't you listen to a thing she says. She's just teasing you about talking to Dax at the cookout.''

"Well, I started teasing," Cambria said with a laugh that didn't hide the sharp interest in her eyes, "but I swear if I hadn't seen him leave with Will before anybody else, I might wonder exactly why you're so heavy-eyed this morning.''

From her years in advertising, Hannah knew a few things about damage control. She'd found it worked best to meet a situation head-on.

"Cambria, I'm surprised at such subterfuge from you. You're usually more straightforward.''

Irene murmured something that could have been "like a sledgehammer." Cambria made a face at her stepmother, who smiled back serenely, but Hannah ignored the byplay and kept on.

"If you want to know what happened with Dax Randall last night during our walk, I'll tell you. We talked— briefly—about where we'd lived our lives. And about the weather—even more briefly. And he asked me out.''

"He *did?*''

"Well, I'll be.''

After a lifetime of being called "wholesome," Hannah didn't harbor particular sensitivity about her appeal to the opposite sex, but she still felt a flash of thankfulness that their utter disbelief was so clearly aimed at *Dax* asking someone out, and not at his asking *her* out.

"I'm glad, Hannah," Cambria said. "We're all so used to Dax being solitary, maybe we'd given up on him, but he's a fine man, and you two—"

"I said no."

Cambria and Irene exchanged a long look, and Irene murmured, "Well, I'll be," again before starting to hum under her breath as she had last night.

"He also said," Hannah continued with the authority she would use to restore calm when a production meeting threatened to fall apart or the twins squabbled, "that he wasn't interested in anything serious. And, while I admire his honesty and I agree with him on that point, I'm also not interested in a vacation romance. In fact, this isn't even a vacation. I came here to work." She took a last swallow of coffee and stood. "And I'll get started if you can tell me where Boone is."

"He's working on our house. That's why I'm here, to drive you up." Cambria also stood, though a little awkwardly.

"Will you be back for lunch?" Irene asked.

"No, we'll have lunch up at the house, then I'll drop Hannah off on our way to Sheridan for my doctor's appointment."

"Fine." Irene wore an abstracted, dreamy smile. "I have some things I want Hannah to see this afternoon."

"What a waste," came a whispered female voice from somewhere behind him.

"Yes, indeed," agreed another from the depths of Jessa Tarrant's sundries store in Bardville. "That Dax Randall's one hunk of man to be going to waste."

Dax dug in his pocket for money to pay for his purchases while cursing under his breath that nature hadn't fixed it so force of will could prevent heat from rising up his neck and no doubt staining his skin an even deeper color than the sun had managed.

It made it no better that the whisperers hadn't meant him to hear or that both whisperers were grandmothers. It made it a sight worse that the comments had also been heard by Rita Campbell, behind the cash register, and Sheriff Tom

Milano, who appeared to be doing nothing more than hanging around Rita.

Some might say Milano was entitled, since he would retire as sheriff in less than two months, and, after more than a decade of being a widower, would marry Rita the weekend after that. Dax thought sourly that a grown man could find better things to do than moon around after a woman.

"Don't let it rattle you, boy," the sheriff said, though at thirty-six Dax Randall hadn't thought of himself as a boy for nearly two decades. "There's scientists say nature abhors a vacuum and sets to filling it up. I couldn't rightly say about that, but it's sure that women abhor an unattached male, and set to getting him attached."

Didn't he just know it.

Dax couldn't think of an unattached female in the county who wouldn't have taken him up on his invitation last night—every one of them hoping it would lead to more. And that wasn't vanity, it was experience. A good number of them had been as subtle as a thunderclap in angling for that very thing.

But not Hannah Chalmers.

She'd turned him down flat.

She'd looked at him seriously then, but most other times a smile had flirted with her mouth. Sometimes, a quick, nervous kind of smile. But then, a real smile, like the one when she'd looked down at the creek. A smile that dropped a shallow dimple on the left side of her mouth and crinkled up her hazel eyes. She had a way of tipping her head a bit to the side, too, that made a man feel she was truly interested in whatever fool thing he might find to say.

"Pay him no heed, Dax," instructed Rita, with heightened color disappearing under the fringe of her graying hair.

As Dax stuffed his change into a pocket of his jeans, he caught the long, smiling look Rita sent the sheriff, which he returned in full. A smile like that would suit Hannah

Chalmers's sweet mouth. Hoisting the box of supplies to his shoulder, Dax blocked the view and muttered a farewell.

"Dax! Dax Randall, wait."

Jessa's voice calling from the back of the store stopped him. He let the street door swing closed and turned back. Jessa had been the only unattached female around Bardville less interested in getting attached than he was, so they'd gotten along fine from the time she opened her store a few years back. But now she was attached herself—attached with a vengeance from what he'd seen of her and Cully Grainger.

"Hey, Jessa."

"It was great to see you last night, and Will. I've missed him. He hasn't been around here to the shop with the other kids lately. And it seems like I hardly ever see you. Sorry we didn't get a chance to talk."

If her sentence ended with the slight lift of a question, as if inviting him to confide in her about his attentions to Hannah Chalmers, he chose to ignore it.

"Yeah. Nice evening. But—"

"And nice to meet Hannah, too, wasn't it?"

That was too direct to ignore completely.

"Yeah." It had been nice to meet her, to shake hands with a woman with a good grip. Firm, but not like she wanted to arm wrestle. Her hands were soft but not so delicate he feared crushing them. And she was forever using those hands to try to bring order to her hair. He could have told her that was a lost cause in a Wyoming breeze. "Yeah. I gotta go—"

"That book you ordered for Will finally came in. I can't believe it's taken so long." The hole in his memory must have been apparent, because she added, "Remember? The one you ordered at the start of summer. The one about the early space program."

She held out a hardcover book and he took it in his free hand, the other still balancing the box on his shoulder.

The Right Stuff by Tom Wolfe. He and Will had rented

the movie back in the winter. Will had been so taken with it, he'd gone right to the battered encyclopedia that had been out-of-date when Dax had used it for homework. Frustrated there, he'd gone to the library and taken out an armload of books, including this one. He'd checked it out from the library so often that Dax had figured Will should have his own copy.

"Something wrong, Dax?" Jessa asked.

"No."

Something *was* wrong. Something was wrong with Will.

His son had lost his enthusiasm. Not just for learning about the space program, but for everything. He had turned into a stranger. Listless, moping. The boy who had once been as happy amid a crowd of friends as he was with the two of them on the Circle CR, now seemed sullen and restless when he was alone with Dax, yet he avoided the company of kids he'd known all his life.

"That was the book you ordered, wasn't it?"

"Yeah, that's it. Thanks. Put it on my account, will you?" he added as he headed out. "Gotta get to Westons'. See you, Jessa."

But he sat awhile in his truck, staring at the dust-caked top of the windshield where the fan of the wipers never reached.

He knew his son, and he knew what he had to do.

Even if Hannah Chalmers had it right, and Will didn't much like the idea of his father going out with her, that didn't matter. It was for Will's own good.

As for Hannah not wanting to go out with him...well, he hadn't run a ranch all these years by giving up easy. He'd change her mind.

Hannah entered the open barn door on a whim.

Returning to the Westons' with Boone and Cambria, she'd felt restless and decided to take a walk, while they went in to visit with Irene awhile before going to Sheridan.

At the other end of the barn's length from where she'd

entered, the double doors opened wide into a corral, with sunlight and a cool breeze streaming in. A horse stood in the wide aisle, a length of rope hooked to its bridle at one end and a post at the other. A man held the horse's left rear hoof in his angled lap as he bent over his work.

Dax Randall.

She knew it immediately. Perhaps from his voice—gravelly, low, calming—as it crooned nonsense words to the animal.

All she could see of him was the back. That was plenty. His movements pulled the faded dark plaid shirt tight across his back. He wore chaps, with the straps buckling at the back of his powerful thighs and spotlighting his buttocks. The smooth-worn denim cupped his muscled rear end.

Hannah swallowed hard.

The animal became aware of her presence first, turning its head to look past Dax to where she stood. If it hadn't been a horse staring at her, Hannah might have taken the look to be the jealousy of one female not wanting to share the attentions of a male with another.

"Hold still, you bag of bones." Dax's tone never changed.

The horse shifted restively.

"Hold, there," Dax murmured. Still without changing tone, he added, "Who's here?"

"It's Hannah. Hannah Chalmers."

His hands seemed to still, but not for long.

"I'm sorry if I'm interrupting. I'll go—"

"No." The strength of the word had both the horse and Hannah staring at him, but only the horse could see his face. "Better stay. Leaving might spook 'er."

The animal seemed awfully calm to Hannah, but what did she know about horses?

"May I talk?"

"Low," he instructed.

"You're changing his shoes—I can see that—but why?"

"It's a her. I'm getting Jezebel ready for bringing the cattle down."

"Jezebel? That's her name?"

"Yeah. What's so funny?"

Hannah stifled her chuckle. She doubted he'd understand if she said she'd guessed the horse's gender based on a jealous look. "Bring the cattle down from where?"

"From up top. Up the mountain." He jerked his head to the west, toward the Big Horns. "There you go, Jezebel."

He released the horse's hoof and watched as she shifted her rear end away, tamping her foot lightly, looking for all the world like a human testing the fit of a shoe. Then, still crouching, Dax pivoted to face Hannah and sat back on his heels in a way that made her thighs ache just to watch.

His hat was tipped back, revealing his dark eyes pinned on her. They were a powerful weapon.

A smudge angled across his jaw, like a thumb swipe. She had the urge to wipe it clean with her fingertips. Or her tongue.

"Up the mountain? Why are the cattle there?"

She hoped desperation didn't seep into her voice. That tingle had returned between her shoulder blades, and she couldn't deny its cause any longer. Dax Randall was one powerfully attractive man.

That was the problem. She wasn't ready for a powerfully attractive man. She'd been off the slopes so long she'd be a fool to try skiing a double black diamond trail her first run back down the mountain. She needed to find herself a bunny hill.

"Better grazing in summer. Come cooler weather, we bring 'em down closer. So we can feed in the worst weather. Hannah, is something wrong?"

His abrupt change of subject threw her for a second. "Wrong? No. Why?"

"You're twitching your shoulders like something's biting you."

She almost laughed. She could just imagine Dax's face

if she told him that what was *biting* her was the sight of him.

"Mosquitoes," she muttered obscurely. "So why're you shoeing the Westons' horses?"

"That's the way around here. I know shoeing, so I do that for some folks. Others know other things and help me out in return."

"You've got more horses to do?"

"Um-hmm. First Midnight, then Snakebit."

"Midnight's the one that was mean before Cambria got him?"

"Made mean."

"I don't understand."

"Horses aren't usually born mean. They're made mean, most often by one of two things—bad shoeing or bad people."

He stood slowly, and she couldn't take her eyes off the powerful, effortless movement as his thigh muscles shifted under the leather chaps. He stepped toward her. She backed toward the door.

"I better get going. Leave you to your work."

"No need."

"I have to… Um, I'll see you later, Dax."

"If you're going by the house, ask Cambria to come out would you? She's done a lot with Midnight, but I'd feel considerable better with her holding his head."

"Sure. I'll do that."

"Thanks. Then come on back."

Hannah had no intention of going back.

She had a cup of coffee with Irene, chatting about life after teenagers, while Cambria and Boone went to calm Midnight so Dax could shoe him. When Irene decided to go to Sheridan with Cambria and Boone, Hannah went to see the color chips and fabric swatches Irene had collected for redecorating the spare bedroom. "Cambria says you have a fine eye for color,'' Irene had said in urging her to review her choices.

An hour after they left, Hannah caught herself flipping through ranching magazines she'd found stacked on an end table in the back bedroom, and wondering about the life Dax Randall led.

That propelled her out of the room and four feet down the narrow, dim hall before the object of her speculations brought her up short. She recoiled from their near collision automatically, but still caught the scent of horse, clean sweat and sun-warmed skin, overlaid by freshly applied soap and water.

"Whoa, you okay, Hannah?''

All she could think was that the smudge on his jaw was gone.

"Hannah?''

"I'm fine. You startled me, that's all. I thought the house was empty. Everybody went to Sheridan.''

"I know. I wanted to check on you before I left. I thought you'd come back.''

All she'd said was "see you later,'' as meaningless a phrase as "I'll call you.'' But she could see he'd taken her at her word. And it occurred to Hannah that she faced a man who truly would call if he said he would.

"I was—'' She gestured toward the half-open door of the guest room, then clasped her hands in front of her. "Irene asked me to look at some paint colors she's trying.''

He showed no sign of interest in paint colors. She had the impression he had something else in mind, and she had the further impression that Dax didn't get easily side-tracked.

"I wanted to talk to you about last night.''

"You don't have to—''

"I didn't want you misunderstanding. About Will.''

"About Will?''

"It wasn't anything personal, his not looking happy about me taking an interest in you.''

"There's no need to—"

"Will doesn't want me to hold on too tight, but he's not ready to let go himself entirely."

"I know exactly what you mean." Their eyes met, sharing this understanding. "Mandy and Ethan went through the same thing the year they were fifteen. Mandy, especially. She was hardly home at all herself with all her activities at school, but she wanted to know that whenever she *did* come home, that I'd be there."

"Probably specially with your folks getting killed sudden like that."

"Yes, I'm sure that had a lot to do with it. But how did you know about...?"

"June."

"Oh." She nodded. "She does ask a lot of questions."

He gave a dry chuckle. "She could do security clearances for the CIA."

She smiled, and he returned another of those smiles that transformed his face. Her throat went dry; her lungs burned.

He stepped close enough to slide his warm hands around her elbows, then stroke the bare skin of her forearms. The tingling there bolted along her nerve endings, knotting the tips of her breasts and pooling at the pit of her stomach.

"Hannah."

He didn't ask a question, but he waited. For her. For a sign from her. Because he was about to kiss her.

Hannah stepped away so abruptly, his hands remained extended between them before they dropped to his side. His eyes burned hot for another instant, but what replaced it appeared to be a rueful sort of disappointment.

"Dax, I thought we had this clear last night."

"We had it clear you didn't think it was a good idea because of Will, but we've settled that. And you thought you'd be too busy working, but judging by today you'll have plenty of free time. So what's left is your not being comfortable with me, and that's—"

"It's not—"

"'—my fault for making a mess of asking. I know I'm a rough sort of man. Not like what you're used to."

"Oh, Dax, it's not that at all." If he only knew how refreshing she found his honesty, and how tempting she found him.

"Good, then you don't mind if I keep asking."

"I don't want to encourage you, Dax, when I really don't think—"

"A man who required a lot of encouraging wouldn't last long in ranching, Hannah. There's an expression 'round here, that during the hard times you work from can to can't." His gaze held hers as he tipped his hat, and the tingle returned, extending from her shoulders all the way along her spine and down to her toes.

"I've got a long way to go with this before I come near to can't, Hannah."

Chapter Three

I've got a long way to go with this before I come near to can't, Hannah.

Mighty fine talk from a man who hadn't asked a woman out on what he'd call a real date in closer to twenty years than ten. How could he show his son what an easy and natural thing it was for a man to take an interest in a woman when the woman didn't cooperate was beyond him. Give him a calf to brand, a fence to fix or a cow to doctor any day of the week.

June and her big ideas. Dax should have called her up at two-thirty in the morning and asked for an answer to that one.

Instead, he'd stayed in bed another hour and a half, staring at the ceiling, then got up to start the long, long day of bringing some of the cattle down from the mountains.

By the time he and Will got breakfast, gathered the necessary equipment, trailered up their horses and drove out to meet Ted Weston, Boone Smith and other neighbors and friends, enough light had spilled into the valley to start out on horseback to gather in the cows and start them to the lower grazing area where they'd spend the fall. In another month, he'd separate the calves from their mothers, getting them weaned. But today's business was moving them lower.

Up this high the air was as cold and clear as ice until the sun rose full to a brightness that could dazzle a man—at least a man whose hat brim didn't shade just so and whose eyes didn't tuck into an expert squint. The horses were fresh and eager, the ground solid and familiar, the companions reliable and enjoyable.

It should have been plenty to fill any man's thoughts.

Instead, as he moved easily in sync with Strider to keep the herd headed in the right direction, his thoughts stubbornly slid to a smile, a pair of hazel eyes and a froth of wind-whipped hair.

It didn't help when, along about midday, Boone let it drop that he and Cambria had tried to talk Hannah into joining in today to experience a cattle drive—even a short, partial-day one like this. Cambria wasn't going because of her advanced pregnancy, but Cully Grainger's nephew, Travis, and Jessa Tarrant were joining the riders. Hannah had turned them down.

But Dax had to wonder if she was passing up the experience or him.

Maybe he'd come on too strong. Maybe he shouldn't have let her know so bluntly that he wanted to spend time with her. But, dammit, he'd never been much for playing games or coming at a situation all twisting and sideways.

Still, Hannah Chalmers came from a different world. She probably wasn't used to tough old cowboys smelling of horses and barns, their hands all rough and their manners not much better. He'd better mend his ways if he wanted to spend time with a lady like her.

After they finished the day's work, and all the riders ate a potluck supper at the Circle CR as they'd done the past several years after bringing the herds lower, it wouldn't be real late—supper came early on a day that started with breakfast before five. He would shower and shave, pull on good jeans, shirt and boots, and try to gather his wits and some smooth words and go see Hannah Chalmers.

He had it all planned—except for the smooth words—when he and Will led the caravan of trailers into the open space between the Circle CR house and the barn. His sister and Irene Weston led some of the other women in setting out dishes on the three long tables set up under the line of cottonwoods behind the house.

But it wasn't Irene or June his eyes focused on.

It was Hannah Chalmers.

She wore jeans and a short-sleeved plaid blouse with that same sweater she'd had on at the Westons' cookout thrown over her shoulders. The breeze ruffled her hair around her face—the face she turned away to set another casserole dish on the table.

Her being here sent his whole plan out the window. He should have been disappointed—now he'd face her in all his dirt, smelling like cattle and horseflesh and without even a hope of finding some fine words. Definitely, he should have been disappointed. He wasn't ready to fix a brand to exactly what he did feel as he swung out of the truck cab and headed for the trailer gate to take care of the horses, but he knew it wasn't disappointment. Never in his life had his heart pounded like this from disappointment.

"Will, get started unloading the horses. I'll be right back."

"Where you going?"

Instead of answering, he repeated, "I'll be right back." Just because he was trying to show his son it was okay to be interested in females didn't mean he had to spell it out. Actions spoke louder than words, that's what they said, and he surely preferred actions to words. Usually.

"Dad?"

Dax heard Will's voice behind him, but kept walking toward the knot of activity around the tables.

Hannah turned with her hands full of a stack of heavy-duty paper plates and a plastic tumbler holding plastic utensils balanced on top. Dax Randall stood before her, silent, dark and right smack-dab in the middle of her path to the serving table. So much for thinking she wouldn't see much of him in the swirl of riders and supper-servers.

"Hi, Hannah."

He hadn't shaved. Stubble darkened the sharp line of his jaw without softening it in the least. His jeans were worn, his boots dusty, his chaps scarred. He looked like what he was—a man who'd spent a long, hard day in the saddle. A man used to spending long, hard days in the saddle. A man who liked spending long, hard days in the saddle.

He was the real thing that so many advertisements had tried to capture. Only it had nothing to do with what he wore or how he wore it. It had to do with the stark lines of his face and something in his eyes.

She had to swallow first, but her voice held steady. "Hello, Dax."

"I was going to clean up and come by to see you after supper."

"Oh." *Brilliant, Hannah.* Maybe Mandy was right. Maybe it was time for her to get back into the social whirl. If any man could make her feel this tongue-tied, maybe she did need practice. After all, she had to be at ease dealing with men—all men—in social situations to be effective in her job.

"Would you like to go riding tomorrow if the weather holds?"

"Oh, I..."

"Have you ridden much?"

"No. And not for years." That admission would probably end any thoughts of going riding, so why did she want to snatch the words back?

"Then this would be a good way to start. Not a full tour of the Big Horns like we talked about the other night, but a shorter ride into Kearny Canyon. It's an easy ride and not too long. I've gotta be back in good time to take Will for a meeting at the fairgrounds."

"That's a beautiful ride, especially this time of year," Cambria commented from over Hannah's shoulder.

Hannah moved to the side to let Cambria by. Cambria looked as if she would have liked to linger, but couldn't ignore the message.

With Cambria headed to the serving table, Hannah turned back to Dax. "I'm sure it is a beautiful ride and thank you for offering, but Boone should have work for me to do by then, and that is the first priority of this trip."

With one hand still holding a pair of weather-beaten rawhide gloves, he hooked his thumbs in the front pockets of his jeans. The veins stood out on his tough brown hands. Those blunt fingers spoke of strength and hard usage. They also happened to frame the line of his zipper—unintentionally, she was sure. But intentions hardly seemed to matter at the moment. Hannah swallowed. Hard.

"Sure, I understand."

He started to swing away from her, then stopped abruptly. She dragged her attention from below his belt and followed the direction of his gaze, not at all surprised to find that it led to his son, who had started to back a smoky gray horse out of the trailer.

Dax remained immobile for a moment, then turned to her so abruptly she took a half step back, setting the tumbler swaying atop the paper plates. Dax reached out and steadied the tumbler, an incongruously mundane action for a man with an expression of such fierce determination on his face.

"If Boone doesn't need you, the offer holds good. Show up around one. And if he does need you tomorrow, we'll do it another time."

"Dax, I—"

"Now that sounds like a reasonable offer," Irene said from over Hannah's shoulder. What was going on? Was there a line of people behind her waiting to add a comment to her conversation with Dax Randall?

"It's a very kind offer," Hannah started, "but—"

"In the meantime, Dax, why don't you show Hannah around the place before it gets too dark to see? We're all set here, just waiting for the meat to cook now that you riders are all back," Irene added, stymieing Hannah's protest that she had to help get the supper things ready.

So she turned her appeal to Dax. "There's no need. I know you have things you have to—"

"I'd like to."

"I'll take these—" Irene removed the plates and tumbler smoothly from Hannah's hands "—and you two go look around. We ring the bell when supper's ready. You've got plenty of time."

Dax strode to the gate in the fence that separated the rough lawn surrounding the house from the dirt driveway, and pushed it open. Only then did he look back.

What choice did she have short of being rude? She walked through the open gateway. "Thank you."

"You're welcome. Will!" Dax called out as they crossed to where he'd parked his truck and dusty horse trailer. His son was stepping the gray horse down the final feet of the trailer ramp. Will turned as he and the horse reached level ground, shot her a disgruntled look, then focused on his father's instructions. "Put salve on that scratch on Strider's flank before you let 'em loose. I'm going to show Ms. Chalmers around the place a bit. You remember Ms. Chalmers?"

Will bestowed on her the briefest nod possible, missing eye contact by a yard. "I think Merc's right hock might be swelling again. You better check it, Dad."

Dax immediately moved to the gray horse's hindquarters, said something low-voiced and calm that made the horse turn its head toward him, then turn away in trusting unconcern. Dax put his hand on the horse's rump, then ran it slowly over the animal's hip and down to what Hannah would have called the knee portion of the horse's back leg. He bent over, the line of his jeans drawing tight across his rear end.

Hannah turned away, determinedly smiling at Will Randall even though he couldn't see it with his back to her. "Hi, Will. Please, call me Hannah."

Dax frowned as he straightened, but she thought it was at Will's barely mumbled answer, not at her suggestion or his horse's condition. "Feels fine to me," he said to his son. "Did you hear, Will? Say hello to Ms. Chalmers, er, Hannah."

"Hello." It wasn't much above a mumble.

"It's nice to see you again, Will. It sounds like from what everybody's been telling me that you've had quite a day—up before sunrise and moving the cattle all day."

"Yeah, well, I better tend the horses now."

Dax's frown deepened. Hannah didn't let her smile falter when the boy turned on his heel and walked away.

She chattered on to cover Will's terseness. "So, Dax, what are you going to show me first?"

With a final glance over his shoulder toward Will, Dax tucked his hands in his back pockets as they headed toward the barn. He ushered her through a covered walkway that connected the slope-roofed red barn and a small log building with a pair of dust-dulled windows—the shoeing shed, Dax called it. Beyond that they came to a long, narrow metal building. "The cow barn," he said. "For animals sick or having trouble calving."

"The horses get the other barn?"

"In real bad weather. Otherwise they're in the corral." He dipped his head toward a fenced-in area that one side of the barn opened into, then a separate, large fenced-in area across from the barn. "Or the pasture."

"And the other buildings?"

He ticked down a list of sheds, barns, granaries and fuel

storage tanks as she tried to follow the small tips of his head.

"It's quite a complex."

"Not like big spreads. But even little ones gotta be able to go for a stretch without running to town for everything." He looked around. "C'mon. You can see from up there."

He circled her arm just above the elbow and started her up the incline that rose behind the house. His hand was warm and solid and slightly rough against her skin. If she became this breathless from going uphill, she was out of shape. On the other hand, if she became this breathless and it *wasn't* from going uphill she was *really* out of shape.

"June said y'all do this every year, but— What? What are you grinning about?" she asked. It was more a lifting of one side of his mouth than a full-out grin, but still nice.

"*Y'all.*"

"It's a perfectly good word."

They'd stopped beneath a quartet of cottonwood trees on a leveled-off section. Another incline rose behind them, and below them she could see several more, gentler gradations, like shallow steps for a giant. The single-story frame house and main barn sat on one, then the other outbuildings on the next lower one, and lower again came a stretch of cultivated fields on either side of the road from the highway.

"Sure. It just seemed, I don't know, kind of cute when you said it."

"Cute?" She tried to sound peeved. "Don't let Cully or Boone hear you say that. They're good North Carolina boys and they use it, too."

He grinned at her, full out this time, and the tingle between her shoulders hit full force. "Don't think it would sound the same coming from their mouths."

His brown eyes darkened as they focused on her lips. She couldn't stop the tiny expulsion of air that escaped between them—surprise, she tried to tell herself. Dax blinked, met her eyes for an instant as short and powerful as a shimmer of lightning, then turned away. She thought she'd seen a hint of deeper color across his sharp cheek-bones.

Oh, Lord, she truly was out of training for this man-woman stuff. Her lungs felt as if she'd been running for miles and it took more discipline than she possessed to keep from twitching her shoulders against the tingle. He'd only *looked* at her, for heaven's sake. And she'd looked back.

"Uh, what were you asking?"

Drawn away from other thoughts by his gravel-voiced question, she tried to concentrate. "Asking…? Oh. About this get-together every year with your neighbors."

"More often than every year and it's more than a get-together. A lot of ranching these days can be done without a lot of hands. But sometimes you need more people. Moving cattle's one of those times. So in the spring when we move the cows up the mountains for better summer grazing and come fall when we bring them back down, it makes sense for people to work together, 'stead of everybody thrashing around up on the mountain trying to find only their cows."

"You make it sound like this—" her gesture took in the group gathering amid the tables below them, with called hellos punctuating the general burble of conversation "—is a totally practical thing."

"It is."

Just then a gust of laughter reached them from the group around the fire. She quirked an eyebrow at him. "You're saying they're not having fun?"

"Didn't say that. Practical *is* fun for ranchers."

"Right. So, why does everybody come here to eat after moving the cattle?"

"Now it's because the Circle CR is closest to the mountains, so we can get to the chow faster and no one has to backtrack to get home afterward. Back when I first had Will I think the women worried about him getting enough food. Come to think of it, that might still be the reason. All the women in the valley have always fussed over Will. Feel sorry for him having to rely on me as cook.''

"I can't imagine anyone feeling sorry for Will for having you as a father.'' She hadn't meant to sound so serious, and rushed out a new set of words to lay over those. "I mean, he seems awfully healthy to me. Besides, I suspect Will's not the only reason.''

He questioned her with a look.

"Maybe they're worried about you, too, Dax. Want to check up on you. Want to make sure you're doing okay.''

The idea startled him—that was clear from the arrested expression in his eyes. That was followed by a moment of consideration, as if he might be running back scenes from the past in his mind and seeing them in a new light. He looked over his shoulder toward the gathering near his house that kept growing as riders finished tending their horses and contemplated their own stomachs.

"They know I can take care of myself.''

His words were brusque, a bit embarrassed, but she heard something more in them. Hadn't he ever considered that his neighbors might be truly and deeply fond of him?

Even as he seemed to recognize the possibility, it struck her as sad—and lonely—that he hadn't seen that affection surrounding him before. Why?

Not that it was her place to wonder such things, she reminded herself firmly. She turned and gestured to the house. "June told me that this is quite an old homestead.''

"More than a hundred years. That's old for whites around here.''

"More than a hundred...but the house didn't look anywhere near that old.''

"It isn't. Homestead's the land, not the buildings. This homestead started when the first ranchers came into the area, but my father built this house in the fifties. He made a lot of improvements to the place,'' he said in a neutral tone. A fair man giving credit where credit was due. "Then when I took over, I updated again.''

"Oh, so there's nothing left of the original buildings?"

"Some. But it's hard to see." He tipped his head toward a small barn on the level below the present house. "That's built around the original house. Didn't know it until it needed repairs a few years ago and I found old newspapers tacked on the walls. They used to use that for insulation."

"You'd never noticed the newspapers before?"

"Weren't visible before. Somebody built over the original log walls, inside and out—sandwiched the old building with new walls."

"Why would they do that?"

"Save them having to tear down the old building or design a new one. The danger is sometimes those old walls fall apart or rot away, and they can take down the new construction with them."

"Is that why your father built the new house?"

"I don't know."

And he obviously didn't want to speculate about it. Hannah cast around for something else to talk about. The wind kicked up and she noticed something swaying to the side of the big pasture.

"What on earth is that?"

"It's a bull."

Hannah raised her eyebrows at him. "Dax, I might not know much about cattle, but I do know the difference between a bull and an oil drum strung up between a couple of posts."

He grinned. Oh, dear. She really wished he wouldn't do that. It just wasn't fair.

"A practice bull. To work on technique and keep in shape between rodeos."

"You compete in rodeos?"

"Used to some. Now it's only a few of the local amateur rodeos. Mostly roping. Will's doing some bull riding, though. He uses that to practice."

"I didn't realize…I mean, isn't Will kind of young?"

"Don't let him hear you say that. Besides, boys 'round

here mostly start rodeoing as soon as they can ride pretty good, and some of 'em start riding soon as they can walk."

"Did you?"

"Before I could walk."

She thought he might be joking, but an edge to the words made her unsure. She usually read most people well, figured out what they thought beneath the surface of what they said. She had to in her job, to assess how someone truly reacted to a slogan or a copy block or a campaign. But Dax Randall wasn't most people. And she had a feeling that, in addition to not saying much in the first place, he didn't let many people figure out what he truly thought.

It was an unsettling feeling, like being a lost tourist in a foreign country where she didn't understand the road signs.

It also made the insights she'd gleaned a little unnerving. Had he purposely let her see more deeply into him? No, she didn't think so, though she couldn't have said why. So if she'd read those signs right, how had she done it?

"Rodeo's part of the life out here," he said more easily. "Bet you had a basketball backboard in your neighborhood back in North Carolina."

"In our driveway," she said with a smile, happy to be led away from her own thoughts.

He nodded. "Oil drum bulls and wood pieces knocked together to look like a calf's head to practice ropin' show up in yards here the way you'd see basketball hoops back East. Part of the landscape."

"Do you get back East often?"

His mouth twitched, quirking up slightly on one side. Or was that the trick of the changed light as he turned from the red glow dropping behind the Big Horns to the west and stared off to the darkening eastern horizon? "Well," he drawled. "I get back to Nebraska now and then."

She spluttered with laughter, then caught herself with a choking sound as his face remained absolutely deadpan. Oh, no, he meant it, and she'd laughed in his face, she'd—

No, wait. Was his mouth twitching again? And there,

deep in those solemn brown eyes, was that a glint of deviltry?

If not, then she was about to end her internal hemming and hawing about whether she wanted Dax Randall's apparent interest in her to be real or not. Because nothing could end a man's interest in a woman faster and more completely than laughing in his face when he was serious. He would recoil. Get huffy. Find a sudden need to change the oil in his truck. Anything to get away.

She stopped holding back, and her laughter spilled out.

Dax didn't laugh. He didn't smile. He didn't grin.

But she saw the glow in his eyes. She saw it clearly because he'd moved closer. Very close. Close enough to…

Her breath hitched as another spurt of laughter—did it sound a bit nervous to him, too?—swayed her away from him. For an instant, he paused. Then he lowered his head, pursuing her lips.

He was going to kiss her.

Their noses met before their mouths. A flash of fear that he'd give up then, daunted by the awkwardness, disappeared when he changed the angle of his head and put his mouth over hers.

She'd had better kisses. She was sure she had.

Practiced, smooth, well-thought-out-in-advance kisses. In far more romantic surroundings than by a patch of weeds under some scraggly trees, with barn smells filtering into the crisp air. They'd bumped noses, for heaven's sake. Not a slight jostling, but an honest to goodness thump. Hard enough that she still saw stars behind her closed eyelids…or had they come after his mouth covered hers? Things were a little vague. The sensations were not.

His mouth pressed firmly against hers. Slightly dry at first, with a faint taste of trail dust not completely washed away. Then the taste was purely Dax, both complex and straightforward. His beard prickled under the palm she put to his cheek, too strong to tickle, yet too gentle to hurt. The sound of it blended in her ears with the rasp of his breathing and a faint, rumbling sound from deep in his chest.

The kiss was like Dax—a little rough, a little awkward, a lot confusing. But also honest and appealing and drawing her deeper and deeper. Until she felt limp and breathless.

He released her mouth as they both gulped in air, taking in each other's oxygen, but he didn't straighten or move away. His body and the brim of his hat, tilted from the angle of his head still poised to kiss her, cocooned her. She felt an urge to bury her face in his shoulder and feel his arms go around her.

"Hannah."

She'd expected some reflection of her own confusion in his eyes. Instead, she saw a heat that burned away everything else. Including her protection.

She stepped back.

His eyelids lowered, remained down for half a dozen heartbeats, then raised to reveal a wariness as deep as the first time she'd met him.

She swallowed down an unreasoning sadness and said, "We'd, uh, better get back."

"Yes."

The bell calling everyone to dinner rang as they weaved among the parked trucks and vans in silence.

Kissing Hannah was a mistake.

He should have quit while he was ahead.

Hell, he would have been better off if he'd quit while he was behind.

He almost had. He'd asked, she'd said no, and he'd started to walk away, telling himself that he'd tried. He could be content with that. He could let it go with some vague comment about another time, and be out of the whole thing.

Then he had caught sight of Will by the horse trailer, looking their way and pretending not to. Will watching how he got on with a female. And what would he see? His father turning tail at the first opportunity.

He hadn't taught Will to give up easily, not with a horse or a math problem or roping a calf or fixing an engine. Females were no different. One try didn't cut it.

So he hadn't given up. And she hadn't said no—at least not absolutely.

Then Irene had given him the chance to talk to Hannah some more alone. And it hadn't been going too badly. Nothing to spark a range fire, but he hadn't tripped over his tongue, either.

Until she laughed.

It was like that time at Bardville Elementary when Mrs. Brachi played the *Hallelujah Chorus* the first time he ever heard it and it didn't matter it was on that tinny portable record player, the music went straight down his backbone. So had Hannah's laugh. He'd wanted to be part of it, to taste it, to taste her.

He'd been as awkward as a schoolboy with that kiss. Fumbling like he'd never had his mouth on a woman's.

But that wasn't why he shouldn't have kissed her.

It was because of what happened when their mouths did meet. The heat that roared through his blood and shimmered in his muscles.

No, he shouldn't have kissed Hannah Chalmers. It had been a mistake.

He wondered if he'd have the chance to make that mistake again.

Chapter Four

"You should take Dax up on his offer." As she gave the advice, Cambria looked over her shoulder to where Hannah sat at the Westons' kitchen table. Then she turned back to pour Hannah a mug of coffee and herself a mug of herbal tea.

"I'd have to be crazy to consider, even for a second, getting involved with someone in a vacation romance—not that I'm on vacation, because as I've told Boone, I fully expect to work my regular hours while I'm out here. But he isn't giving me enough to do. Maybe I should call the office—"

Cambria clunked the mug down in front of her. "Forget the office. Get back to the topic at hand."

"Topic at hand?"

"Dax Randall."

"Oh." She took a long swallow of very hot coffee. Great, now she had a burned tongue, watery eyes and a too-interested-for-comfort Cambria Weston Smith—and that could definitely come under the heading of playing with fire. Cambria didn't miss much, and she didn't pull her punches. Hannah shook her head and repeated. "I'd have to be crazy to even consider *thinking* about such a thing."

Talk about playing with fire...

Dax Randall definitely qualified. Or at least her reaction to him qualified. One kiss, and she'd been burning.

"Hmm." Cambria considered Hannah over the rim of her mug as she sipped the tea. "I meant Dax's offer to take you riding up into Kearny Canyon today, but apparently he's been making much more interesting offers, too."

"No, no—you're right. Riding..." Hannah said, feeling incredibly inept. "That's what I'm talking about, too. His offer to take me riding today. But with work and all, I really don't think—"

"I don't want to butt in." Cambria seemed not to hear Hannah's involuntary snort. "But I like you and I like Dax. I don't want to give you the wrong impression about him. What I said about it being strange that he took such an interest in you at the cookout—I didn't want you to misunderstand. Usually Dax stays to himself when it comes to women. Sometimes he's sidestepping someone chasing him. I can tell you, I've known him most of my life, and I have never seen Dax Randall go after a woman the way he's pursuing you."

"Oh, surely that's an exaggeration," Hannah said with a fair assumption of airiness. Curiosity tempted her into adding, "He must have pursued the woman he married, Will's mother."

Cambria snorted. "It's real clear you never met Elaine Mansson Randall, or you'd know different."

Cambria took a swallow of tea, and Hannah expected that to be the end of it. Cambria didn't indulge in gossip. Neither did she. Sure, she was curious about the woman Dax had married, but she wouldn't pry.

So she kept silent while Cambria gave her a long, assessing look, then transferred her gaze to the contents of her mug while tapping a fingernail against the side.

When Cambria started talking again, Hannah found herself holding her breath. "Elaine went to school over on the other side of Sheridan, but her aunt lived in Bardville, and she spent a lot of time in town. I was a few years behind Elaine in school, and she was a couple years behind Dax. He came home from college one Christmas and she hit him like a Mack truck. Not long after, she told him she was pregnant. He married her. Before long he knew she'd lied, but by then he'd taken her to Dallas, then Denver. At first she was satisfied because getting to a city was what she'd always wanted."

A guilty internal voice told Hannah she should stop Cambria from telling her these things about Dax. She felt almost disloyal to him for listening.

"That didn't last long. With Dax still trying to go to school part-time, money was short and that didn't suit her. When she got pregnant for real, he quit school, but then Elaine got the jolt of her life when Dax laid down the law, making her take care of herself during her pregnancy—no drinking, no staying out late—and coming back to the ranch when his father died and left it to him. That happened right after Will was born.

"Elaine walked out when Will was not even a year old. She never came back. Never had any contact with Will. Word came about eight years ago that she'd died in an accident."

Hannah wrapped both hands around her coffee mug, trying to draw some warmth from it to combat the chill inside at the thought of Will—and Dax—being so thoroughly deserted by a woman who should have loved them.

"Dax was never one to chase the girls, but after Elaine... I'm not saying he's lived a monklike existence," Cambria added dryly. "But he's kept a thick wall up against nice, eligible single women. Until you."

Despite herself, hearing that his overtures to her were

something extraordinary brought a deeper, richer warmth to Hannah's blood than coffee had ever managed. How tempting to think she was special to Dax Randall. Even though it was foolish.

"Cambria, it's not like that. He's nice to me and he answers my questions about ranching and asks about my life—" *And when his lips touch mine I forget not only what we're talking about, but where I am and complex things like how to stand and breathe.* "And even if it were, uh, like that, I wouldn't be interested. I'm not prepared to get involved and I'm not interested in a vacation fling."

"Sure, sure, you told me that before." Cambria tilted her head slightly and raised her eyebrows. Hannah had once seen a cat who'd cornered a mouse with that identical expression on its face. "But since it's not *like that,* there's no harm in taking him up on his offer to go riding, is there? It's a great way to see some beautiful country. It's as simple as that."

Hannah perused the big-boned spotted horse in front of her from its black-splotched nose to its scraggly tail. In between came a very broad—and very high—back. She was expected to sit on that? Even when it moved?

How had she let Cambria talk her into this? True, her boss's wife's logic had backed her into a corner and her boss had thrown away the key by declaring he had absolutely nothing for her to do this afternoon. But that didn't mean she had to actually drive to the Circle CR and present herself at one o'clock with a declaration that she intended to take Dax up on his offer to show her Kearny Canyon.

It had seemed brave and devil-may-care at the time, and a way to prove to Cambria that her suspicions were totally unfounded. Now it seemed like one of her less successful decisions.

"He's awful big."

"Spock's the mildest horse we've got."

Dax sounded reassuring, but he hadn't looked at her directly since she'd first driven up. Maybe that was just as well. He'd rather unnerved her when he'd slowly turned at the sound of her car climbing the incline to the barn area. He'd watched the car—or maybe her inside the car, she hadn't been able to tell—with a steady, complete stare until she'd gotten out and started toward him.

"Spock?"

"'Star Trek.' The ears. Will named him. Then he started naming horses after space missions. Mercury, that's his gray mare. And that—" Dax tipped his head to an adjoining corral where a young horse of a burnished red watched them with great interest "—is Apollo."

"So Will's interested in space?"

"Was. You ready?"

She was nervous, but not nervous enough to miss that switch of subject. But it could wait. She had more immediate concerns. She eyed the distance from the ground to the stirrup and from the stirrup to the horse's back.

"Do you have something I can stand on?"

"Me." Loosely holding Spock's reins in his left hand, he moved beside her, bent one knee and squatted slightly, presenting his well-muscled thigh as a nearly level surface. He patted the denim faded nearly to gray better than halfway up his thigh. "Right here."

"I don't think—"

His right hand wrapped around her upper arm and drew her toward him.

"Left foot. Now."

She succumbed to the command in his voice and put her left foot where he said. Her hand went to his shoulder automatically for balance. Just as automatically, she recognized the solid power that rested below her hand. As she bent her other knee to get more lift, her toes nearly nestled in the crease between his thigh and crotch. Between that and his straightening as she started to jump, she had more than enough lift.

She dropped in the saddle with a soft "oof." Spock

twitched his tail and sighed patiently. Hannah found that
very reassuring. She took the reins from Dax and searched
for the stirrups with her toes. He tugged on the straps of
the saddle and stirrups, checking the fit, while she carefully
did not look at him. He had swung up into his saddle and
maneuvered the tan horse with the black tail and mane that
he called Strider next to her before she settled.

"We'll take it slow, Hannah."

For an instant, she thought his words referred to something other than their ride. Then he went on.

"But if something happens, hang on to the horn and
Spock'll find his way home."

Startled, she looked up. "What could happen?"

He shrugged. "Probably nothing. But you can't count on
probably. If you're on foot, follow the water." He gestured
toward the line of water parallel to the road that she might
not have noticed amid clumps of pasture grass if it hadn't
enjoyed the company of cottonwood trees in spots.

"The stream?"

"Irrigation ditch." Count on Dax Randall not to pretty
up the terminology. "'Round here, long as you follow water, you'll 'most always come out somewhere. There's not
so much water that we can let any go nowhere."

"Now you're really worrying me."

"No need." He tipped his head back. "Clouds look
clear."

"You read clouds?"

"Folks out here do. You *should* be worried if you went
off with someone who didn't respect the sky and land. And
real worried if you went off with someone who didn't tell
you how to get back on your own."

The corner of his mouth tucked in and a gleam of amusement glinted from his dark eyes. Oh, yes, Dax Randall was
one attractive cowboy when he let himself be.

Spock's loose, slightly rolling motion let her relax
enough to expand her field of vision farther than between
his ears.

They headed west, toward the rumpled spine of the Big Horn Mountains. Sweeps of green fir trees jostled with patches of silvered tan of dried range grass. At the peaks, she noticed splotches of white. Snow. It was hard to remember on a golden, warm day like this that fall approached. Occasional slashes of rock's lighter color indicated the canyon clefts left by eons of that melting snow.

Movement caught her eye and, for an instant, she thought she was seeing things—that one of those green sweeps shifted places on the mountain. Ah, now she saw that the patch of dark was the shadow of a cloud passing silently across the blue sky. It fascinated her. She watched the shape shift and change as it flowed over the rolling ground, disappearing behind the rise in front of them, then bursting over it and engulfing them.

The air around her cooled, but only for an instant, then the shadow moved on and sunlight bathed them once more. Twisting in the saddle, she watched the cloud and its shadow continue their busy progress. When she turned back, she realized she was smiling. She would never use a moment like that in an advertising campaign—it was too ephemeral, too vague, too odd. But she felt connected to this land in a way she hadn't a few minutes ago.

"How long has your family had this ranch?" She had turned to face Dax to ask the question and found him watching her.

"Nearly fifty years this time."

"This time?"

"My great-great-grandfather started this ranch. He homesteaded the land from there—" He pointed behind them to the skeleton of a huge cottonwood, still impressive despite broken off limbs. "To the road. The next couple generations added to it some, mostly up." He tipped his head toward the mountains that rose above and around them. "Valley land cost more."

He appeared totally at home on horseback, his rear settled well into the saddle, his back straight but relaxed, his leg slightly bent at the knee, the reins resting in his left hand. He looked around, apparently at ease as Strider walked along beside Spock. Yet she sensed that one sound, one movement, one thought, could spark both horse and rider. She was almost tempted...just to see it.

"What happened?"

"My great-grandfather built the place up, then my grandfather sold it and moved his family to town when my father was a teenager. He swore the day they moved that he'd get the place back, and he did. But he didn't forgive his father. Claimed my grandfather sold his birthright because he wanted an easier life."

"How old were you when the family moved back to the ranch?"

"Happened before I was born."

"Your father must have loved this land."

"More than anything living."

The way he said it chilled Hannah. Totally uninflected, as matter-of-fact as if he'd said the sky was blue. Not a bitter or harsh note crept in, yet he had as good as said that his father had loved the land more than he'd loved his family.

"So that's how you learned about ranching, by working with your father?"

"Until I was old enough to leave."

"But you came back because you thought it was the right thing to do for Will?"

"Yup."

A single, laconic syllable that somehow told the story of a man who dearly loved his son. If he thought something was the right thing to do for Will, he needed no more reason to do it. The missing element in his accounting remained Will's mother.

And for that matter, what about Dax's mother? She lived in town with June Reamer, that's what Irene Weston had said, so why didn't she figure into Dax's history? What had happened to her?

"You must not have hated ranching too much if you came back to bring your son up here."

"Never said I hated ranching."

No, he'd escaped his father, not this land, during the years in the city he'd told her about the first night. That was clear. And very sad. Hannah thought of her father, of strong hands wrapped gently over hers to teach her how to grip a tennis racket, of a beaming face in the audience of her sophomore play, of a strong arm under her hand as she walked down the aisle to marry Richard.

The man beside her apparently had no comparable memories.

"June and your mother live in town together, right? So you must see your mother—"

"Gets steeper here, we better go single file. I'll lead."

And that just goes to show that Dax Randall is fully capable of slamming a door in your face even in the middle of the great out-of-doors, Hannah thought.

The path narrowed to a track worn deep into the rock and barely as wide as Spock. On their right, rock rose in a hillside topped with what resembled the works of a mad stone mason with pretensions of topiary—her imaginative eye spotted open archways, gigantic toadstools and crumbling castle towers.

The trail curved away from the water, circling a boulder about the size of a house. When they came back to the water, the continued irrigation ditch had widened and grown noisier. It rushed over a rock-strewn bed, protesting the impediments in its path vocally and with froths of irritation. Hannah saw that the irrigation ditch they had followed was a minor offshoot of this stream. The water came down from the mountains to their right, dividing behind the huge rock they'd circled, with the main part curving to the south and the ditch heading east.

"Thought we'd rest here awhile. If you want," Dax added as an apparent afterthought.

"Yes. This is lovely."

He dismounted in one fluid motion, then held Spock's head while she slid down with considerably less grace but no catastrophes.

"There's a blanket and some food in here," he said, handing her a leather pack he unstrapped from behind his horse's saddle. He also unhooked a canteen, which he set on a well-shaded rock. "I'll tend the horses."

She stood where he'd left her, and watched as he led the horses through the rocks bordering the water. When they'd had their fill, he took them to an open area to one side of where she'd left him but within sight. He squatted down, first by Strider's front legs, then by Spock's, doing something with lengths of leather with a series of buckles. When he straightened, she saw he'd hobbled their legs, limiting their wandering ability.

Only then did he turn to her.

He frowned slightly, apparently in puzzlement. "You okay?"

"I'm fine, why?"

"Thought maybe your legs…? Thought you'd have the blanket spread and the food out."

"Well, my legs do feel as if they're having trouble adjusting to no longer being molded to that saddle. They're not used to being in that position." As soon as the words left her mouth, she knew they were a mistake, sparking images of what might put her legs in a similar position. He flicked a look at her, but said nothing. He didn't have to. Her face burned and that blender kicked up a fuss in her stomach. "I mean they're sort of wobbly, but I guess I just didn't know the chores you expected me to perform. The women's work, I suppose."

Being careful not to make eye contact, she pulled the blanket from the top of the pack and shook it out. Dax caught the opposite side in midair and stretched it so it came to the ground smoothly.

"Hannah, I didn't mean—I'm no great talker. Never have been, and now I'm rusty—"

"No, I'm sorry, Dax. I shouldn't have snapped at you. I got caught up in watching you—what you were doing," she added hurriedly. Her leg muscles protested as she sat tailor-fashion on the blanket, then relaxed. The guilt of taking out her embarrassment on him would take longer to ease. "Why not tie their reins to a branch?"

"You can lose a lot of reins that way. If anything startles them enough to run, they'll snap leather reins." He handed her a small apple he pulled out of the pack as he spoke. "And anything that moves can startle them."

He bit into his own apple, then held it between his teeth as he pulled out a large plastic bag filled with nuts and dried fruit, then a plastic bottle of water. He handed her the water. "June thought you'd prefer this to a canteen." Before she could answer around the bite she'd taken of her own tart, juicy apple, he went on. "Ninety-nine leaves can blow across their path without any bother, and the hundredth one comes along and you'd think it was a tornado, fire and flood rolled into one."

"Can't they wander away?"

"Yeah. Some even get pretty good at running with hobbles. But usually slows 'em down enough that you can catch 'em." The twitch at the corner of his mouth appeared. "Especially Spock."

She grinned at him. "Just my speed."

They finished their apples without conversation, but not in silence. The water, the breeze and the birds had plenty of comments to fill their ears. She started to tuck the apple core into a plastic bag to throw out when they got back, but Dax stopped her with a hand to her wrist.

"We've got our own recycling system out here. C'mon." He stood easily and tugged her wrist so she joined him, still holding the sticky core between her ring finger and her thumb. His hand easily encircled her wrist. His touch was warm and firm.

Spock lifted his head. Strider kept grazing.

"Hold your hand out," Dax ordered. She hesitated. She

had the oddest urge to hold her wrist immobile, as if moving it might break some invisible force field. He clearly had no such qualms. He molded his big palm across the back of her hand and tipped it so the core faced up. "Put it in your palm." The core dropped to her palm. "Keep your hand flat. Like this."

He curled the tips of his fingers over hers and bent them back gently, so her palm arched up, offering the apple core to Spock. Soft, moist lips with tickling whiskers brushed across her palm and delicately removed the core.

Without releasing her hand, Dax put the remains of his apple, which he'd held in his other hand, onto her palm. "Now Strider."

The horse raised its head at hearing its name, or perhaps at sensing the potential for plunder. Before Hannah could blink, Strider's black-maned head swooped down and she felt the same sensation of soft, moist lips and tickling whiskers across her sensitive palm, but this time a new sensation followed, like being attached to the business end of a vacuum cleaner.

Half startled, half amused, she made a sound, and Dax immediately cupped her core-offering hand protectively in his and stepped between her and Strider

"You okay?" he demanded.

"I'm fine." She chuckled as she straightened her hand, still resting inside Dax's. "He obviously believes in the motto 'good to the last drop.' I don't think he left an atom of that apple."

Dax stroked the pad of his thumb slowly across her palm. Maybe to make sure it was okay, the same way he'd run his hand down the leg of the horse named Merc yesterday evening. But she was positive Merc hadn't reacted the same way—with a shiver that skittered from her palm, up her arm, across her shoulders, then straight to the tips of her breasts.

"Greedy." Dax's voice came as a low rumble. His eyes met hers a moment, then his gaze dropped. She couldn't be sure where he focused, but her nipples tightened abruptly, as if *they* were sure.

"Wha—what?"

Dax cleared his throat. "Strider. He's greedy when it comes to apples."

Hannah muttered something she suspected was both unintelligible and unintelligent, withdrew her hand from Dax's unresisting hold and wiped it down the side of her jeans. That removed the slight remnants of apple stickiness and horse kiss, but it did not stop the tingling.

Rusty, he'd said? Maybe. But beneath the rust, Dax Randall had plenty of top quality raw material to work with.

As they returned to their seats on the blanket, she looked around to keep herself from considering that raw material too closely.

Bushes and trees turning to autumn shades of gold and lemon with flashes of orange hugged the creek's banks, apparently more grateful for the water than the boulders and rocks that battled it. At a curve in the creek, a lone tree leaned over the water as if trying to reach the other side. Rough, sage-speckled slopes rose sharply, stepping back so the sky opened wide above them.

The sunlight glowed off the bright-colored vegetation like a beacon and glinted clear fireworks off the water.

She lifted her face to the sky. A speck in the clear blue left a thin trail. A jet heading west.

"Think of everything those people are missing."

"What people?"

She gestured to the jet. "The ones who consider anything between New York and L.A. fly-by territory. The ones who think it's all a wasteland of boredom to be suffered through with drinks, phone calls back to the office and free movies they belittle. The ones like my ex-husband."

Odd how she could see her ex-husband more clearly from here than she had even from North Carolina. Maybe the deep hurt and disappointment had clouded her vision of their past, even after the twins filled her life.

"What's he do?"

"Advertising."

"Like you, huh?"

She sat straighter. "No."

Her vehemence didn't seem to bother Dax, but it surprised her. Everything inside her objected to his thinking she was like her ex-husband, someone she'd once been so sure she loved. *How sad.*

On the other hand, as a sign that she was well and truly divorced emotionally from a marriage that had probably been over even before Richard had given her the ultimatum of caring for her brother and sister or staying married to him, it felt a lot more final than any legal papers.

"I'm not like him at all," she said firmly.

"Guess advertising's a pretty high-powered business."

"It can be, but it's not all high-powered."

She saw his skepticism in the tilt of his head.

"It's not. Not what I did. Richard used to say I was to advertising what legal-aid lawyers are to the legal system. To his mind, we both dealt with the dregs."

"Richard." He didn't make it a question; in fact, he gave the word no inflection at all. Maybe he wanted to know about her ex-husband, maybe not. It didn't matter. Such a beautiful a day shouldn't include talk of Richard.

"I *liked* representing the nonprofits. It was rewarding to sell a product I believed in. So what if the resources were thin and everything had to be done on the cheap? I liked the challenge. And when a campaign succeeded, I felt good, really good. No twinges to the conscience like when…"

"Like when what?" He settled his hat brim low over his eyes.

"I guess like when I started. When I worked for a big firm." Where she'd met Richard. Where he continued to ascend the ladder. Why hadn't she seen how uncomfortable the atmosphere where he thrived had made her from the start? She had been naive and blind to ever have thought she could change him.

"It's like judging all of Texas on that old TV show 'Dallas.' There's a lot of Texas that's not like that."

"Some is."

Lord, the man was stubborn. "But not me," she said, answering his real question. "I don't want to be on that jet, sipping scotch, wishing it would go faster so I could get to the next power lunch or client dinner. I'm happy to be right here."

She dropped back against the blanket with her hands crossed under her head. The earth held a summer's worth of warmth to cradle her back, the sunshine rested on her skin like silk, the sky dazzled her eyes. She was completely happy.

"This is the kind of day I'd like to bottle up and save," she said.

"If you bottled it up, it wouldn't be the same. It has to be wide-open like this to be real."

She shifted and squinted against the sun, but she could see only his profile. "You're right, Dax. You're absolutely right."

"Happens like that by accident sometimes."

She laughed, and when he turned and looked down at her, with the shadow cast by his upper body and hat shielding her eyes from the sun, she knew he was grinning even though she couldn't see his face. "I think it's more than accident. I think it's a matter of somebody paying very close attention to what's around him."

"Could be something in that. There're a lot of lessons nature can teach if we're paying attention."

She was paying attention. Right this moment. To the part of nature that hummed through her nerve endings and pulsed in her blood. She became aware of her breasts rising and falling with each breath. A flash of an image heated her mind, of what it might feel like if he leaned down, his weight pressing against her breasts, his mouth—

He twisted around, so he faced off to the distance, and the sun dazzled her eyes.

"Some of the lessons are hard." His voice rasped with a note that hadn't been there before. "On a day like this you can forget the days when the land and the weather and the animals all seem like they're out to bring you to your knees if they don't kill you outright."

She sat up. It felt safer. "But you stay, anyway."

"Only thing I know how to do."

She peered into the shadow cast by his hat. "You'd really want to leave?"

"Only in a pine box."

"That's what I thought. That's the feeling I get from Ted and Irene Weston, too. But if it's such a hard life...?"

"It's hard all right. The land's hard. But it's mostly fair. It doesn't make promises it won't keep." The bitter note echoed deep in his voice again, and she wondered what broken promises had spawned it. "And there's something about it—it's you and nobody else. You're responsible. You carry the load. When you're out here you can see what life's really about, see how it all fits together. I can't explain it."

She thought he explained it beautifully, but she feared if she said anything, if she moved, if she let the tears pooling in her eyes fall, maybe even if she breathed, he'd remember he had an audience beyond himself and he'd stop.

"You're producing something real, seeing it grow, knowing it will feed people out in the world, not just line your pocket. End of the day comes and you're feeling like you haven't got a bone that's not weary or a muscle that's not griping, but your body's more tired than your spirit. Because your spirit filled up with the day, it didn't get emptied."

He'd been running his mouth on like one of those fools on a TV talk show. Those people who told the world their problems and begged for sympathy. Might as well have called up Sally Jessy Raphael and asked to spill his guts before God and everybody.

It was Hannah's doing. She kept asking those questions. Not pushy ones, like a talk-show host, but quiet ones. She'd told him things about herself, too. And she'd looked at him like she really was interested in his ramblings. Things he thought about when he was out alone except for the animals, the land and the sky.

She hadn't even gotten huffy when he'd finally shut his trap and said it was high time they got back.

She'd smiled at him and got on her horse, aided by a boulder, sparing his body another blast of heat. Now she rode along beside him in silence. Not the kind of silence that could hide hard words, but the kind of silence that enjoyed the soft sounds of quiet. He could tell from the way her eyes sparkled as she watched a soaring hawk. He liked listening to the small sounds, too. The rustle of the grasses in the breeze, the steady, slow tread of the horses' hooves, the sliding creak of the leather saddle, the quick call of a bird warning its brethren of their approach.

He'd never have expected someone like Hannah to pay much heed to such simple things. Someone from back East. Someone who held a high position in a big company. Someone so pretty. Someone who probably had men falling all over themselves trying to get closer to her, trying to stir that sweet smile—

"I'll get the gate."

Hannah's voice jerked him away from frowning contemplation of unknown men hovering around her as thick as flies. Lord, he'd lost track entirely of where they were. They'd reached the gate to cross the pasture nearest the house, and she'd nudged Spock ahead to deal with it, while his mind wandered.

"Hannah, I can—"

"No, it's okay. I watched how you did it. I think if I—"

She leaned sideways from the saddle trying to catch the wire loop that hooked over the gatepost and fence post. Like a driver learning to park, she'd left Spock a good two feet farther from the fence than necessary. Rubbing against it wouldn't have hurt the animal any, but Hannah had been overly cautious. So now she had to stand in the stirrups and stretch for all she was worth.

The movement tightened her jeans across her rump and pulled the fabric of her blouse snug against her breasts. His jeans developed a sudden tendency to fit snugger in a certain area. He swallowed.

"I think I've got it... I... Yeah!"

Her celebration of success ended abruptly as Spock pretended to be startled by her voice and backed away a second before Hannah could lift the loop clear.

Half laughing, Hannah called out, "Whoa!" as she stretched dangerously from the saddle, barely grasping the loop between her fingertips.

"Here, let me get in there."

He maneuvered Strider in next to Spock. Shifting the reins to his right hand, he reached between the two horses with his left for the wire loop. Now that backing up would have contributed, Spock moved closer. And Strider stubbornly wouldn't give an inch.

Hannah's right leg rubbed against his left one as the horses shifted, then his slipped behind hers, snug and comfortable, as perfectly aligned as two spoons. Dax felt as if a line of fire had erupted all along his leg and spread into his groin.

He dropped the wire, not bothering to see if it fell back in place on the upright or not.

"What—?"

Her question evaporated. Laughter still lit Hannah's sun-blushed face. Her mouth curved with it, her eyes sparkled with it. Deeper in her eyes, though, he caught something else, a glitter of awareness, a haze of smoke from the fire churning in his gut.

He reached for her. His left hand spread on the side of her neck, the pressure of his fingers drawing her to him.

In the first instant her lips were sun-warmed, laughter-molded. Then they softened, parted, meeting the demands and desires of his. He tested the seam of her lips with his tongue. They parted slightly, and he took that opening, stroking and exploring, with leisured thoroughness.

She smelled soft, real. Her hand curved around his forearm. Holding on, not trying to draw him away, he realized with a rush of pleasure.

Spock shifted his weight to his outside legs, rolling her saddle slightly away from Dax and his hold on her nearly dragged Hannah from the saddle. He had to end the kiss to let her right herself, but he didn't release her.

"Whoa, whoa," he murmured, not sure if he meant the words for the horses or himself.

Perhaps catching his uncertainty, Hannah slanted him a small, wry smile as she shifted more securely in the saddle. His eyes followed the movement, then came back to the smile. And he was lost.

The reins slid across his open palm unheeded as his right hand trailed down the side of her neck, then under the collar of her blouse to grasp her shoulder. He took her mouth with urgent greed. His tongue sliding deep and slow. Letting her know. Letting her feel what he felt.

She gasped, producing a sensation as hot and sharp as lightning inside him.

Her tongue answered his. The pull of her blouse bound his wrist, then it gave as a button slid free of its hole. His hand cupped over the point of her bare, soft shoulder, his thumb delving deeper, stroking the smooth skin, absorbing the softness that swelled above a line of simple lace edging. Then dipping under the lace. His rough thumb sliding over a softness he'd never imagined.

He wanted more. Heaven help him. He wanted more.

He'd wanted it sitting on that blanket in the sun. And he'd wanted it lying alone in his bed last night. He wanted more than the taste of her this time. He wanted the feel and weight of her.

Barely holding on to each other, on the backs of two shifting, twitching, tail-swatting horses, and he wanted to pull her fully into his arms, and know the sensation of her body pressed from shoulder to toes against his. He wanted—

"Dad?"

The shout floated across the air, faint, familiar and in this instance terrifying.

Dax might have flinched. Or maybe Strider reacted to Will's call on his own. Either way, the horse took a step forward. Dax felt the saddle moving under him, but still he didn't let Hannah go. Didn't even stop kissing her.

Not until a second "Dad?" and a second step by Strider. Dax, stretched like a trick rider, could do nothing but let her go and mutter dark curses under his breath while he waited for his body's demands to subside from a pagan roar.

Hannah drew a deep breath and let it out slow. If that was all it took for her to settle herself back into calm she was a damned sight cooler than him, he thought sourly.

"Dad!"

Will's call vibrated with impatience now.

"Be right there!" Dax shouted back. Both horses shifted uneasily, putting a little more distance between them.

He risked a glance at Hannah. She was fastening the top button below the V of her blouse, covering the smooth, pale flesh there. Another streak of lightning shot through him. He knew the feel of that flesh now. No matter how much she covered it, the imprint of it remained on his skin. And deeper.

She finger-combed her hair. More than sun blushed her cheeks. Her lips were full, damp, swollen.

"We gotta leave for town in twenty minutes." Will had come around the corner of the barn and glared at them all the way across the pasture, hands on hips.

"All right. We're coming." With an unfamiliar guilt, Dax wondered if Will had seen them. He hoped not. He didn't want Will asking the kind of questions that might raise. But he also didn't want that moment between him and Hannah to be anything but private.

Hannah looked up, their eyes snagged.

Damn.

He jerked around to break the connection. He snatched the loop and backed up Strider with more authority than he needed, opening the gate for her and Spock.

After closing the gate behind them, he trailed her across the open ground, making no move to come up alongside her.

His thoughts were grim enough without getting another dose of those eyes.

Damn.

He wanted this woman. Wanted her in his bed, beneath him, holding his body, taking him inside and slaking his hunger.

This wasn't supposed to happen.

Chapter Five

Hannah's knock brought a gray-haired woman with lines etched deep around her eyes and mouth to the front door of the tiny house on the east side of Bardville.

"Hello, I'm Hannah Chalmers. Irene Weston asked me to drop some things by for June. June Reamer?" she added after a moment, because the woman's continued silence made her wonder if she had the right house. Irene had given precise directions, Bardville didn't provide many possible wrong turns and the dark green house with the fading marigolds out front matched her description.

"Yes, she's my daughter. Come in. I'm Sally Randall."

Hannah followed Dax's mother down a narrow hall. The woman paused at the doorway to the living room, then continued on to the kitchen. Her slow and cautious walk favored her left leg. She gestured for Hannah to take a seat on the bench by the table and she took the chair opposite, a slight sigh escaping as she settled into the seat.

"You're staying at the Westons'?"

"Yes. I work for Boone in North Carolina, and he had me come out here. I've gotten to know June through them and Dax—" Hannah's attempt at breeziness evaporated as Sally Randall's face changed. Such a small movement. Not even a wince. But it made Hannah realize the lines of pain in the older woman's face did not all arise from physical causes. She cast about for something more to say. "And I've met Will and—"

"Will's a good boy." A faint smile curved Sally's mouth. "Now that he's in high school he comes by nearly every week. Not often a boy that age takes the time." Sally stood slowly, resting one hand on the table for support. "Would you like some coffee?"

"Yes, thank you."

Hannah's mind was whirling, trying to piece together scraps of conversation and half seconds of looks. A rift between Dax and his mother, that's what she came up with. But why? And how could she avoid saying anything that might hurt the older woman when she didn't know the details?

"Will seems like a very nice boy," Hannah agreed. *Even if he does freeze me with every look.* Then again, maybe that was only fair since his father's looks were anything but cold. "Uh, mature for his age. And it sounds like he knows so much about ranching and horses, especially for someone so young."

"Born to it," Sally Randall said with pride. The pride remained, but her voice added more complicated notes as she added, "Just like his father."

The back door opened, saving Hannah from having to try to formulate an answer.

"Mama! What are you doing?" June Reamer demanded. "You're supposed to be in bed, resting your back and leg."

"I'm making coffee for our guest." The coffeemaker made familiar hissing and rumbling sounds.

June peered around the door. "Hi, Hannah. Nice to see you. But I'll make the coffee, Mama. You get to bed."

With minimal fuss, June herded her mother out of the kitchen, barely allowing her to exchange nice-to-meet-yous with Hannah. From down the hallway, Hannah heard Sally's fond grumble. "You're a tyrant, Juney."

"Benevolent despot," her daughter replied.

June returned in minutes, talking as she entered the room. "Now, I'll get that coffee and we can have a nice talk."

"Thank you, June, but there's no need. I'm dropping off these dishes—" Hannah gestured to the shopping bag at her feet as she stood "—for Irene, and I'll be on my way."

"Nonsense. No need to run off. The coffee's finished. You're having a cup."

And with that, June turned to the coffeemaker, clearly expecting Hannah to fall in with her plans. At the moment, Hannah could see a strong family resemblance between brother and sister. No wishy-washiness in the Randall family genes.

"June, really, I—"

"I can use a cup myself after running around all morning handing out leaflets. Campaigning for Cully Grainger." June brought filled cups to the table, then retrieved a plate of sugar cookies from the counter. "You know Cully?"

"A little. I understand he stayed with the Westons last spring."

"Yeah, but now he's renting a house just outside town. It's closer to Jessa's place and easy for Travis—his nephew—to get to school. I figure before long, he and Jessa will be looking for a new place for the three of them. You knew Cully's running for sheriff of Shakespeare County?"

"Yes, I heard that. When he came out of the army, he joined the police in the city where I live. A lot of people there thought very highly of him. I hope he wins."

"Oh, I expect he will. On the surface he might not seem a real good fit, not being from this area and not having stuck long with his other jobs, but folks 'round here are pretty good at looking beneath the surface." She squared off to stare at Hannah and added, "How're you at doing that?"

"Beg your pardon?"

"How're you at looking beneath the surface? Say with my brother."

As Hannah recovered from her initial jolt at June's demand, she put herself in the other woman's shoes, and realized she might be as protective of Ethan in a similar situation, though—and she almost smiled at the thought—she hoped she would be more tactful.

"June, I think you've misunderstood," she said gently. "There's nothing going on between your brother and me."

Not a lie…not exactly. Sure, those kisses on horseback had rocked her so badly that the rubber in her knees when she'd dismounted had not been the sole fault of Spock's broad back. Dax's touches had burned her skin nearly as much as the hunger in his eyes had heated something deep inside her.

But that didn't mean anything—*couldn't* mean anything.

"Why not?"

With two words, June scattered Hannah's assumptions like dust. "Why…? *Not?*"

"Sure. You're both healthy, attractive, unattached and young enough. Unless—you're not attached, are you?"

"No, but—"

"Then what's the problem? Dax is no smooth Don Juan—"

He didn't need to be. He did just fine, Hannah thought.

"But even a sister can see he's got his points. And I can tell you he'd sooner cut off his arm and even more vital appendages before he treated a woman rough. He's not swimming in money, but he owns his land and he's a reliable kind of man. He's not going to be running off to Vegas to gamble the grocery money. And—"

"Whoa, whoa, June!" Hannah laughed with an effort. "You sound like you're trying to marry him off. I'm only here for two weeks."

"Now you sound like Dax. Two weeks can be plenty long enough sometimes."

"But—"

"Six days it took me to know my Henry was the one for me and vice versa. But I don't expect Dax to be that smart. Not with his feelings about women." She openly studied Hannah. "You know about that?"

She considered hedging. For about a second and a half. Then she realized the futility of it. "I've heard how Will's mother got Dax to marry her, then how she left them."

June nodded. "She was a bad one," she said unemotionally. "The kind another woman would spot a mile off. A lot of men might have seen her for what she was, too. But Dax didn't have a chance. He doesn't know women and, after Elaine, he's sure he doesn't want to. Oh, he gets along fine with women like Irene and Cambria and Jessa, because he sees them as neighbors rather than women. But for a *woman*...well, Elaine confirmed his suspicions, but they started a long time before Elaine came slithering on the scene."

June paused and Hannah knew if the other woman didn't keep talking on her own, she'd have to drag the information out of Dax's sister. No way could she walk out of here without knowing what June Reamer meant.

"It started when our parents separated. Guess it had been brewing for a long while. Pa wasn't an easy man, not by anybody's yardstick. Mama came to town and Pa stayed on the ranch. I was eighteen, working as a waitress over by I-90. But Dax was a boy. He loved the ranch and had already made it stark clear that's what he meant to do with his life. I can't imagine him ever living in town."

Hannah remembered the disdain in Dax's voice as he spoke of his grandfather giving up the ranch for an easier life in town and the peace in his eyes as he'd looked out over the land, and she agreed with June. Dax Randall belonged nowhere but on his ranch.

"I suppose that's why Mama left him with Pa. Trouble

is, from that time to this he's kept Mama at arm's length as much as he can manage. When Pa was alive it didn't take much doing, because he wouldn't let Mama see Dax. But Dax could've got around it the way he did to see me. He didn't want to. As he got older, Dax did his own part in freezing her out. We argued about it 'round and 'round, how he wouldn't let her get within arm's length of him.''

"But Will...?"

"Oh, Dax doesn't stand in the way of the boy seeing his grandmother—he wouldn't deprive Will of a grandmother. But himself, that's a different story. As if he doesn't think he—"

June broke off, almost as if she'd come near betraying a confidence. But how could that be when she'd been so willingly telling the family history?

When June went on, Hannah forgot that question. "Even now that Mama's living with me and her health's not the best, when Dax comes by to do repairs and such around the house, he keeps his distance from her. She doesn't say much, but I can see it breaks her heart. Lord, he's one stubborn man. He's holding on to a grudge he started nursing when he was seven.''

Seven. Sympathy welled in Hannah both for a boy separated from his mother at that age and for a woman who had suffered the consequences of a decision made thirty years ago.

From the outside, she might find the decision hard to understand, but looking from the outside didn't always give a clear picture. From the outside, Richard had seemed a perfect husband—spending generously on their home and entertainment. She would need a calculator to total up the times their acquaintances had said how lucky she was to have Richard and then how foolish she was to give him up.

But those were people looking from the outside. Only from the inside could anyone know how hollow a marriage could be. Or how an imperfect decision could be the best of a bad set of choices.

"That's a shame," Hannah said at last, wincing at the words' inadequacy.

June nodded. "That's what it is, all right. And it set the tune for Dax's thinking about women. What the lughead needs is someone to set him straight. Gentle, but firm. The way a good trainer can turn a rogue horse."

The older woman looked at Hannah so expectantly that she had to fight the urge to say she knew nothing about training horses—or setting men straight. Much better to pretend she didn't know what June hinted at.

"I hear Cambria's worked miracles with Midnight," she offered brightly, then pursued her turn of conversation with such doggedness that June couldn't get in a word. From Cambria's training of the difficult horse, to the house she and Boone were building, to Hannah's own work with Boone, to June's work. Until Hannah could excuse herself politely—and safely—without another mention of Dax.

But as she drove back to the Westons', Hannah's thoughts returned to the painful split in the Randall family.

What a shame that someone couldn't help bring Dax and his mother together. She didn't doubt for a second that June told the absolute truth about his stubbornness. But he wasn't a mean man. If he spent enough time with his mother, he would see her pain at their estrangement and that might be the first step.

Maybe she could change his mind about—

"Oh, no!" Hannah whispered to herself in the solitude of the car. "Not again."

She had sworn, during that painful period after breaking up with Richard and before totally accepting it, that she would never again try to change a man. Never.

She had wanted to change Richard to a man who would match her ideal, to someone who would be the kind of husband she'd hope for. A man who would share with her so much more than *things*. She recognized the selfishness in that now. Her motivation with Dax was more altruistic—wanting to change him so *he'd* be happier—b... was surely equally foolhardy and probably more danger...

Yes, Dax most definitely posed a threat to her peace ... mind, not to mention her hormones, so she had to be very careful.

"I hear you took Hannah riding."

Dax eyed June. "Yeah. This window needs replacing."

He'd come by his sister's house to put up the storm windows for her. As always he timed it for a day his mother would be having physical therapy.

"Order a new one from Al at the hardware store, then."

He grunted an acknowledgment.

"That's good," June added. "I mean, you taking Hannah riding, not the window needing replacing."

"It's just part of what we talked about—showing Will it's okay to be interested in a female."

"That's why it's good." She sounded real smooth and sincere. His suspicion didn't buy it. "And how's it working?"

Dax shrugged, the question reminding him of the testy exchange he'd had with Will on their way into town yesterday, followed by twenty-four hours of mostly bleak silence.

"Is he back to being part of that crowd of friends he always had?"

"I wouldn't know. He's not talkin' to me like he used to. And when he does, it's mostly to sharpen his horns on me."

"That's natural for a boy that age. He should've been doing it before. That's part of the problem."

Dax expelled a disbelieving *huh.*

"Boy's got his nose out of joint, that's all," June went on. "He's used to having you to himself. This is good for him, too."

Dax narrowed his eyes at his sister. "What do you mean, *too?* This is *all* for him."

nat I mean is besides showing him it's okay to be
.ested in a girl, this is also weaning him from being so
d to you."

"You make him sound like a calf," Dax grumbled.

"And you made him sound like cattle—*sharpening his horns*. Now, he's bullheaded enough to be your son, but he's not full grown yet. Sometimes I think you forget that, Dax. Just because you turned into an old man before you'd ever been a kid doesn't mean he's doing the same."

He ignored the jibe at him. "Will's got a good head on his shoulders. He's mature."

"In some ways. In others he's—well, I wouldn't say a calf. More like a yearling colt."

"Bull."

"It's not. He needs to break away from you more, Dax. That's not an easy thing—ask the parents of any teenagers."

"I don't like to see the boy unhappy."

"I know you don't, Dax. That's one of the things that makes up for you otherwise being as cuddly as prickly pear." June patted his hand. He grumbled, but didn't move away from the touch and she didn't stop. "Of course, you could always decide not to see any more of Hannah Chalmers. That would make him happy—at least short-term. Is that what you want to do?"

"No." The word hung in the air for a full second before he realized he'd said it. "It's just what you said—that's the short-term. And it would defeat the whole idea. We started this, might as well see it out."

"*We* might have started it, but, my dear brother, you're the one who's going to be seeing it out to the finish. All by yourself."

With the fire alarm bell shrilling behind him, Will filed out of the high school with his classmates and stepped into the sunshine. Any doubt that this was a drill ended when he saw the principal talking so calmly to a man wearing a windbreaker with Fire Marshall emblazoned across the back.

Jerry Poolter and some of the other guys stood over by the fence, way off to the right, along with three girls. But not Theresa Wendlow. Jerry waved, but Will pretended he didn't see. Jerry hung around Theresa's friend Ashley all the time these days and acted like a total idiot.

Will found a spot alone, sitting on the concrete base of the Bardville High School sign. Facing away from the school. Then Theresa started past him, probably on her way over to Jerry and Ashley and that group. She paused.

"Hi, Will."

"Hi."

"Guess this is just a drill, don't you think?"

"Yeah."

Theresa glanced at the building, then studied the toes of her tooled leather boots for a while. He didn't mind. It gave him a chance to look at her from the corner of his eye without getting caught. But when she glanced over to the group she hung out with, he stopped watching her. Why didn't she just go with those fools if she wanted to so bad? He hadn't asked her to come over here.

She drew in a breath, and he expected a quick goodbye. Instead, she said in a rush, "I saw your dad with that new woman, that Hannah Chalmers who's staying out at Westons'."

"When?"

"Driving back from Sheridan to the meeting at the fairgrounds about Shakespeare Days. We came the back way and saw them riding. Looked like they were headed toward the barn."

"Oh. That's okay, then."

"Aren't you glad your dad's seeing her? She seems real nice."

"She's okay, I guess."

Theresa sat beside him, and for a moment he couldn't

breathe, much less move. Only a couple inches separated them.

"She was great to me. You know, for that paper on professions for Mrs. Grabhern's class? I'm doing advertising, and I called Hannah Chalmers out at Westons' and she said she'd let me interview her this weekend. And just over the phone she gave me all this great information, and the names of some books to check and people I can write to in New York. It's going to be great."

"You don't need all that New York stuff."

"It'll make the paper better than having only local stuff."

Will mumbled something. Maybe he could find something at the Bardville Library about ranching in other parts of the world to supplement what he'd found out about ranching in Wyoming.

"Anyway, everyone's been talking about Hannah and your dad."

"Bunch of busybodies." Even with his head turned away from her he sensed her attention zeroed in on him. And as much as he didn't want to, he had to ask the question—his dad had taught him to try to know everything he could about a problem before tackling it. "What're they saying?"

"Well, I heard Rita Campbell telling Sheriff Milano how she heard from Jessa Tarrant that your daddy and Hannah Chalmers seemed to hit it right off and how well they're getting along."

He faced her then, and said with more confidence than he felt, "That doesn't mean anything."

"Don't you want them to like each other? I don't understand. You and your dad always seem to get along so well, not like most of my friends and their parents. It's one of the things I…I, um, thought we had in common. Because my parents are usually pretty good, too. And it seemed like you and your dad had the same thing. You know, liking each other."

"We used to."

Her eyes, wide and sad, seemed to swallow him up, making his insides feel like they did the moment after a horse had thrown him and before he came to the hard earth.

"Oh, Will…"

So what could he do then, but blurt out a question about if she'd like to walk over to the library after school to work on their papers? And when she said yes, his head buzzed so loud he hardly knew when they started ringing the bell to signal everyone should return to the building.

Dax was scraping mud from the bottom of his boots on the metal rectangle set by the back porch for that purpose when Will came out the back door in his stocking feet with the backpack holding his schoolbooks dangling from one hand and the morning paper folded back to the sports section in the other.

"I'm heading to Lewises' to do their shoeing this morning," Dax said. "I can take you by school if you'd like."

Will hesitated a moment, coloring up at the same time. "No, thanks. The bus is fine."

Dax dropped his head as if concentrating on his task. He suspected what was *fine* about the bus these days was that Theresa Wendlow rode it. But a grin now could make a mess of everything. It almost had last night at supper.

First, he'd been so pleased that Will had been almost his old self, answering Dax's questions about his day and his schoolwork with more than grunts. Then Dax had nearly blown it when Will let it slip that he'd gone to the library after school with a girl—Theresa Wendlow. He'd almost grinned. Just in time, he'd noticed his son's challenging look, and he'd hidden any sign of amusement behind a long, long drink from his glass of water.

So maybe his being around Hannah had produced the effect he'd hoped for. The only fly in the ointment, with Will acting more normal, was he'd have to tell June she was right.

Will cleared his throat, and went on. "There's a football game in Sheridan on Saturday night we could go to, Dad."

Dax's bubble of well-being didn't burst, but it developed a dent. This was awkward. "I, uh, thought I'd take Hannah to a movie Saturday night."

Without a word, Will dropped the paper and backpack to the porch floor, grabbed his boots from beside the door and started jerking them on.

"Look, Will, I know it's been the two of us for a long time. But it's not always going to be that way." *Not as you grow up, and go off and find your own life and, God willing, a woman to love.* Not that he'd be saying that out loud—no sense scaring the boy to death with a future that right now he couldn't imagine wanting. "But that doesn't mean things have really changed between us."

His boots on and the backpack retrieved, Will spun around to face his father. "Yes, they have. You're spending all your time with *her.*"

"Her name's not *her.* You either call her Ms. Chalmers like you've been taught or you call her Hannah like she says."

"I don't want to call her anything."

Will started to walk away, but Dax snagged his arm sharply enough to pull the boy around.

"You don't walk away when I'm talking to you, boy."

"Why not? That's what you're doing. Your own kind of walking away. Just like my mother, deserting me. Only you've worked it so you don't have to leave the state to do it."

"Will!"

The claw of pain in Dax's gut was worse than any he could remember. Because it was more than the pain inflicted by Will's words. It was the pain he knew his son must be feeling to say such words.

And Will's feelings went a whole lot deeper than confusion and jealousy over his father spending time with a woman. Dax knew what it was like to grow up knowing your mother had walked away from you. You didn't shake that at fifteen. Not at thirty-six, either.

"Will, I won't ever leave you. Not ever. Someday, you'll be leaving me, but I'll always be here for you. And if you need me, I'll be wherever it is you need me. Like I've always been. You've got to know that."

With a relief that almost left him light-headed Dax saw that, beneath the anger, Will did know that. But the anger and confusion remained.

They stared at each other for another tense moment. Dax swore a bit under his breath, then dropped his hold on Will's arm. He gave a tired sigh. "I'm doing this for you, boy."

"That doesn't make no sense."

"*Any* sense. But you're probably right. Look, it seemed like you didn't feel real comfortable with girls, so I thought if I could show you it wasn't such a hard thing..."

Hell of an idea that had been. It *was* a hard thing. Early or late, being with a woman meant pain. Just because it hadn't been that way so far with Hannah didn't mean anything. Or, most likely, it meant the pain would be sharper when it did come.

Will's eyes went wide. "You mean, she's sort of a practice for you?"

"I wouldn't say that, because I'm not looking to do this for real. It's more like..." Intensely uncomfortable with this conversation, he rustled around in his memory for something to liken this to. "Remember when I first taught you how to ride and I had Buster throw me to show you how to fall?"

Will nodded.

"It's like that. I'm showing you a bit of how to go about it, 'case you want to, but I'm not saying you should, and I'm not saying I plan on getting thrown anytime soon, myself."

"So you're not thinking about marrying her?"

"Marrying? Good God, no." Dax recoiled from the thought. "Where'd you get that idea?"

"It's not something I made up," Will said, a little defensive.

Dax narrowed his eyes. "Has your aunt said something?"

"Aunt June? No. But Rita told the sheriff you two got along real good, and I heard Irene Weston tell Wanda at the library she hasn't seen you take a shine to a woman like this since my mother."

Dax got a strange feeling up his back, the kind that June used to tell him as a kid meant someone had walked over his grave.

"Well, now you know why. And now that you do, I can quit pestering Hannah. She didn't want to have anything to do with me in the first place. And now I can leave her in peace to enjoy her vacation the way she wanted to from the first. Starting right now, I'll quit..."

Quit seeing her. Quit kissing her. Quit touching her. A burn lit in his gut that Dax translated into anger.

"It was a damned far-fetched, lamebrained idea in the first place, and I have your Aunt June to thank for it. From now on you can figure out how to get along with females on your own, without me showing the way. And all this nonsense is forgotten. Now I've got irrigation pipe to move, and you've got that bus to catch."

Chapter Six

"Uh, Dad...?" Will's voice came from the doorway that led from the barn to the corral where Dax had nearly finished saddling Strider. Will already had Merc saddled and waiting to take him out to a pasture by the creek where they'd put some heifers they needed to check to see if they were pregnant.

"Yeah?"

"I've been thinkin'"

Dax had been thinking, too. All day. He'd been thinking it was just as well this fool idea of June's had blown up. He'd kept separate from women around here for good reasons, and those reasons hadn't changed. Even if Hannah Chalmers was a near stranger who'd be leaving in a week and a half, it was...*dangerous.*

He'd had to remind himself of that real hard on his way back from the Lewises'. The damned truck had almost turned in the Westons' road by itself. He'd ended up stopped dead in the highway, talking himself out of stopping to say hello to Hannah. Good thing nobody had happened by. He'd have looked a damned fool.

"I suppose it wouldn't hurt. I mean, if you went around with, uh, Ms. Chalmers some more. I mean, she's leaving and all in a couple weeks, right?"

"Yeah."

"And you seem to like her, I mean being around her. You've been smiling and all."

"That's so?" Dax asked, a frown tugging at his forehead.

Will, clearly intent on his own thoughts, appeared at the open door of the stall, his eyes wide-open the way they used to get as a toddler when he wanted to pretend he hadn't done some bit of mischief.

"Yeah, and I suppose it couldn't hurt, I mean, if you don't think she'd mind too much if you kept seeing her and I sort of see how you, you know—" he gave a wave of his hand, as if plucking an idea out of the air "—asked her out or something like that."

Dax put the stirrup on his shoulder to keep its strap out of the way and tightened the cinch on Strider and wondered how long Will had thought about asking Theresa Wendlow out.

"And then I could watch how you, uh, do things, I mean on a date and such. So—" Will drew in a long breath and finished in a rush "—if you want to keep being around, uh, Ms. Chalmers, and bringing her around here, I won't raise any more fuss."

Dax studied his son's face, but apparently he meant exactly what he said. Dax didn't want Will to be thinking about the sort of things Dax and Hannah had been doing out by the pasture gate and especially not about the sorts of things Dax had wanted to do. Will had a lot of growing up to do before he tried wrestling with those sorts of impulses. Hell, Dax was a man and he hadn't come close to winning against those impulses.

In fact, the memory of Hannah's smooth, warm skin under his hand and of her pliant, sweet lips under his mouth sent a surge of heat through his body.

"I suppose it couldn't hurt," he agreed at last.

That was a lie. It already hurt.

"Oh, Hannah, it's so good to hear your voice."

The uneasiness that bloomed in Hannah the instant Irene had told her she had a call from her sister calmed when she heard Mandy's tone. Whatever Mandy had called about wasn't catastrophic.

"It's good to hear yours, too, Mandy. What's the matter?"

"Nothing's the matter. I was thinking about you."

"You're okay? Ethan's okay?"

"Yes, yes, we're both fine. And having a wonderful time. I told you, I was just thinking about you."

Hannah perched on the arm of the easy chair in the family room and looked out the window. A breeze ruffled the pages of the professional journal she'd left on the porch swing when Irene called her. "You're not supposed to be thinking about your old fuddy-duddy sister, you're supposed to be staying up all night talking over the problems of the world. Didn't anybody tell you that's what college is for?"

Mandy brushed aside the old joke between them. "Yes, you did. But I've been thinking about you, Hannah."

A dusty midnight blue pickup with the Circle CR brand painted on the door pulled to a stop in the yard outside. The pulse in Hannah's throat jumped. When a broad-shouldered, lean-hipped figure in worn jeans and a faded denim shirt got out, she felt the muscles clench south of her stomach.

"Hannah?"

"What?" she muttered.

"Are you listening? You're not an old fuddy-duddy. At least you wouldn't be if you gave yourself half a chance.

Promise me you'll do that—promise me you'll give yourself a chance.''

Dax's survey of the area honed in on the picture window. There was no way their eyes could have actually met. Not at this distance. Not with him looking from the sunshine outside into the shadow of the house. But tell that to her pulse.

Dax settled back against the truck, his arms crossed comfortably across his chest, one booted ankle over the other. A man who'd found what he sought and had settled in to wait.

"Give myself a chance at what?"

"At *love*."

"Love? What on earth brought this on, Mandy?" Hannah turned away from the picture window.

"An assignment for that class I told you about—on understanding the history of North Carolina through writings of ordinary people. I read this journal by a woman who lost her fiancé during the Civil War—so *sad*. He was a Yankee—they met when she visited up north before the war, and they fell in love. When the war came he asked her to come north, but she said no. He joined the Union Army and she nursed Confederates. But he kept writing to her and she still loved him, you *felt* it reading her journal. The war had nearly ended and he wrote that they'd be together again. But—" A sniffle came over the long-distance line. "He was killed. Oh, Hannah, it was so sad. It broke her heart. And she never gave herself another chance to love. She closed off her heart. The rest of her life was a waste. It was...*tragic!*"

Hannah cast her eyes to the heavens. Her sister's flare for the dramatic had earned her the family nickname of Bernie—short for Bernhardt, as in Sarah—so this didn' surprise her. "It does sound sad, but what does this have to do with your course?"

"The professor's using it to talk about how women

coped during the war and after—this Mary Albert started schools in a coastal area and improved sanitation there.''

''Doesn't sound as if her life was a waste, then,'' Hannah said dryly.

''Well, maybe not in a practical sense, but her personal life... That's what made me think of you.''

''Thanks a lot, Mandy.''

''I didn't mean it that way. It's just...it's just you gave up so much to take care of Ethan and me, and—''

''Mandy Chalmers, stop right there. I never gave up anything I didn't regain a thousandfold. In fact, this talk of giving up something and repayment is nonsense. We're family. It's as simple as that. And if I *had* given anything up, it certainly wasn't my life's love. I am not pining for Richard in any way, shape or form. In fact...''

''In fact what?'' Mandy said with an eagerness that stopped Hannah's impulse to tell her about Dax Randall. Mandy would blow it out of proportion.

''In fact, I've realized what a good thing it is that I finally saw his true character when I did. If that hadn't happened, I might still be stuck in that marriage, not knowing why I was growing more and more miserable every day.''

''Really?''

''Really.''

''Okay. But still...could you promise me something?''

''What?''

''Promise you won't give up on love. Promise you'll get out there and meet men and give them a chance to fall in love with you now that you don't have Ethan and me underfoot all the time. Promise me that, okay?''

Hannah's gaze flicked to the figure outside the picture window. ''Okay. I promise.''

After they hung up, Hannah added another promise to herself. She would be careful with this love business, because it could be as explosive and devastating as nitroglycerin.

She didn't pine for Richard the way Mary Albert had for

her love, but that didn't mean that sort of heartbreak couldn't happen to her.

"A movie Saturday?" Hannah repeated.

"And dinner," Dax added.

Dinner and a movie. About as innocuous as a date could get, Hannah thought. She'd been on hundreds of dates that included dinner and a movie. She knew how to handle that.

Unlike a horseback riding outing.

Surely that's why the kisses they'd shared on horseback had shaken her so badly—she'd been out of her element. But dinner and a movie—that she knew how to handle.

Dinner and a movie... The sort of date she needed to help ease back into the social whirl.

"Thank you, Dax. I'd like that."

Hannah ignored the tingle of nerves between her shoulders—nerves, surely—when she opened the cabin door to Dax on Saturday night and let him in with a smile.

She had prepared for this date the way she prepared for business meetings.

Talking to Theresa Wendlow this afternoon about advertising for the high school girl's paper on the profession had helped get her in the right frame of mind. She had mentally prepared a list of topics she wanted to cover, considered several approaches to each, then visualized how the whole encounter might go and finally willed herself into a state of serenity. She had dressed for the part, too. She wore a straight-line denim jumper that buttoned from the hem to its deep V neck over a collarless white blouse of washed silk, flats and nylons, and plain hoop earrings.

She'd balanced the line between too casual and too dressed up, and that boosted her confidence. She could do this. She could definitely do this.

"I'll get my purse and sweater, and we can go."

He mumbled something she didn't catch, but thought

might have been his saying she looked nice. When she turned to face him after gathering her things, however, she couldn't mistake the expression in his eyes. She'd seen it when he'd kissed her on horseback. The tingle between her shoulders spread down her arms, then pulsed with a new heat when he touched the small of her back to guide her from the cabin to the passenger door of his newly washed truck.

It took several minutes of silent self-lecturing to drag her serenity out of its hiding spot. But by the time Dax cleared his throat and spoke, she felt back in control.

"Thought we'd get some dinner first, then go see a movie."

"That would be nice. Which one?"

"We can decide when we get there, if that's okay with you."

"Of course."

She smiled straight ahead and brought up Topic Number One, the history of the area that Zeke, the one-time ranch hand at the Westons', had told her about at the cookout. Dax didn't chatter, by any means, but he contributed a couple anecdotes, and she started to relax.

When he got on I-90 and headed north, she quelled momentary uneasiness. The only movie theater she'd seen in Bardville had been boarded up, so they must be going to Sheridan. A little more time in the truck alone with him than she'd initially figured on, but that didn't pose any great problem. She could adjust. She often had to do that in meetings. No big deal.

Then they passed the last exit to Sheridan.

"Uh, Dax, where are we going?"

He looked over at her, a faint cast of surprise showing under the brim of his hat. "Billings."

"Billings! But that's...that's in Montana."

"Uh-huh," he agreed politely.

"It's got to be—what?—an hour away? And—"

"Closer to two."

"It's in another state for heaven's sake."

"Yeah, it is. It's got the best choice of movies. And there're nice restaurants. Not fancy. I said dinner and a movie. What did you think?"

"I thought, Bardville or maybe Sheridan."

He eased his foot off the gas pedal and pulled the truck onto the shoulder of the highway. When they stopped, he glanced at her, then returned his attention to the view through the windshield. "We don't think anything of going to Billings, so I didn't think to spell it out, Hannah. Do you want to go back?"

Her list of topics wouldn't last until dinner, much less getting to a movie and the return trip. This wouldn't be like any other dinner-and-a-movie date she'd been on, because none of them had included a four-hour round-trip commute. They would be in uncharted territory, beyond her preparations and planning.

"I'll take you home if you want, Hannah," he added gruffly, still speaking to the windshield.

Did she want that?

"No," she said slowly. "It's all right. We'll go to Billings. I was, uh, surprised. I overreacted."

He'd glanced over at her first few words, and the lines around his mouth eased. "Interstate dating can do that to you."

He said it solemnly enough, but she caught the glimmer of amusement in his eyes. Settling back into the seat as he pulled onto the road, she felt an answering grin tugging at her mouth.

"Interstate dating, huh? Pretty fancy description for dinner and a movie."

They never made it to the movie.

In a booth along the side of the narrow, storefront restaurant that she finally got Dax to say was his favorite for its generous portions and plain cooking, they talked. Mostly about Will, the twins and the pitfalls of teenagers, but also about ranching, advertising, horses, dogs, mountains, small towns and a little about her childhood. Though she would never describe Dax as a talkative man, he mostly held up his end—except when it came to their childhoods. On his, Dax remained silent.

With Dax, conversation was almost leisurely. As unhurried as the frizzy-haired blond waitress who cheerfully refilled the coffee cups they sipped to emptiness several times after she cleared away their plates. When they looked up, it was too late to make the last show of any of the three movies they'd discussed—to Dax's obvious chagrin.

"We could go get a drink," he offered. "Or I could take you dancing."

She shook her head.

"Or...or bowling."

He sounded so desperate she laughed a little. "No, Dax. There's no need, really. I've had a very nice evening."

"We'll go someplace else for a nice dessert, then. Anywhere you want. You choose."

She chose an ice cream stand, and he grumbled that he would bet she'd never gone on a date in New York City that included ice cream cones. But he didn't scoff at her choice, he didn't try to change her mind and he didn't blink when she ordered two scoops. In fact, he ordered three himself.

As they sat on a bench eating their ice cream, a teenage couple parked nearby, pausing to neck briefly but passionately before getting out to order their ice cream.

An intent expression settled onto Dax's strong features as he stared at them, following their progress to the window, with the boy's arm hooked around the girl's neck.

"Thinking that will be Will in a few years?" Hannah asked before she took a long lick of her dwindling cone to keep it from dripping.

"What?" He sounded slightly dazed.

"Or maybe I should say are you worried that will be Will in a few years?"

She noticed his intent stare zeroed in on her mouth. She probed the corners of her mouth with her tongue, checking for ice cream smears. He swallowed hard and seemed to jerk his attention back to the present.

"Believe me, I know it's tough when they're teenagers, and especially when they first get interested in the opposite sex, but it's all part of the natural process. Every kid goes through it. And they seem to come out the other side pretty much intact. Some of them even grow up. It's a rite of passage."

"Yeah," he said with an odd note of grimness in his voice. "A rite of passage."

They started back soon after that, the conversation desultory now. The ease and comfort of their silences combined with the mesmerizing rhythm of the road to lull her until her bones felt heavy and her muscles utterly relaxed.

When they continued on the highway past the turnoff to the Westons' and again past the Circle CR she started getting curious. Only after they had climbed enough S-curves to keep a snake vocal for a week did Dax slow almost to a stop and take a sharp turn into what seemed a wall of trees.

"Hang on. It's a rough road."

From the jouncing and jolting not a road at all, but a boulder field.

"Where are we going, Dax?"

She'd asked that same question some seven hours before, in daylight and on an interstate highway and she'd been worried. Now, in the dead dark and with no idea where she was, she was simply curious.

"I promised a movie. Least I can do is show you something worth seeing."

Her assurances that she didn't mind missing the movie died as the pickup left the canopy of trees and the windshield filled with a vista of stars.

"Oh, my."

"Best view for miles. But it's better from outside. Wait a minute."

While she gawked, he turned the truck and backed nearly to the end of the small, level outcropping jutting from the mountain. He led her to the back, helped her step onto the truck tailgate, then arranged a cushion for them to sit on, with their backs against the cab. Somewhere deep in her mind a voice suggested she should beware this setup, but it sounded very faint against the hum of her comfort with Dax and her pleasure at the view.

Besides, Dax simply sat beside her, making no move to touch her, except that when she tilted her head back to look at the stars directly overhead, he nudged her to use the support of his hard shoulder. If she forgot to move away, if she thought she felt the brush of his mouth across the top of her head, what did it matter?

"This is amazing, Dax. It feels like we're sitting in the middle of all the stars. I've never believed in that stuff about the stars telling our future, but seeing them like this... Can you read stars the way you read clouds?"

"Nope. Not other than finding the North Star and some of the constellations. Mostly I get the feeling they know more than we do."

"Yes. That's it, exactly. How did you ever find this place?"

"Riding the cattle up here as a kid one summer, I chased a cow into those trees back there, then followed her out onto this ledge. She stood there quiet as you please, waiting for me to toss a rope. Almost like she'd led me here."

The final words were so soft, Hannah barely heard them.

"I come here if I need to chew on something. A few years back, I cleared a few trees so the truck could get through, but mostly I still ride up here."

"Alone?"

"Usually. I've brought Will here a time or two, but that's all."

Hannah folded her lips tight. But her mouth wouldn't

stay closed. Something in her had disconnected her mind and manners from her mouth. "Not even your wife?"

"Especially not her."

Hannah heard the echoes of pain, anger and disappointment in his sharp words and still couldn't deny the ripple of pleasure that went through her. She was the first woman he'd brought here.

Dax cleared his throat. "Guess that sounds harsh."

"No. I know exactly what you mean, and I can understand why you kept this place to yourself. Everyone needs someplace to get away from tensions, especially if a marriage is in trouble. At least I did. It got draining being around someone so unhappy."

"She was never happy," Dax said. Hannah thought he was surprised to hear himself make the statement, but he didn't stop. "Wasn't happy when we lived in Denver, wasn't happy on a ranch, wasn't happy being pregnant, wasn't happy being a mother and most of all wasn't happy with me."

"Sounds like it didn't have much to do with you. She didn't know how to be happy." She knew the type. She'd married one, too.

Richard had made an avocation of being dissatisfied. With the table in the restaurant. With a job title. With his salary. With her clothing. With the social cachet of their guest list. He said it made him strive for more, better, bigger. She'd believed that at first. By the end she'd recognized his attitude wasn't a motivator—at least not for her—but a malaise.

"Maybe," Dax conceded. "But this is a hard life on women. Even women brought up to it like her. I brought her back here when Will was about three months old. Shouldn't have done that if I wanted the marriage to last. Guess I didn't want the marriage to last as much as I wanted Will brought up here. When the first snow flew, so did she. No big surprise."

Hannah shifted away in order to see his face better, but

the brim of his hat dropped shadows over everything but his hard jaw. "But her son...?"

"She wasn't interested. Not when she was here, and not after. Least she never got his hopes up any. Will always knew exactly what to expect from her—nothing."

"So you had the ranch to run and a baby to care for all on your own. How on earth did you manage?"

"June. Wouldn't have made it without her."

He sounded so gruff, Hannah almost smiled at him in the silky light of the stars. Did he think gruffness hid his deep gratitude and great affection for his sister? It only made it more obvious, at least to her.

"And your mother?"

Without moving, he seemed to pull back from her. Or maybe from her question.

"She helped some. But mostly June. June was here all the time. Sometimes when Henry went out on runs, she'd stay for a week at a time, taking care of Will." He might have heard the same belligerence in his voice that she detected, as if someone had argued that he possibly owed his mother gratitude, too, because he seemed to collect himself, even as he repeated, "Wouldn't have made it without June. Or—" His mouth gave a tiny, telltale twitch, though it looked forced to her eyes. "Or without disposable diapers."

Once again, he'd turned the subject away from his mother. And she let him, because she didn't like his discomfort. "Disposable diapers?"

"Yes, ma'am. They might not be the best thing for the environment, but I don't think it'd be great for the environment to have more crazy people roaming around, either, and that's where I'd have been headed without disposable diapers."

She asked him questions about Will's early childhood, and he answered more expansively than usual. She suspected that had a lot to do with the topic. But she wondered if relief to leave the earlier subject and determination not to return to it also had something to do with his filling in the silence.

One phrase from his earlier comments kept running through her head.

Least she never got his hopes up any... There was a clue there. A clue to Dax's dealings with his own mother.

That was why, when he brought the truck to a stop in front of her cabin, she asked him if he'd like to come in for a cup of coffee. She had a clue, and now she could follow it up.

Chapter Seven

"Make yourself comfortable," Hannah offered as she dropped her purse on the end table by the couch. "I'll make the coffee." *And try to think of how to pump you for information without you knowing you're being pumped.*

Instead of sitting, he roved the room, picking up an item here and there. As she kept track of him with glances over her shoulder, she noticed he unerringly picked up things that belonged to her personally, a large-scale map of Wyoming, a paperback by John McPhee about the history and geology around southwestern Wyoming. Maybe he knew the cabin well enough to know what she'd added, but she didn't think so.

He put down the book and picked up a framed picture. "This is Mandy and Ethan?" He hardly made it a question.

"Yes." With the coffee machine making familiar noises from its spot atop a bookcase, she went to his side to look at the eight-by-ten she'd had blown up from a snapshot of the twins and her. In the corner of it she kept a smaller, older snapshot of the whole family from the Christmas before her parents died.

"You take this with you everywhere?"

"Um-hmm. I like to have them with me."

"Nice to feel that way about your family."

"Yes, it is. What do you think of them?"

She expected him to say something about what a good looking pair they were. That's what most people said.

"Mandy looks like she's happiest with the bit between her teeth."

Hannah laughed, surprised and oddly pleased. "She wouldn't care for being likened to a horse, but you're exactly right. And Ethan?"

He studied the picture a moment longer. "Solid."

She sighed. "Yes. I'm afraid he didn't have much choice."

"He doesn't look like he minds much."

"I hope you're right. I hope he's having fun in college now. When I went off to college, my mother told me to behave and my father told me to have fun. Now, when I talk to them, I always tell Mandy to behave and tell Ethan to have fun." Interesting, but not surprising, that he chose the picture without her parents in it. He wasn't going to open that door to a discussion of his parents. "I guess your mom and dad must have given you advice when you left home, too, huh?" she asked.

He put the photo down carefully. "Not really."

Then he went to the couch and sat. End of discussion. So much for getting him talking about his mother—or his father. But the weave of her disappointment carried another thread, and she realized she would have liked to have known what he thought of her picture.

The coffeemaker emitted a finishing gurgle, giving her a reason to move from where he'd left her standing. When she came to the couch with the two mugs of coffee, he sat on the edge of the seat with his elbows on his knees and his hat in his hands, turning it slowly.

She sat beside him, but all the way back against the cushions. They didn't touch, but if one or the other of them reached out, they could.

"It's getting late." He didn't look at her, didn't touch the coffee.

"Yes."

"I better get going."

"Okay."

Neither of them moved, except he kept turning his hat, and she watched it, turning between his tough, battered hands.

"I still owe you a movie, Hannah."

"No movie could have matched those stars, Dax. I had a wonderful time."

He turned his head to look back at her, his brown eyes as dark and mysterious and overwhelming as the Wyoming night sky.

A rustle of sound reached her. She had only a moment to realize he'd let the hat drop out of his hands to the floor. And then he was kissing her and his hands were in her hair, cupping her head.

She'd missed him. His taste, his touch.

What a strange thought. It had been only five days since he'd kissed and held her. But she had missed him.

She put her hands along each side of his jaw to follow the curved lines that traced from the corners of his nose beyond the corners of his mouth that even now pressed against hers.

His breathing changed, dragging in harder and faster.

He enfolded her, his strong hands open across her back, drawing her tightly against him. Yet, for all his strength, she knew his restraint, too. She felt his tight control in the tenor of his touch and the tautness of his muscles, and it frightened her just a little because it hinted at what could be if he let go...*when* he let go? Did she want that?

She only knew she wanted this. Right now. Right here. The mouth she'd watched all night opened against hers and he claimed hers with his tongue. The chest she'd leaned against to watch the stars was revealed as a texture of hot, muscled flesh when her questing fingers flicked open the snaps on his shirt—and they opened so easily. The hands that had offered polite assistance with a guiding touch to her back or a steadying hold entering the truck now sculpted her body in sensation.

From where he touched, heat flashed to the pit of her stomach, pooled there, gaining strength, then flowing throughout her body.

He stroked gently from her throat, over the hollow at its base, and down into the V of her blouse, dipping into the valley between her breasts. It was a wordless request, an asking of permission. Her body gave its eloquent *yes,* arching her back, offering him more.

She wasn't aware of specific movements of buttons opening or material parting, only of the intoxicating expansion of his touch. And then of his kiss.

His lips brushed the swell of her breast above the line of her bra as his thumb brushed her nipple. Then he covered the hardened peak with the moist heat of his mouth and she moaned. The flick of his tongue through the clinging fabric was a bolt to her core.

More...more... No need to say the words aloud, because he knew. Somehow he knew. Or else he felt the need as strongly as she did. Drawing down the covering of her bra, holding her, so carefully in those hard, gentle hands.

He was carrying her down, pressing her to the cushions and aligning his body with hers. She felt his weight and strength against her, fitting to her, promising—

Rattle...crash!

They held for an instant, immobile, perhaps the possibility of ignoring the interruption streaming through his mind the way it burst into hers.

He moved. Lifting up without looking at her.

"The coffee."

Frozen by the rush of air that replaced his heated presence, it took her a long moment to straighten. He was sopping up the dark liquid off the bare wood floor as best he could with the small napkins she'd used as coasters under the mugs, now a jumble of broken pottery on the floor.

She tugged her bra up and drew her blouse closed without taking time to button it, before dashing for paper towels. "We must have both kicked the table when…"

When we laid down on the couch, a few minutes away from making love.

She lowered her head and sopped up coffee.

She would have made love with this man. She would have taken him inside her body and given a part of herself that went so much deeper even than that most intimate of physical acts. A man she'd known barely a week.

And she didn't know if she regretted the interruption or not.

Dax just stopped his hand from stroking the tangled hair obscuring Hannah's downturned face and wished nature had fixed it so a man really could kick himself, because he sure deserved it. What had he been thinking of, treating a woman like Hannah like that? She wanted more than the sex, she wanted the emotions—the love and commitment. The things no woman would get from him. So he had no right…

How could he apologize when she wouldn't even meet his eyes? Not that he blamed her. Bulls had more finesse than he'd shown in the past few minutes.

He was doing this for Will. He had to remember that. That's what he'd kept telling himself while they sat looking at the stars and the sweet weight of her head rested against his shoulder and his arm followed the curve of her shoulders. Her hair had felt as silky as the smooth material of her sleeve. Her hair had smelled good, too. A familiar scent he couldn't name. It swirled around in his mind as he grasped for the name and came up only with *Hannah.* Something sweet and clean. It made him feel good. And it made him feel hot and hard.

That was damned near a permanent condition. Desire kept tugging at him like an undertow since Hannah had arrived. Hell, more like a damned riptide in an ocean of confusion.

"I think we got it all," she said, balling the wet paper towels together and putting them on a cloth towel.

Finally, with both of them sitting back on their feet leaving them knee to knee, she looked up. And she smiled at him. That smile that added a shallow dimple beside her mouth and crinkled up her eyes.

He wanted to taste that smile again. To feel the curve of her lips against his own. To touch his tongue to that indentation.

He wanted to hold that smile in his soul.

And right this moment, it didn't matter that he couldn't ever give what a woman like Hannah wanted. It didn't matter that he'd vowed not to get involved with a woman again. It didn't even matter that she was supposed to be the perfect stranger who passed through his life, then kept going.

He raised up on his knees before her, cupped her face in his hands and kissed her.

He touched his tongue to her lips and they parted. Still holding her face, he plunged inside her mouth. She met him. He changed the angle of the kiss, deepening it. He drew in the scent of her skin, that sweet, familiar scent, and knew if it were liquid, he would happily drown in it.

Going down once...

Still kissing her, he put one hand under her bottom and the other on her back and urged her up. She rose to face him, and he brought them together from knees to shoulders, absorbing the softness of her against him.

Her hands slipped under his shirt, charging the skin of his back. Their tongues met, retreated, rediscovered, and the beat of it set the pulse growing stronger in his groin.

Going down twice...

The fabric of her blouse and jumper parted under his

hands as if it had been waiting for him. Her skin was warm and smooth, so smooth. He bent his head to take her in his mouth again. So sweet. So blood-burning sweet.

He slid a knee forward, taking the small gap she'd left between her knees for balance, and widening it, pressing through the layers of fabric to the juncture of her thighs. Her hands curled into his back and she gave a little gasp.

If he laid her down now, the ceiling could crash on them, the floor could turn to rubble and it wouldn't matter.

Going down the third time...

He pulled back, with the last shreds of self-control, resting his forehead against hers as he pulled in breaths that carried too much of her scent to bring much sanity. But enough...just barely enough.

Carefully, he put his hands to her shoulders and guided her back to sit on her heels. Then sat back himself. He made himself look at her.

"Hannah."

"Yes, you're right."

She said it quickly, too quickly. Like someone who'd been thinking of saying the opposite, but was not willing to risk it. Or was that wishful thinking?

"I better go."

"Yes."

With quick pulls and tugs she had her clothes mostly back in order before they even stood. He fastened his shirt and tucked it in with reluctance as they headed to the door. He would have liked one more touch, one more brush of skin to skin.

"I'll take you to that movie tomorrow night."

"Dax, there's no need—"

"I want to see you, Hannah." He didn't have the strength in him to not say that.

She drew in a deep breath. "I want to see you, too."

Digging in his bottom drawer for the new shirt he'd bought on a spring trip to Denver, Dax came across the old black-and-white photograph.

He squatted there and stared at it the way he used to as a kid, the way he had that last night before he'd left home for good, never to return until his father's funeral.

A dark-haired woman with a smile that came from her eyes sat on the narrow porch step that used to lead to the back door before he added a full porch when he moved back. The woman wore a checked dress and an apron. She had both arms around a little boy of maybe five in denims and a plaid shirt who sat on her lap. Her cheek rested on the top of the boy's head, the shadow from her face obscuring the child's.

For no reason he could name he thought of the photographs of Hannah and her family he'd seen last night. In those pictures, everything was clear—the faces, the connections and the love. The features of her parents blended well in their children, so each resembled the others, yet carried a distinctive cast.

Seeing that in Hannah's photographs should have made the uncertainties and isolation he'd always found in this photograph hurt more. It didn't.

"Dad?"

Dax dropped the photo into the drawer, pushed it closed and rose before he turned around to face his son.

"What's up, Will?"

"What're you doing?"

"Getting a clean shirt." He bent to retrieve the shirt, setting off the telltale crinkle of tissue paper as he squeezed it.

"New shirt? What for?"

"I'm taking Hannah out tonight." He pulled the straight pins that had held the sleeves folded in place, shook it out and hung it up, running a hand down its surface in a rough ironing motion. Would Hannah run her hand over this fabric tonight? Would she slip a hand under the fabric and touch his skin? His lower body stirred at the thought.

But he wouldn't let it get carried away. He couldn't.

"Again?"

"Yup. It's what happens when two people have a good time together. If she lived around here, I'd go slower, but she's leaving in a week..." That was his safety net.

"You're not wearing the new shirt for the roping Friday?"

"Thought we'd wear the green, if that suits you." He crumpled the paper and sent it toward the wastepaper basket. It hit the rim and went in.

"Should've been all net on an easy shot like that."

"Lucky or good, two points are still two points."

Will grinned. "Guess it's a good thing you're lucky, then. Uh, Dad, Mr. Weston called and asked if I would come help them for a couple hours closing up some of the cabins for the season. With Pete at college, he said they could use some help—Travis Grainger's going to be there, too—and Mr. Weston said he'd pay us. My chores are done."

Dax understood the lure to Will of working for the Westons—they paid him. All the work Will did around the ranch earned him only rare extra cash. Will hadn't ever asked for a whole lot, and Dax had always been ready to give him money for a movie or a book or some candy in town. That needed to change. Will needed to be making more of his own choices, setting more of his own priorities about money. God, his son was really growing up.

"I thought we were going to practice roping?"

"I'll be back by five. We can get in an hour before supper."

And at seven-thirty he'd pick up Hannah. Strange the satisfaction that thought brought. "Homework?"

"Mostly done. I'll finish the reading tonight."

"Okay. You need a ride?"

"Nah, I'll ride Merc."

"Okay. See you at five, then."

"Bye."

Will headed out, but before Dax followed him—at least as far as the desk in the den where a stack of paperwork awaited him—his gaze went back to the bottom drawer of his dresser.

The picture doesn't hurt the way it used to.

But he'd still hidden it from Will.

Hannah slept in Sunday, and that was entirely Dax Randall's fault. First for keeping her up so late and second for invading her dreams.

But she wasn't about to tell the Westons that when she emerged from her cabin after noon. The less attention she drew from the group gathering by the main house's porch to prepare the unoccupied cabins for winter, the better. Besides Irene and Ted, Boone and Cambria, she saw Jessa, Travis Grainger and Will. Cambria for one wouldn't hesitate to ask about her evening with Dax, a question Hannah didn't want to answer, especially in front of Will.

"Hannah," called Irene. So much for slipping into the group unnoticed. "We saved you breakfast. It's warming in the oven."

"I had coffee. I'm ready to help. I just…I didn't, uh—"

"Nonsense, dear," Irene kindly cut her off. "Coffee is not enough. Come on, I'll get your plate, and then we'll catch up with these folks."

So Hannah was led off, with all eyes on her. That did not, however, kill her appetite for Irene's apple bread, scrambled eggs, crispy bacon and orange juice. While she ate, Irene talked about the tasks of draining water pipes, sealing windows and protecting furniture in the cabins.

"We'll get half done today, then next week's the festival so we'll have guests in the bunkhouse and a couple other cabins. But that's really the last of the season."

"Festival?"

"Shakespeare Days. A local celebration."

"Oh, yes, Boone mentioned that when we scheduled this trip."

"Next weekend is the rodeo and fair. So the rest of the cabins will wait until the weekend after. Although if you wanted to stay…"

Stay? Hannah pushed the idea away from the threshold of her mind and swallowed a bite of apple bread. "I have to get back. Boone isn't letting me do any work here, but I do still have a job I'm being paid for."

Irene sighed. "Then the cabins will all be empty and we'll finish week after next. I tried to get Cully to stay on here with Travis, but he wouldn't hear of it. Said he didn't want to impose. *Impose.*" She blew out an indignant breath. "I like having people around. Travis is staying with us tonight. It'll be like old times getting a boy up and out for the school bus tomorrow. And it's nice having Jessa and Travis and Will here to help today. Though it does seem strange without Pete. With him off at college, I guess a lot of things will be strange without him until he comes home for Thanksgiving."

"Have you heard from him?"

"Oh, yes, we e-mail and talk on the phone, but it's not like having him here. He's my baby, after all. It'll be good for Ted and me to be away awhile later this fall—in North Carolina when Cambria has the baby."

"That will give me a chance to repay some of your hospitality."

Irene smiled a bit absently. "That will be lovely, dear." Her gaze focused to a laser. "You've thought about having a baby, haven't you?"

"I, uh…" In the early days with Richard she'd longed for one. Since then? Had she thought about it? She wasn't sure she wanted to answer that question to herself, much less anyone else. "It's like you told Cambria at the cookout, Irene, the first step should be finding the right husband."

"Yes, of course." Irene wrapped the remaining apple bread, then put the orange juice and butter in the refrigerator. Hannah carried her empty plate and glass to the sink. "How is Dax?"

Hannah's fork rattled against her plate as she sputtered for an answer. Irene certainly had a knack. Her implication was clear, but couldn't be disputed without making a big deal of it. Hannah bent to load her dishes in the dishwasher. "He's fine, I guess."

"Yes, he is a fine man," Irene said, serenely misunderstanding. "And he's been such a good father to Will. It would be wonderful to see him have more children. He should have a baby, too. With the right woman, of course."

Was she the right woman? The question exploded in her mind before she could hope to defuse it. The image followed of a brown-eyed baby with a killer smile that wouldn't be as rare as the father's. And then another image—of her and Dax and methods of conception.

Oh, my.

"Someone who appreciates more about him than his tight buns. Someone who gets him to enjoy more in life, like a beautiful day or a starlit night. He deserves more happiness in his life."

Hannah knew she was gaping and blushing, and she couldn't stop either one. Irene looked so unthreatening, but she'd lobbed a half-dozen hand grenades into Hannah's stomach. *The right woman… He should have a baby, too… Beautiful day…starlit night…*

"There," Irene said briskly, surveying her tidy kitchen, "Now, we'll get you started helping Jessa with covering the furniture."

Hannah docilely followed Irene's instructions and stepped into a cabin in time to take the fluttering end of a sheet Jessa was shaking out over an overstuffed chair.

"Thanks. Glad to see you, Hannah," Jessa said as the subsiding sheet revealed her dark hair, then her smiling face. "I thought— Now tuck it into the crease of the cushion, then under the feet. I thought Irene might keep you in the kitchen bending your ear. But you weren't in there above twenty minutes. Although you do look a little…''

Hannah kept her head down as she secured the sheet under the chair foot. "There. Now what?" Her cheerfulness echoed hollowly in the partially shrouded room.

"The bedroom. Strip the bed, then cover the furniture with these." She hoisted a stack of covering sheets. "Are you okay, Hannah? Did Irene say something to upset you?"

Jessa sounded so concerned and the last thing Hannah wanted to do was malign Irene—even by omission. Besides, it was not what Irene had said but her own reactions that had her reeling. Irene had made a general observation, and she'd made it personal—very personal. Irene talked about Dax's baby, and Hannah had made it her baby, too. Like a schoolgirl combining her first name with her boyfriend's last name.

Hannah Randall.

No. *No.*

She wouldn't do that.

And she wouldn't confide in anyone like a schoolgirl, either—especially because she wasn't sure *what* she would confide if she did. She searched for something truthful, innocuous and not too revealing.

"She said…she said Dax has tight buns."

Jessa stopped dead with a pillow in one hand and the pillowcase she'd pulled off it in the other. "*Irene* said that?"

Hannah nodded vigorously. "She said *tight buns*. I'm not making that up."

"Tight buns…" Jessa shook her head in obvious bemusement. Then she giggled.

It was infectious, and a delicious release of the lingering aftershocks from Irene's hand grenades as Hannah broke into answering laughter. They both dropped onto the bed, laughing.

"Irene never ceases to amaze me," Jessa said, using a corner of the pillowcase to dab moisture from her cheeks.

"Though, I must say, she's right. Dax does have tight buns, along with some other very nice attributes. Oh, don't look at me that way, Hannah. There's never been anything like that between Dax and me."

"I didn't…I mean, it wouldn't be any of my busi—"

Jessa ignored her. "But you know, it's an odd thing—Cambria told me that getting together with Boone made her more comfortable with other men's attractiveness in some ways. You should have heard her on Cully." Jessa's slightly glazed expression made Hannah suspect Cully's fiancée was not remembering Cambria's comments, but the original model. "I've noticed it, too. It's like you know you've got the whole package that's the best for you, but that doesn't mean you don't admire individual points on other men. Dax has a lot of points worth admiring." She sighed and stood. Hannah helped remove and fold the spread and blankets, then piled the linens for washing. "It's just a shame no one's really seen beyond his tight buns to the whole man."

"That's what Irene said. 'Someone who appreciates more than his tight buns.'"

This effort to deflect the conversation failed. Jessa gave her a steady, serious look. "And someone who wouldn't disappoint him. He's had a lot of hurts."

Hannah drew a steadying breath. "Yes, I hope he finds that, too. It's been a pleasure to get to know him this past week and I hope to enjoy his company for the coming week, but then…"

"You might come back."

"Maybe." Hannah reached for the covering sheet to go over the now bare mattress, "but my life is in North Carolina."

"Lives can be moved. Believe me," she said, reminding Hannah that Jessa had moved to Bardville a few years ago. "Cully's doing it now. So's Travis for that matter. It's a tradition of the West. Maybe because not so long ago—in historical terms—everybody was new to the area, even most of the Native American tribes that are here now."

Hannah jumped on the opportunity to turn the conversation and peppered Jessa with questions about the region's history. She learned a lot of interesting information as they finished that cabin and moved on to three more. She also avoided uncomfortable questions and thoughts.

"You've been great, Hannah. I'll put the linens in the laundry room, then be on my way. I have to get cleaned up before Cully and I go out to dinner—a rare treat during campaign season, let me tell you."

"I've enjoyed it, Jessa, but I think you should let me take the linens in, because someone's waiting for you." Hannah nodded to a figure leaning against a four-wheel drive parked beside Boone and Cambria's.

Jessa turned around, then surrendered the armload of sheets and towels without an argument.

The tall man with the easygoing air took off his sunglasses and, as he focused on Jessa, Hannah felt a shiver zig down her back. When it came to this woman, Cully was not so easygoing, after all.

Was it possible for a man to be different with one woman?

She heard Jessa say, with a laugh, "You were supposed to meet me at the house, Cully. I'm a mess. I need to get out of these dirty clothes and take a shower."

Hannah thought Cully's low voice answered, "We can take care of that."

They put their arms around each other and kissed.

"There they go again," said Travis as he joined Hannah walking toward the house. His words, while filled with a twelve-year-old's disgust for such matters as adults kissing, also carried acceptance. As their path took them near the couple, he added, "Glad I'm staying with Irene and Ted tonight."

"Me, too, Trav," Cully said with a slow smile, his arm around Jessa.

With pinkened cheeks, Jessa put her palm to Cully's chest and rubbed lightly. "Feels like I haven't seen you in ages."

"This campaigning…"

"You're going to get elected. You don't have to campaign so hard." It wasn't a complaint, but a reassurance.

"Maybe. But I want people to know what they're getting. That way they're more likely to stick with the bargain when things get rough."

Everyone else seemed to show up at once, all eager to say hello to Cully. Hannah took the opportunity to slip away, depositing the linens, then heading back toward her cabin.

She had her own cleaning up to do before Dax arrived.

But she found herself thinking about Cully's words: *I want people to know what they're getting. That way they're more likely to stick with the bargain when things get rough.*

That was part of what had gone wrong with Richard. Neither of them had been truly honest in showing the other what they were getting. Richard had thought he was getting someone who enjoyed ambition and high living as he did. And she'd thought she was getting someone who could change to the warm, family-oriented man she'd wanted.

And when things got rough, they hadn't stuck with the bargain.

Dax Randall would always let someone know what they were getting, wouldn't he?

"Uh, Ms. Chalmers…?"

Caught.

Trying to forget she'd been indulging in more foolish schoolgirlisms, she straightened her shoulders and, with a determined smile, faced Dax's son by the empty camp fire circle. "Why don't you call me Hannah?"

"Okay. I, uh, just thought I should say—I mean, I *want* to tell you, it's not just I think I should." He ducked his head, then raised it and met her eyes straight on. "I'm sorry. For being such a jerk to you."

Hannah felt a bloom of warmth unfurl in her chest. The evening with Dax had been one of the best of her life. She felt comfortable talking to Dax; more important, she felt comfortable being silent with him. She'd known long before he'd kissed her—a kiss good-night that had come so close to turning into their saying good morning—that she felt more for this man than she had expected to.

As much as she'd tried to be sensible, she'd begun to hope Dax felt the same. What he'd told her about his exwife and raising Will had fueled that hope, for he clearly confided in few people. And the chemistry between the two of them could fuel a laboratory. Maybe Irene and Jessa were right. Maybe it wasn't outrageous to hope.

Will's blatant disapproval, however, posed an insurmountable obstacle. She wouldn't come between father and son, even if she could.

Now that obstacle stood contritely before her.

She smiled at Will. "I wouldn't say you were a jerk. No need to apologize. You weren't so bad."

"Yeah, I was." The stubborn lines around his mouth said he would take his punishment whether she wanted to dish it out or not. He looked very much like Dax at the moment. "I was a real jerk about you and Dad, uh, sort of seeing each other."

"That's natural, Will."

He shook his head. "Maybe so, but it wasn't right. Especially not since you're really...you know..." Red rushed up his neck and he ducked his head again. "Helping me out."

She didn't know. Helping him out? "I'm not sure I understand."

"Because Dad knew I didn't—I mean, to sort of show me what..." He shrugged, then added as if it said everything he could possibly hope to say. "Girls."

"Girls?"

"Yeah." His heartfelt syllable conveyed deep appreciation that she agreed with him. She still didn't know what he was talking about. Or rather, she didn't know what it had to do with her and Dax. "You know, how to talk and be around them and even, uh, ask them out on, uh, dates. Not that I'm going to do that," he added hurriedly.

Before she could ask for clarification, he launched on a spate of words that had her head spinning and her heart shriveling.

"Dad told me how you didn't really want anything to do with him in the first place and how you wanted to spend your vacation in peace, but you've been seeing him, anyhow. And he's been taking you out and all to help me out. That's how it's always been with him and me—he's always shown me how to do stuff. Like riding and roping, but other things too, you know, homework and such. He says that's what a father does for a son. But you didn't have to do any of this, and I wanted to tell you I'm sorry for being such a jerk when you were taking time from your vacation and all. And…and…well, thank you. That's all."

"You're welcome." The words came automatically. Automatic reactions were all she had left.

When Will said goodbye with the great cheer of one who'd successfully discharged his duty, she answered that automatically, too.

Then she retreated to her cabin, to wait until Dax arrived for their second try at seeing a movie.

Chapter Eight

Dax smiled at her when she answered the cabin door. A warm, slow smile. A little shy, a lot personal. As if he was remembering. As if it was drawn from him just because he was glad to see her.

She wanted to throw something at him. She wanted to slam the door. She wanted to cry.

But, no, she would deal with this in a straightforward, adult manner, no matter how she felt inside. No outbursts of tears or temper. If she'd been misled, she'd gone along more than willingly.

"You ready? Sheridan okay with you tonight?"

"Dax, I'd like to talk to you." She pushed the screen door open and stepped out.

His smile dimmed. "Something wrong, Hannah?"

She sidestepped the hand he would have put on her shoulder. "Let's go sit on the bench." Without waiting for an answer, she led the way to a bench not far from the footbridge over the stream.

He sat beside her, a frown in place and his brown eyes as grim as the night she'd met him. "What's this all about?"

She drew a deep, steadying breath.

"I want to ask you if the reason you started showing interest in me and asking me out is that you're acting as a kind of role model to your son—that you're using me to show Will how to get along with girls."

He stilled, and his eyelids lowered to half cover his eyes. The grooves by his mouth etched deeper. After a moment, he swallowed, and she knew she was about to get her answer.

She braced for the evasions, the half-truths, the self-serving, self-excusing, convoluted explanations and rationalizations....

"Yes."

She hadn't been braced for that. Not the single word. Uncompromising. Spare. Unvarnished.

A strangled laugh caught at her throat, but it came from surprise not amusement.

Maybe she'd been hoping, just a little, it wasn't true. And that he'd somehow convince her it wasn't true.

"How'd you...?"

"Will." She saw the grim lines in Dax's face tighten, and she quickly added, "He thought I kn-knew." Dax shifted as if he would reach for her and she held out a hand to stop him. "He was thanking me."

He remained at the distance her gesture had left him, but his low voice seemed to reach out to her.

"Hannah."

She didn't think she'd ever had a more eloquent apology. He hadn't meant to hurt her. But he had. And he was sorry.

"Why?" she asked when her voice cooperated.

"It's like I told you." Jaw tight, voice grim, he presented the picture of a man determined to tell an unpleasant truth about himself. "I haven't dated women around here because I don't want anything permanent, and no matter what they say, that's what they'd be thinking might happen, and then it gets to be a mess. So I steered clear.''

He regarded her from under the lowered line of his brows as if searching for understanding, and she found herself nodding.

This was a man she could trust. The thought slid into her mind. She considered it.

A man she could trust? He'd hurt her, hadn't he? He'd used her.

But he wouldn't pull lines on her—he certainly hadn't to this point. And the first tough question she'd asked him, he'd answered with unflinching honesty.

"That's been fine for me. But not for Will. Problem is, Will took my way of livin' to mean he shouldn't have anything to do with the girls 'round here, either. He got left out. Worse, he was cutting himself out. Settin' out all the dances on his own. He needed something to get him started, to help him jump in the ring. To see it was okay to try.''

Beyond his deep voice, she heard the familiar light tones of her sister telling her it was time to start her life again. Time to regain a social life. Time to open herself to certain possibilities again. Then Cambria's voice joined in, talking of babies and two-by-twos. And Irene's phrase about an empty nest.

And her own, inner voice, spoke up, though softly.

This was a man she could trust.

"A stranger seemed the answer. Somebody who wouldn't be around long, wouldn't get the wrong idea. After meeting you, June thought you'd be the perfect stranger—" The lines around his mouth dug deep and his lips thinned. "It was a damned fool idea. Not that I'm laying this off on June. I decided. I mean, I...well, I, uh, I thought you'd be the perfect stranger to show Will I didn't have anything against...you know...''

"Okay."

She hadn't known she was going to say it herself until

it came out. Since Will's words this afternoon, she'd been teetering between denial and a hurt she kept telling herself she shouldn't feel so deeply. Dax's forthrightness had ended the denial and somehow taken away the bitter taste of the hurt. Yes, she still felt disappointed that the possibilities she'd let herself dream of, though briefly, weren't going to come true. And, no, it didn't escape her that there'd been an element of using her in Dax's plan.

But he'd certainly come clean now.

This was a man she could trust.

She liked him. She trusted him. She enjoyed his company. And now, he was safe. *She* was safe from getting too involved.

She would leave in eight days. And after what he'd just told her there was no danger that she would really fall for him. An opportunity like this to ease back into dating at practically no risk was unlikely to ever come again. Could she afford to pass it up?

After all, didn't this situation with Dax show how dull her social instincts had become? She had been on the verge of falling for this man, when he'd viewed her as a partner in a demonstration for a teenager.

It was laughable.

Almost.

"Okay," she repeated. "Let's do it."

"Ma'am?"

"Let's show Will how it is." She wasn't sure if his stare meant he was simply stunned, or also shocked. Maybe decent women in his world didn't consider dating under these circumstances. "Unless you don't want to?"

He looked away from her for the first time. His gaze seemed to be pinned on the small stream. His big hands clenched, then released. He cleared his throat and said, "I...I'm not going to marry again."

Now she felt awkward. "I wasn't...I didn't mean..." Protesting made it worse. She swallowed and drew in a deep breath. "Dax, let's lay our cards on the table here.

You said I was the perfect stranger to help you give your son some lessons on how a man and woman..." She bogged down on the terminology. "Or, uh, a boy and girl, sort of, get together."

"I wouldn't say lessons." One side of his mouth tilted up in a grin as dry as tinder. "I wouldn't be one to be giving anyone lessons. More like if he sees me doing it, he'll see it's all right for him to be doing it, too."

Their eyes locked, and the phrase *doing it* seemed to echo between them.

Hannah watched Dax swallow hard and knew the only reason she didn't do the same thing was her throat muscles seemed to be frozen. Her imagination, however, was in fine form. Dax's touch, stroking, testing. Dax's mouth on her, tasting, delving. Dax's body above her, heating, claiming. Her hands on his broad chest, sliding down it, discovering the landscape of his muscles. Then lower, to his waist. And lower still...

"Being interested in a girl, I mean," Dax said at last.

Hannah's thoughts jerked back to the present and reality.

"Yes. Of course. Well, anyway, you said your sister said I was the perfect stranger to suit your purposes. Well, you're the perfect stranger for me, too."

He frowned.

Apparently it hadn't previously occurred to him that turnabout could be fair play or the sauce that spread over the goose could suit the gander just fine, too. From his expression he didn't particularly like the idea. Too bad.

She sat up, feeling a new enthusiasm for her idea. He'd viewed her as the perfect stranger, why shouldn't she view him as a practice run? A trip around the dating block with training wheels before she ventured out to try the real thing with a man who might stay in her life longer than two weeks.

"Raising my brother and sister, along with earning a living hasn't left me much free time. You must know how that is, with the ranch and Will." The barest dip of his head signaled his agreement. "I haven't had, uh, much of a social life. Everyone's telling me it's time I get back out there—into the dating whirl. But taking that first step…well, maybe this is a good way to do it. I leave in eight days. You don't want to get involved. I don't want to get involved. We get along okay."

His dark eyes met hers again, and the heat of them recalled the moments they'd spent on her couch less than twenty-four hours earlier. *Get along okay?*

She licked her lips, and his eyes followed the motion. "I leave in eight days."

"You said that."

"What?"

"'Bout you leaving in eight days. You already said that."

"It's worth repeating," she said, defensively. "Because it means there can be no misunderstandings—about the future or anything. We can go on as we were, and everybody wins. You can help Will feel comfortable with girls, because he sees you doing—uh, I mean being with me. And it could help me get my feet wet with dating again. So what do you think?"

Before he could answer, another thought occurred to her. *Go on as we were…* Going on as they were included last night on the couch. Going on as they were meant his mouth tempting her lips to open to his tongue, his hands skimming across her skin, his body heating hers. Not a good idea.

"I don't mean a fling, Dax. I'm not looking for a one-night stand or a vacation romance that gets all involved, uh, physically." Her cheeks were blazing. Too bad. For him to truly be the perfect stranger to get her started back into dating, she had to make this clear. His face remained impassive. "Do you know what I'm saying?"

"You're saying you don't want to go to bed with me."

Heat bolted through her as her unruly imagination flashed visions and sensations of lying beside Dax Randall's tough body in a wide, sheet-tangled bed. Oh, my. *Didn't want to go to bed with him?* She couldn't say that. Not without lightning coming down and striking her, to burn her outsides the way her thoughts had cindered her insides.

He saved her from lying, evading or worse—telling the truth, by adding bluntly, "You mean no sex."

"Right," she agreed with the enthusiasm of relief that his second, more clinical description produced no mind pictures. She hoped her dreams would be as cooperative. They sure hadn't been G-rated last night. "Pleasant companionship. An easy reintroduction to dating. No stress, no strain. Platonic. That's what I mean. The sort of relationship you'd like to show Will. If you still want to."

He hesitated so long she'd started to imagine how awkward the next eight days could be if he said no.

"Yeah. I want to."

Pleasant companionship. No stress, no strain.

She had made him sound like an ancient horse good for nothing more than ending its years out to pasture, or a white-muzzled dog that spent the day dozing in the sun. No, she'd made him sound like a young boy, Will's age.

Well, his hormones felt about that lively lately. Brushing arm to arm during the movie last night had had him in a sweat.

She'd gone along when he insisted on taking her to Sheridan for the movie. He couldn't have said what the movie was about to save his soul. She'd said she had a good time when he brought her back to the cabin, walked her to the door and saw her in without setting foot inside himself. It hadn't even been eleven o'clock.

He'd been left to a long night of trying to sort things out.

He was still trying Monday morning as he drove into Bardville.

They'd show Will the way of getting to know a

woman—Dax's hands tightened on the truck's steering wheel—in a social sense, not a biblical sense. And there'd be no danger of it going beyond that. Not now that her opinion of him had dipped below a snake's belly, and with good cause.

Not only had he sought her out at the Westons' for the sole purpose of flirting with her, but he'd gone way beyond that with kisses and touches that had nothing to do with wanting Will to know it was okay to be interested in females. And now that it wouldn't be happening anymore, the knowledge that he wanted Hannah in his bed was as stark and clear as if it were written on the windshield before his staring eyes.

The first part had been wrongheaded. Going beyond that had broken all his rules.

So it was a good thing—no matter what his gut felt like—that Will had spilled the beans and everything came out in the clear. No danger of him getting in any deeper this way. Much better this way.

"Much better," he murmured as he turned off Bozeman Avenue and onto Buffalo Street.

Dammit—he just wished she hadn't sounded so damned eager to agree when he'd said "no sex."

But that was foolhardy. Hannah Chalmers wasn't the kind to go to bed with a man she wasn't involved with. And he wasn't a man to get involved. She'd said it, she wasn't interested in a one-night stand. Not even an eight-night stand.

One night down. He suspected he was in for seven more very frustrating nights.

"June!" Dax swung open the back door of the small house where his sister had lived for thirty-one years, first with her husband, Henry, and after his death with her mother, Sally Randall.

"Quit your bellowing, Dax. You sound like a weaning calf." She came in carrying a divided plastic tote brimming with cleaning cans and rags in one hand and a broom in the other. "I'm in the same county, you know—and close that door before the wind blows in all the dirt I spent the morning sweeping out."

He marched over to the coffeemaker and poured himself a cup. "I wish you weren't."

"Sweeping? Pour me one, too."

He obeyed and June took a seat on the bench under a window facing the backyard. He leaned against the counter.

"In the same county. Then you couldn't butt into my life and I might get some peace."

"You don't need peace. You need a good shaking up," she said sternly. "Sometimes you need a good kick in the head."

He grunted and swallowed from his cup.

"Ah." June sat back in her chair. "Now I get a good look at you, I'm thinking maybe you got that kick in your head, and since you treat your horses too good to deserve it from them, I gotta think a woman did the kicking, and it musta been Hannah Chalmers, since she's the only candidate." She tilted her head. "Guess she's got a good, strong leg on her."

"You sound damned pleased."

"I am. So what happened?"

"Your great plan turned out not so great. She figured out I'd asked her out just to help out Will."

"Just to...? Dax Randall, you don't need a kick in the head, you need a house falling on you. That's what you told her?"

"Well, she asked," he said defensively. "I wouldn't lie."

"Of all the stupid—you're hopeless. So she tore a strip off your hide and now she won't have anything to do with you, huh?"

"No."

"No? No what?"

"She didn't tear a strip off my hide and turns out she's

in the market for a perfect stranger herself. We're going to keep seeing each other—as friends.''

June gave a snort of laughter.

''June, you—''

The back door opened, and a woman with gray hair and slightly halting walk came in. She smiled when she saw him.

He pushed away from the counter. It was Monday. One of his mother's days for physical therapy on her hip. What was she doing here?

June echoed his thoughts, though not his sentiments. ''Mom, what are you doing home? Something wrong?''

''Nothing's wrong—not with me. Sylvia, who does my therapy, came down with the flu and had to leave. Irene Weston had stopped by the hospital with some supplies for the volunteers, and she brought me home.''

''I gotta go. See you later.'' Dax gave a nod and headed out past Sally Randall.

''Dax—?'' his mother said from behind him.

He kept going.

Dax didn't feel much like conversation, but Will didn't deserve to suffer for either the mood that had dogged him since this morning or the mess he'd gotten himself into with Hannah. So at supper Dax asked, as he always did, how things had gone that day at school.

Will's fork, which had been making round trips from his plate of June's reheated lasagna to his mouth with enthusiastic regularity, stopped abruptly in midair. Dax counted himself lucky the fork was empty. Tomato sauce was one of those laundry mysteries neither he nor Will ever solved.

''Well, how'd it go?'' he repeated.

''Fine.''

''What's up, Will?''

''Nothing's up.''

Dax sighed and put his own fork down. ''How bad is it?''

"What do you mean?"

"Expelled? Suspended? Flunking?"

Will's defensiveness evaporated under the heat of outrage. "No! Why would you think that? A stupid project is no big deal, and it's all under control, so I don't know how you can start thinking I'd get expelled or be flunking."

"I don't think that. I'm just putting it in perspective. So what's the project?"

"It's on the different flora and fauna in our region. You know how you're saying that right around here we have near desert and grasslands and foothills and mountains and river bottoms and all that."

"Yeah. So what's the problem?"

"Each pair got assigned an area."

"What did you got?"

"Shell Canyon."

The canyon cut into the Big Horn Mountains by Shell Creek on the other side of the range, feeding into the Big Horn Basin to the west, but it wasn't that far beyond where they summer-grazed cattle, and he knew the area well. Dax shrugged. "Okay, I'll drive you up."

"Not just me." Will sent him a pleading look that Dax didn't understand. "My partner, too."

"Partner?"

Will colored up from the opening of his shirt to the tip of his ears. "Theresa Wendlow."

Ah. Now Dax understood everything, including the pleading look. It had meant, please don't tease me about this. *I wouldn't do that to you, Will,* he silently pledged.

"No problem, I'll drive you both up."

"That's just it, Dad…having my father drive us up and hang around all the time, it'd be so *lame.*"

"It's too far to ride and unless you can wait until you're old enough to drive to do this project, I don't see how you're going to get around it."

"I thought…I thought if you asked Hannah—Ms. Chalmers—we could all go up. You know, sort of like you talked about. Besides, then you'd have somebody to hang around with while we took notes and stuff, and it wouldn't be so weird. It'd be more like…I don't know…normal."

God help him, a double date. With his son. Taking out the woman who had him feeling like an edgy stallion, but swearing to behave like a twenty-year-old gelding.

Only for Will…

"I'll ask her."

Chapter Nine

At the sight of Dax Randall standing at the bottom of the steps outside her cabin Tuesday morning, Hannah stopped dead at the edge of the porch.

The cabin's outer door slammed shut behind her, and she jumped. At least it got her moving again.

"Good morning, Dax."

"Morning. Hope it's not too early."

"No. I was going—" She gestured toward the Westons' kitchen door. "I'm sure Irene would love to give you some breakfast."

"No. Thanks. I can't stay. I wanted to catch you before you got tied up for the day. But…are you okay?"

"Fine."

"You sound kind of hoarse."

Lack of sleep or reaction to seeing him? Neither alternative would she confide to him. "I'm fine. What is it, Dax?"

"I didn't expect this to come up so soon, but…" He

hooked his thumbs in his front pockets. He'd done that other times when he was uncomfortable, but she wished he'd break the habit. The pose unintentionally framed the region around his zipper—and that made *her* uncomfortable. "Will's been assigned a school project and Theresa Wendlow's his partner. He's as skittery as a mother cat and thinks having you along would make things easier—for him."

"On a school project?"

"Yeah. About the plants and animals and geology and history and such of different local areas. They got assigned a spot on the west side of the Big Horns, so I'm going to drive them over. So…would you like to go to Shell Canyon this afternoon?"

"Oh…I, uh—"

"It's a nice drive. The canyon's interesting and there's a waterfall. It's worth seeing. You can ask Cambria or Irene."

"I'm sure it is. That's not—" *—the issue.* But did she really want to get into what the issue was? "This afternoon? But aren't the kids in school?"

"I wouldn't be telling you they'd be going if they were going to be in school. I'm not lying, Hannah."

"I'm not saying—"

"It's Shakespeare Days Week."

"Shakespeare Days Week?"

"Yeah. This weekend is Shakespeare Days—for the county, you know? Shakespeare County. Celebrating the early days of the county. There's a rodeo, a parade, a sort of fair and lots of other things.'

"Oh, yes. Irene told me a little about the festival."

"Lot of the stuff's this weekend, but it starts during the week. When I was a kid the teachers used to keep us in class, but not a lot got done. Now they've decided, since it's so early in the school year, they can cut the kids some slack. Take the younger ones on field trips about county history. Give the older ones special projects and let 'em loose early. Including today. We'll drive to Shell Canyon, let them get what they need for their project, then go for supper at a little place on the creek the other side of the canyon. Should be back before ten.''

"I see." She manufactured a bright smile. "Okay. I'd like to see Shell Canyon, thank you. I'll be sure to bring my camera. Oh, and I'll pay my own expenses.''

"No." He should have been at a disadvantage, still having to tip his head back because he stood below her. But that *no* carried no doubt.

"Since this is as much for my benefit as yours, Dax, it only makes sense," she said with exaggerated reasonableness.

"How's it to your benefit?"

"Like I told you, it's helping me get back into socializing.''

He glared at her—no other word described the lowered brows, tight mouth and glinting eyes. "I asked, I'll pay. And it's mostly for Will's benefit.''

He didn't have to remind her. "Then for Will's benefit it's important to show him that a woman can be independent and pay her own way.''

"A woman can be independent and still be treated nice.''

She opened her mouth, then closed it. It sure weakened her arguing stance when she agreed with him. "So can a man.''

He grunted an acceptance.

"Besides," she added, picking up speed again. "Being treated nice doesn't necessarily mean paying the bills. They're separate issues.''

"Maybe so, but when someone does the invitin' he should do the payin'.''

"All right," she conceded after a moment. "But if I ask you to something, then I pay.''

Silence.

"All right?" she insisted.

"All right. But today I'm paying.''

* * *

The twisting road seemed oddly familiar, though she was certain she hadn't seen these views before—the land dropping off sharply to the east in vistas of rolling, rugged land dotted by the hand of man with threads of roads and flecks of fields and the mountains rising solidly to the west. Fir-tree mantles covered rock shoulders with aspens circling the lower edges like flame yellow fringe. From the top it must seem as if you could see forever.

Of course.

This was the road Dax had taken for the first part of their journey to his overlook the night they'd gone to Billings—just three days ago.

Hurried whispers from the back seat produced Will's request. "Dad, can you pull over at an overlook so we can get pictures?"

"Sure."

They all piled out when he stopped his four-wheel drive in a parking area off one of the switchbacks cutting its way up the mountains. Will and Theresa walked over to read a sign describing the area's geology; he took notes and she took pictures. Theresa was quite pretty with shining light brown hair past her shoulders and bright blue eyes—and she was obviously smitten with Will.

Hannah saw Theresa slip in a shot or two of Will among the pictures she snapped of the area.

Smiling, Hannah turned away to follow the twisting of the road back down the mountainside.

"Is that the Westons' barn?" She pointed to a speck of red.

"No. They're farther south." Dax gestured past a rib of the mountain chain that extended into the valley. "Beyond that. Kearny Canyon, where we rode, is tucked back in there."

"So this is a different angle from your spot?"

He cut a look at her and for a second she thought he might say he didn't know what she meant. In a way she wouldn't blame him. Only three days ago, but another time.

He pointed to a knob of land jutting from a second, taller rib of mountain beyond the one he'd first indicated. "It's more south of here."

Back in the four-wheel drive, they continued up until they reached a relatively level area, then turned south on one highway, while another continued west.

"That's the road to where we graze cattle summers," Will commented as they passed a set of tire tracks worn into the hard ground.

"I read that most of the early grazing up here was sheep," Theresa said. "One of the books I checked out for this assignment said cattlemen came up here first, after farmers started planting more of the grazing land. But before the turn of the century, there were one hundred and fifty sheep for every cow."

"You know about Copman's Tomb?" Dax asked her, glancing in the rearview mirror.

"Of course. I've lived here all my life, Mr. Randall."

Dax seemed inclined to grin at Theresa's indignation. He sent Hannah a look that invited her to share his amusement, then turned away immediately. Perhaps to pay attention to the winding road, but Hannah thought more because he'd remembered they were on different terms now.

It was a good thing he broke the eye contact, because another heartbeat and she'd have forgotten their changed status, too.

"Why don't you tell Hannah about it, Theresa?"

"It's a huge yellow rock. It was named after Jack Copman—one of the first cattlemen to bring a herd up here in the summer, back in the 1880s."

"He was a sheepman, too," said Dax. "His real name was Wolfgang Robert Copman, and he brought a herd from Oregon. Then Copman stuck here. Old-timers' story is he built a model airplane."

"A model airplane?" Will sounded surprised and interested.

"Uh-huh. Kind of a glider, according to the story. He

said if he built a full-size one, he'd take it to the top of what we call Copman's Tomb and try it out. If his airplane worked, he'd fly. If it didn't, then that pile of rock would be his tomb—that's how it got its name. That was in the early 1880s.''

"But…but…"

"That's right. It might have been Wolfgang Robert Copman in the Big Horns instead of Orville and Wilbur Wright at Kitty Hawk if things had gone different.''

"What happened to his plane?" Will asked.

"Nobody knows. Some articles quote old-timers swearing they saw it fly, but nobody knows what happened to his design.''

"We can use this in our report," Theresa said. "What happened to him?"

"He got his own ranch eventually—over on the basin side of the Big Horns. Got married, had some daughters and died. Story is he wanted his ashes scattered up here, but his widow didn't do it.''

Was that a trace of bitterness Hannah heard in Dax's voice? Was he thinking this was another woman who failed her man? Or was she reading much too much into a story of local lore?

"How do you know all that, Dad?"

"You two aren't the first ones to have Mrs. Plankeski assign you a project, you know. I had to find out all about Copman's Tomb when I was your age.''

"And you still remember it?"

"Yeah, I still remember it," Dax said with indignation. "I'm not ready to be put out to pasture yet." He cut a look at her then that Hannah couldn't interpret. But she forgot it when he announced, "And there it is.''

Out the windshield, Hannah saw a flat-topped rock bluff rising abruptly above the craggy ground, its golden surface striated with red and tan and beige. It was nearly bare except for a cluster of stubborn fir trees on its stair-stepped back slope. She focused her camera through the glass and shot several pictures.

Not long after, Dax pulled into a parking area and announced they'd arrived.

Off the main path, signs described some of the plants that dotted the rock-strewn landscape with the green of scrub pine, the silver of fading sagebrush and the gold, crimson and lemon of deciduous bushes and trees. Hannah recognized juniper but not the orange-leaf flecked bush identified as curlleaf mountain mahogany.

"And they use the wood for roller-skate wheels," Theresa finished reading. "This is great. We'll have to take notes on these for our paper, but let's go see the falls first."

As they started down the steep, occasionally spray-slickened steps to the main observation deck, Dax went first. He reached back to take Hannah's arm a couple times to make sure her footing was steady. Hannah noticed Will did the same thing for Theresa, so she knew Dax's gesture was done as an example for his son.

Hannah went immediately to the railing to watch the water take its seventy-five-foot tumble to a steep rock cavern where the water churned and foamed before continuing on its way.

Behind her Theresa and Will moved around, talking about points to make in their paper and questions to answer before they wrote it. Dax remained some three feet behind her and to her right, moving nearer only when she leaned over the railing to take a picture of the water below. He stepped back when she straightened.

She kept busy with the camera, pleased by the rich color of the vegetation and the angles and lines of the rocks. She marveled at the tenacity and ingenuity of nature. A wall of rock presented itself, yet out of a crevice grew a tree. A tree with its roots clinging to an apparently impossible spot yet growing straight and proud, reaching toward the sky and celebrating with a blaze of yellow-orange.

She took many pictures, but she kept coming back to that tree, zooming in on it until it alone filled her lens.

"We're going back to check out those signs, okay, Dad?"

"Sure. We'll be there in a while."

Hannah glanced at Dax, who gave a slight shrug. She supposed he was right—the two kids probably wanted some time on their own. She just wished it didn't leave her and Dax alone, too.

For something to do, she followed them with the camera. "Theresa? Will?"

She snapped a picture of them as they turned back at her call. It would be a good picture, their youth and zest caught against this humbling stark beauty.

They laughed and kept going. She tracked them with the camera, but the curves of the path and the vegetation masked them from view. Instead, she found herself contemplating the jagged wall of rock rising behind them. She wondered how many people ever turned away from the falls to this side of the canyon.

The lowering sun caught the jutting rock formations and cast dramatic shadows into the crevices. That's how Dax's face looked sometimes. In firelight, like that first night. Or when he tried to damp down a strong emotion. It would look more and more like that as he aged, she thought. She wouldn't see it then. But she could remember.

She swung the camera around, hoping to catch Dax unaware. His brown eyes stared directly back at her through the lens. She lowered the camera. But that was worse. Now she no longer had the protection of the lens. Her breath came shorter and shallower.

"Oh, look, Thomas! Now, aren't you glad we stopped?"

A high-pitched voice and heavy footsteps descending the path above them broke the moment. Hannah moved to the far corner of the observation deck, and Dax came to stand about two feet away as "Thomas," a stout man with grizzled hair and heavy jowls, stumped down the final steps, followed by a woman about the same age with a barrel-shaped body over shapely legs. The men exchanged nods and Hannah and the woman smiled at each other.

"Isn't this pretty? Why, my word, do you see that tree growing over there just like it wasn't solid rock? Isn't that something? It would have been a shame to miss this."

Thomas harrumphed. "Ain't what I'd call pretty."

But Hannah noticed he didn't argue that it would have been a shame to miss it and smiled to herself.

Side by side, but with a foot of space between them, she and Dax gazed out at the water rolling, dashing and cascading down the rocks in silence while Thomas and Mrs. Thomas shared the platform with them. When the older couple started the climb back up the stairs, Hannah searched for an innocuous subject.

"Theresa seems like a really nice girl."

Dax grunted without moving from his position—bent forward, forearms resting on the railing, one hand cupped over the other, staring at the water.

"Do you know her parents?"

"Everybody in the county knows the Wendlows. They've got money. Came into the county in the fifties already having money and they haven't lost it. He runs a trucking company that does okay, but family money is how they go to Europe and such."

"What kind of people are they?"

"Nice enough. They're country club. She's always raising money for the library or school trips to Denver to hear a symphony and such. She started giving art supplies to the high school years before Theresa got there for kids who couldn't afford their own. Does it quiet, too. They do most of their spending in town and Sheridan, and when a range fire threatened some houses in Bardville—rundown places, but all those people had—he was out there with the rest of us fighting it."

Hannah murmured an acknowledgment, mulling how much his answer revealed about Dax. He wasn't impressed by the trips to Europe or the country club or even the obvious sharing of their wealth. But he saw their contributions to the local economy as a kind of loyalty. And the individual efforts of Mrs. Wendlow's quiet generosity and Mr. Wendlow's working to help fellow Shakespeare County residents made them okay in Dax's mind.

He judged, and he used tough standards. But not the world's standards. Not money or prestige or power or privilege. He judged on loyalty and generosity and pitching in when you're needed.

The awareness of being watched broke across her thoughts like a wave. She looked up to find Dax had turned his back to the railing; he was resting his elbows on it behind him and unabashedly studying her. Without allowing herself a chance to think about it, she lifted the camera and snapped a picture. No fiddling with the focus or fine-tuning the exposure. When that frame was developed she might have nothing. But then again, she might have something...special.

He said nothing about it, only, "We'd best get going. Light's going to fade fast now. Won't be enough, pretty soon."

"Yes," she agreed.

But as they started the steep climb up, she wished she'd asked if he meant the light Theresa and Will needed for their project, the light she needed for photographs or something else entirely.

"You and your dad seem to be getting along okay." Theresa pulled out a notebook to copy the information on the plaques describing the plants.

"Sure," Will said.

"That's good. Even with...? I mean, because I thought last week... Uh, you didn't seem to like Hannah much."

"I like her okay, I guess. But I don't like everybody marrying my dad off to her with their gossip."

"Oh." Theresa tucked her hair behind her ear.

"It's okay now. They're friends." He didn't know why he felt a desire to explain it to her, but he found himself repeating, "Friends."

She gave him a soft look that made him feel his knees might melt. "You really think so, Will?"

"Yeah." He said it more sharply than he meant to, but she didn't get upset. And she didn't argue.

"Okay." She bent her head over her notebook. "Can you read off that last sentence to me?"

He read the words describing how juniper smelled on a camp fire, which was pretty lame because how it smelled didn't matter in the mountains on a cold night. But his mind wasn't on that, anyhow.

"Oh, here, this will be good." She picked up a twig some passerby had broken off the bush and put it between the back pages of her notebook. "You're my witness I didn't pick it, okay?"

"Yeah, sure. What you said before, about my dad and Hannah...you don't think they're friends?"

"I didn't say that. It's just..."

"Just what?"

"Have you noticed how he looks at her? Especially when he thinks she isn't looking. It's exactly the way Hugh Grant looked at Emma Thompson."

"Who?"

"Hugh Grant in *Sense and Sensibility*. The movie Mrs. Henratty showed us in English last spring, remember?"

Hell, yes, he remembered. "That guy? The one who kept falling over his words and couldn't hold still? My dad's *nothing* like him."

"Oh, no, I'm not saying that. But there's something in your dad's eyes... Well, maybe I'm wrong. You certainly know him better than I do."

"I know him better than anybody does, and he and Hannah are friends, that's all." But he'd pay a lot closer attention to his father's eyes when Hannah was around.

"Okay. It's kind of a shame, though."

"Why?"

"Well, she's nice and your dad…he's been alone for so long."

"He hasn't been alone."

"Oh, I know, but you'll be going off to school in a couple years, and then he'll really be alone."

Will hadn't thought of that before. Sure, he'd envisioned going to college, planned on it, in fact. But the vague images he'd conjured had always been of himself at some movie set college—sometimes a Mickey Rooneyish atmosphere of football games and tree-lined paths, then sometimes an *Animal House*-like series of escapades. He'd never once considered what his father would do when he went to college.

Run the Circle CR, of course. By himself? His dad would have to do all the chores he did now, plus Will's. And face it, his dad wasn't getting any younger.

"He can hire a hand to help him out," he said out loud.

But what stuck wasn't the idea of his father doing double chores. It was his father sitting alone, with no one to talk to at suppertime.

Dax pulled into the circular drive in front of the Wendlows' sprawling, multilevel home and stopped in front of the double doors with the hidden lighting and the bench flanked by pots of chrysanthemums.

"Thank you, Mr. Randall, for taking us up to Shell Canyon and for supper and all."

"You're welcome, Theresa."

While Hannah and Theresa said good-night, Dax gave his son a significant look, and Will slid out of his seat and went around to open Theresa's door.

"Will," Dax said. The boy leaned over and peered in the still-open car door. "We'll wait for you over there."

Dax eased the car a short way farther around the circle, then pulled off to the side into a puddle of shadow and parked.

He stared straight ahead. The lighting caught his and Hannah's reflections in the windshield, curving their images and making it seem they sat so close they nearly touched, instead of with as much of the seat between them as Hannah could manage. With the engine off, it seemed incredibly quiet. So quiet, he thought he heard Hannah's breathing, could almost imagine the sound of fabric brushing against her soft skin as her breasts rose and fell.

He watched the sweet, slow movement in the reflection and his gut burned hot.

"That was nice of you."

At the first sound of Hannah's voice he jerked guiltily. Friends, he'd promised her. Platonic, she'd said. Not sitting next to her lusting after her. Not with all his blood and sense headed south so none remained to fuel his brain cells and he didn't have a clue what she was talking about. How many times had that happened today? More than he liked.

"What?"

"Giving them some privacy."

In the windshield he could see that she'd shifted to look at him. All he'd have to do was turn his head and their reflected images would be mouth to mouth. In reality, he'd have to reach for her. Take her shoulders in his hands and pull her toward him. Press his lips to hers. Open her mouth with the pressure of his tongue. Touch her soft curves—

"You know, Will and Theresa?" She sounded both amused and puzzled.

"What about them?" He sounded as if he'd eaten sandpaper. Felt like it, too. And his arm muscles twitched with the urge to take hold of her. To touch her.

"Giving them some privacy? Pulling over here like this so they wouldn't think we were staring at them, spying on them, as they said good-night."

He stretched his arms and pressed his palms against the steering wheel. The cold, dimpled surface rubbed against his palms.

"I didn't do it for them."

Three days ago his palms had absorbed the sweet sensation of her nipples, hard and warm.

"Oh?" She still faced him.

He slid his hands around the steering wheel, to the bottom. If her eyes followed the movement, her focus would be square on his lap, where there was more to focus on every second.

"A man on a diet who watches someone else eating cake is a fool."

"Oh."

He barely heard that, because she found something real interesting to study in the dark out her side window just then.

He jerked his hands away from the wheel, the left one landing on the door handle, the right one on the seat. The tips of his fingers grazed her thigh and she jumped. His left hand clenched in reaction and the handle clicked as the door opened a crack.

That brought her head around as he turned to apologize for touching her and there they sat, face-to-face. No more than twelve inches from mouth to mouth. The world spun down to the two of them. There was no light except what touched her face. No sound except her breathing. No smell except her spice. No touch except her remembered soft heat.

"Hannah—"

The world exploded in on them. The dome light glared and the door creaked as Will yanked it open with an excess of youthful muscle. The dry earthiness of fall fields and Will's own scent of boy and leather boots billowed into the vehicle as he plopped down in the center of the back seat, slammed the door closed and leaned forward, all beaming smile and wind-mussed hair.

"Thanks, Dad. Let's go."

Dax had driven with twists and strains of every limb and more muscles than he could count, but he couldn't remember in all his born days a more uncomfortable driving experience than this trip. He ached. Inside and outside. And Hannah sat silent and unreachable beside him, while Will hummed tunelessly in the back seat.

"You know, Dad, if you wanted to drop me off first, that would be fine," Will said as they turned onto the highway that led first to the Westons' ranch and then theirs. Will might have meant it as man-to-man magnanimity, though his voice held an odd note.

"I really should get back—"

"No."

His grim negative coincided with Hannah's more tempered response, and that ended the discussion.

So they dropped Hannah off, with twin awkward farewells from the Randall men to Hannah. Dax guessed they were neither one of them sure how to deal with Hannah now that she was a friend.

Though he strongly suspected that Will did not deal with the problem when they got home by stripping down and stepping into a frigid shower.

Chapter Ten

A phone call interrupted Wednesday's breakfast with the Westons. Ted Weston answered.

"It's for you, Hannah. It's a man."

"Why don't you take it in the den, dear," Irene suggested. "You'll have some privacy."

"It's not Dax," Ted added.

Hannah flushed at Ted's implicit expectation that the man who'd be calling her was Dax Randall—and that she would need privacy only to talk to him. But she simply thanked him and went to the den.

"Hello?" She heard the click of the extension being hung up.

"Who's Dax?" came the long-distance question.

"Ethan! How are you? Why are you calling? Is something—"

"Nothing's wrong. I'm fine. Mandy's fine. Who's Dax and why would he be calling you?"

"He wouldn't. I mean he might, but I didn't necessarily expect—"

"Who is he?"

"He's a man out here I've gotten to know."

"Dating?"

"Some. Casually," she added hurriedly.

"Good. Mandy'll be happy."

"Oh, Ethan, don't—"

"Don't tell Mandy? You've got to be kidding."

She'd recognized the foolishness of the request as soon as she heard herself voicing it. Mandy could smell a secret a hundred miles away, and she and Ethan rarely kept any from each other. "I don't want her making a big thing of this."

"Mandy? You've got to be kidding," he repeated, this time with a big dollop of sarcasm.

Hannah laughed. "She called me last week all wrapped up in a story about a woman from the civil war she's studying in a class."

"Mary Albert. Don't I know it. I've been hearing about Mary Albert for weeks."

"The best thing is, Mandy's got one of her notions that I could be headed for the same fate."

Instead of a laugh from Ethan, Hannah heard silence. "Ethan?"

"She's worried about you. We both are."

"There is no cause to be worried about me. I'm fine."

"Don't you get lonely, Hannah? I mean, without—"

"Oh, Ethan, of course I miss you and Mandy, but I've hardly had time to get lonely. You've hardly been to school a month and what with work and this trip..."

"I wondered about...Richard. Do you regret—"

"Never. You and Mandy have this crazy idea I somehow sacrificed myself for you. That's absolutely not true. As for Richard, one of the things I've realized out here is that that time of my life is absolutely behind me, and so is he, and I'm glad."

"Does this Dax have anything to do with that?"

"I told you, it's nothing serious." For half a heartbeat an impulse to tell Ethan the whole story tempted her. The notion that she didn't tell him because it might be disloyal to Dax she dismissed as quickly as the original thought. It simply wasn't Ethan's business. "Casual, that's all."

"But you don't want it to be?"

The question stopped her. She was surprised Ethan would ask it. Shocked she didn't immediately know the answer. "I'm going to be here only a few more days."

"So?"

She could have told him he sounded like several people here in Bardville, but that would have meant more explaining than she intended. "He's a very nice man. I'm getting to see some of the area—oh, and Ethan, it's amazing country. You'll have to see it someday. It's incredible."

"And how about this very nice man named Dax? Will I meet him someday? Any chance he'll be visiting North Carolina?"

"No," she said firmly, because she knew what he really wanted to know. If there was a future. "But speaking of visiting, when are you and Mandy going to come home for a weekend?"

As the conversation shifted to the activities that would keep her siblings on campus until Thanksgiving, Hannah felt a pang and wondered if she'd told a lie when she said she wasn't lonely. Or if it was only regret at having to so firmly kill the image that had sprung to life of a Thanksgiving table with Mandy and Ethan joined by Dax, Will and June.

Only later, walking along the stream behind the cabins, did she think of the face not included in that image—Sally Randall.

Dax kept such a solid wall between himself and his mother it even influenced her.

Now, that was interesting. Because Hannah had learned that if someone didn't care about something, they didn't bother building walls against it, they walked away. Only strong emotions needed walls to hold them in—or out.

Why did Dax need such a strong barrier?

She considered what Irene, Cambria, June and Dax had said about his childhood and marriage—and what Dax *hadn't* said.

The realization burst across her brain like a fireworks display.

Dax kept away from his mother because he didn't trust his defenses against wanting his mother's love. A love he didn't believe in and didn't trust.

As long as he kept distance between them, Sally Randall posed no threat to the wall he'd built around his heart. But if he'd thought the wall was unbreachable, he wouldn't have minded seeing her. So, if someone threw the two of them together and let nature take its course...

Surely that wasn't trying to change the man. It was simply letting the true man come out of a self-imposed exile.

The knock on the cabin door shortly after one in the afternoon startled Hannah awake from a doze. She hadn't slept well the past week, especially not since Sunday, and this was not the first time she'd dozed off on the couch while reading professional journals—the only work Boone appeared willing to have her do. It was also not the first time Dax had invaded her dreams, with his dark eyes, roughened hands and firm mouth.

It *was* the first time she woke to find Will Randall standing on the cabin porch, with fist raised to knock on her door again.

"Will?"

She paused in the motion of running her hands through her hair and looked from the boy to the man who stood behind his right shoulder on the porch. For a disorienting second she wondered if she'd conjured him up from her dreams. The same tough body, the same sun-streaked hair and the same steaming heat in his eyes.

But no, he couldn't be a remnant of the dreams that plagued her. He hadn't been wearing anywhere near as many clothes as the work shirt, faded jeans and beat-up boots he had on now. Though he had, come to think of it, had his cowboy hat on at times.

"Uh, Hannah? I wondered if you could maybe do me a favor?"

Will's voice cleared her mind of confusion—the boy had certainly never appeared in any of those dreams—and broke whatever had riveted her eyes to Dax's.

"Come in. Come in, both of you." She backed into the small living area of the cabin, scooped up a fan of advertising journals from the couch cushions and dropped them on the low chest that served as a coffee table. "Have a seat."

Will followed her gesture to the couch, but Dax went across the room, took a chair from the square table, turned it around to face the room and sat down, one booted ankle over the other knee.

Reading all this to mean that Dax wanted Will to handle this on his own, Hannah sat in the corner of the couch, angled to face the boy. That left Dax also in her line of sight. She concentrated on Will, but remained attuned to his father. Dax seemed decidedly grumpy for some reason.

"What kind of favor, Will?"

"It's a... I thought—I hoped—maybe you could, er, would..."

Will checked over his shoulder to his father, and her eyes followed the same path. "His idea," Dax said, his low voice barely a rumble. What was with the man? He might want Will to run this show, but he didn't have to be such a bear about it.

"I'm sure we can work something out, Will," she said with a soothing smile.

He looked at her anxiously for a moment, as if trying to gauge her sincerity, then drew in a breath, set his jaw just like his father did and said, "It's about going to supper at the country club."

"The country club?" she repeated, not following this so far.

"There's a big party there every year the Saturday of Shakespeare Days Week. They have a real good view of the fireworks from the county fairgrounds and I guess they have dancing and this big, fancy supper. Only it's not a supper, it's a *dinner*."

He emphasized the last word as if it should explain his whole problem to her, but her face must have shown it didn't. He started toward his father again, then stopped himself.

"Theresa asked if I wanted to go this year—you know, sit with her family and all. I wasn't thinking—she caught me off guard—and I said yes. And now I can't say no."

"You weren't thinking about what, Will?"

"I don't know anything about fancy dinners. I'd be sure to do something wrong in front of...of everybody. I hoped maybe you'd teach me about what I'm supposed to do, so I won't mess things up in front of everybody."

Especially Theresa and her family. Sympathy welled in Hannah.

"You won't do anything wrong, Will. At least not anything major. The first thing to remember is the idea is to have a good time."

"So, you'll help me?" His eyes, so like Dax's, gleamed with hope.

"Absolutely. I could set up a table like you're going to see, so it would be familiar Saturday night, and go over what utensil you use for what." Her planning aloud hit a snag. "If I had a formal place setting here. Maybe the Westons—"

"You mean fancy forks and knives and stuff? We've got that, don't we, Dad?" Will eagerly turned to his father for confirmation.

Dax grunted an affirmative. "Family stuff."

"A whole cabinet of it," Will added. "We had to take it all out to move it once—silverware and dishes and fancy glasses. I'd never seen it before that."

A whole cabinet of family tableware packed away as thoroughly as Dax had packed away his thoughts of his mother. A plan started taking shape in Hannah's mind. A plan that involved more than teaching Will the niceties of place settings.

"How would you like to have a practice, Will?"

"A practice? What do you mean?"

"A sort of dress rehearsal. Instead of just showing you how the table would look, we could have a real dinner. Let's see…if we polish the silverware and get the dishes ready, you'd get to know the pieces. Then I could cook, and we could have a real practice dinner—like it'll be at the country club. So you'll have already gone through the whole thing once before Saturday's dinner."

"That'd be great."

"Hannah," Dax said in that gruff voice that meant he was uncomfortable, "you don't want to be doing all that work."

"It would be a pleasure." Polishing wasn't her favorite activity, but in this instance, it would be a pleasure—for Will's sake and for Dax's.

"I thought you'd show him some things about forks and such and that would be it. Not polishing and making a meal and all."

He couldn't possibly know what she had in mind for him, but something had him growling. Perhaps he picked up warning signals the way he read clouds.

"This will show Will how it works a whole lot better, and I'd like to do it." She paused, then looked from Will—who'd paid little attention to the adult's interchange—to Dax. "Unless you'd rather I didn't do it?"

At that, Will spun around to his father. "Dad…"

He didn't plead, he didn't whine, but he made his desire clear. Hannah didn't see how Dax could refuse.

"I don't think we should impose on Hannah—"

"It's no imposition. In fact, I'll be imposing on you, taking over your kitchen on Friday and—"

"Not Friday," Will interrupted. "Friday's the rodeo for the locals. Dad and I'll be competing."

"I didn't realize... How about Thursday—tomorrow? Is that okay?"

"Yeah," Will said with enthusiasm.

"Dax? Will it bother you if I take over your kitchen?"

"That doesn't matter. It's you working so—"

"Good, then it's settled."

Will waited until Dax gave a grudging nod of agreement, then faced her. She expected a smile; instead, she saw earnest concentration.

"I was thinking, Hannah. Uh, about what you said about this being a rehearsal?"

"Uh-huh."

"And I wondered, maybe...you know, a rehearsal needs more people there."

Hannah went absolutely still. How could he possibly know her plan? If he gave it away now, it would never work—

"So I wondered what you'd think about me maybe inviting Theresa," Will finished in a rush. He consulted his father over his shoulder again. "If that's okay?"

"Don't ask me," Dax grumbled. "Hannah's the one who'd be cooking for her."

"I think it's an absolutely marvelous idea." Relief had Hannah gushing, and she didn't care. "That will be terrific. You and Theresa can have the date Thurs—"

"Not a date." Will sounded horrified, or maybe that was terrified. "It's not a date. Not the country club dinner, either. It's because of working with her on the Shell Canyon project. It's not like we're *dating*."

"Oh. I see. I shouldn't have jumped to conclusions. But even so, the practice dinner Thursday will make you more comfortable with the situation and more comfortable with each other and that will make Saturday more fun—even though it's not a date," she added hurriedly.

Now Will did smile—in fact, he beamed. She beamed back at him.

"So it's all set," she added. "I can come over this afternoon and we'll get the dishes and everything ready. Then I'll shop tomorrow morning and cook in the afternoon."

She and Will discussed what time he should invite Theresa, then they all headed toward the door. Will left with repeated thanks and cheerful goodbyes. Dax stopped in the open doorway, next to where she stood. He stared straight ahead.

"You shouldn't be going to so much trouble."

"It'll be fun."

"Anything you spend on this, you tell me. I'm paying. And—"

Now he did look at her. Her pulse jumped and the spot between her shoulders tingled so much she longed to rub it against the edge of the door. How did the man do that?

"You shouldn't swing your door wide open like that before you know who's there. Not even in Wyoming."

Then he marched out, boot heels clomping on the wooden porch.

A fool could see she'd just woken up. The way she'd blinked slowly against the light. The flush across her cheeks, especially on one side where it had rested against something. The way her clothes were slightly rumpled.

It made a man feel soft inside. Like he wanted to stand and watch her sleep so nobody rudely woke her up.

Then she'd put both hands up to try to tame her tousled hair, and her blouse had tightened across her breasts, and a man felt anything but soft.

"This could be okay, you know, Dad?"

Dax dragged his thoughts from something far better than *okay*. "What?"

"This whole dinner thing at the country club. I didn't

want to hurt Theresa's feelings, since she was pretty nervous about asking me and all, but *geez*... But I think it's going to be okay now."

His son's recognition of Theresa's feelings made Dax proud—and a little awed. Wasn't easy for any male to figure a female's feelings, but at fifteen it had been damned impossible for him. "You'll have a good time."

"Hannah is nice, Dad."

"Yeah, she is."

"You know...I, uh, what I said about you seeing her, back at the start, and then when I said you could keep on seeing her to sort of help me out, I know that's not true."

"What's not true?"

"Both."

"Will, I'm not following you. What're you saying?"

His son sighed the sigh of a teenager dealing with a dense adult. "It's okay with me—you seeing Hannah. I was a jerk before. A baby. That's what I'm saying. And I know you're not seeing her just because of me. That there's, you know, something going on with the two of you. Maybe something serious."

Dax opened his mouth to repeat the reassurance he'd given Will last week—he wasn't getting serious about anybody—but before he could, his son rushed on, "I'm not saying that's bad. It's kind of weird, but I guess it's natural that you might still be interested in women. You're not all that old."

Torn between laughing and groaning at Will's views on his age and the fact that lately he'd been feeling about fifteen himself, at least in one department, he kept to the main trail.

"There's nothing serious between Hannah and me."

"But...I see the way you look at her. And you're happy when you're going to see her."

"I enjoy her company." He swallowed and strained to keep his voice as even as possible. "She's a fine woman.

But she's leaving in a few days, going back to North Carolina.''

"Oh." Will's voice was very small.

He couldn't tell his son that her leaving had been his reason for choosing Hannah to ask out in the first place— that got entirely too complicated. And he sure couldn't mention the strange fragments of thoughts surfacing in his mind the past few days on the subject, because that was even more complicated.

"So you see," he said flatly, "serious can't come into it."

Dax hadn't cleared his mind of that conversation when he walked into his house that evening. Even if he hadn't seen her car in the drive, he'd known Hannah would be there.

She'd called not long after he and Will got home, and said she'd talked over the dinner plans with Irene, and they wanted to come by right away to see what he had in the way of supplies and equipment.

Fine with him.

He'd stayed away from the house all afternoon. He could have stayed away this evening, too. He should have.

She had Will there to help her and keep her company. He could have driven into town and caught supper at the café if he'd a mind to. Or, if his conscience shuddered at that much indulgence, he could have worked until the light held. Or later, since his never-ending list of chores included upkeep on shoeing equipment stored in the lighted shed.

So, why he didn't head that way when he got out of the truck, he couldn't say. But he found himself stepping inside his own kitchen, and stopping dead still.

It felt warm.

Surely warmer than when he'd checked the clean tile floor and unencumbered countertops before leaving this afternoon to be sure they were passably clean. But that was pure nonsense, because he'd wager a year's feed money that Will was too oblivious and Hannah too polite to think of turning up the thermostat.

Maybe it was the clutter.

A stack of cloth-draped items hip-high leaned against the blank wall opposite the U-shaped work area of the kitchen. A trio of baking sheets, a pair of rectangular glass pans and a freestanding mixer sat on the counter. Bread crumbs and shreds of lettuce scattered across the counter by the refrigerator most likely indicated Will had made himself a sandwich. A hot pad and a small square pan with something crusted inside sat atop the stove.

Maybe it was the sensation.

His hand connected with something soft yet faintly scratchy. He looked down to find his hand stroking what hung over the protuberance of the inside doorknob. Hannah's sweater. He snatched his hand away, but it didn't seem to matter to the nerve endings in his hand.

Maybe it was the smell.

He drew it in hesitantly. Something sharp, like…like cheese after it melted and just before it burned. And more. He breathed in more deeply. The rich, round scent of cooked apples with a punch of spice of some kind. Cinnamon. And something else. Something familiar. Something he connected with Hannah. Something that had his lower gut tightening. Something…he still couldn't name.

Maybe it was the sound.

Muffled voices. Not the tinny sound of radio or TV, but the mellow strains of real, live voices. Dax leaned against the door and tried to remember the last time he'd walked into this house and heard voices before he called out a hello to Will.

He couldn't.

Surely, sometime, June had been here with Will, talking to the boy when Dax came home. Sometime there'd been this same murmur of life within this house when he walked in.

Not when I was growing up.

No. But since he'd brought Will back, surely it had been different. Surely... He searched his memory. Its answers were quiet and cold.

But that didn't mean a woman was the answer. Elaine had lived here eight months. Yet there were no memories of her bringing this kind of life into the house. Screaming, crying, self-pity, accusations. Those were the sounds he remembered from that time.

But that didn't mean Hannah was the answer, either. Even if she somehow filled a house with warmth in an afternoon. A single afternoon. A few hours... *A few hours. A few days. Two weeks.*

Two weeks nearly gone.

She'd leave come Monday and she'd take the warmth with her. Unless he could get her to stay.

No. He'd have to find another way. He'd have to figure out this warmth stuff himself or keep on living without it. Because he didn't need a woman in his life. Never had. Never would.

Chapter Eleven

Hannah looked up from polishing a soup ladle to find Dax in the dining room doorway staring at her. The man made her heart beat faster just by *being*. The moment stretched and stretched, as she wondered a little desperately what was going on behind those brown eyes that studied her so intently. When he finally opened his mouth, she held her breath.

"What's that smell?"

Air came out of her in a rush that blended a snort and a chuckle. The perfect antidote to her waywardly romantic imagination.

"Silver polish. After seeing the state of your silver, I'm not surprised you're not familiar with the smell."

"It's not my silver."

"Your family's."

He shifted his right shoulder, as if shaking off any association with his family, and leaned the left one against the doorjamb.

"Will's been telling me how your great-great-grandmother received this silver as a wedding present from her parents and she brought it all the way out here when she and your great-great-grandfather homesteaded here."

"And then after the big die-out the winter of '86–'87 she took it back to St. Louis and sold it to get the money to keep the ranch going," Will took up. "And the first thing Casper Randall did when he had the money was go and buy it back for her."

"Can't say I've heard that story," Dax replied.

And he didn't sound all that interested. So she had no reason to tell him, Hannah reasoned, about the linen table-cloth and napkins she and Irene had found, lovingly folded away between layers of tissue paper and ready to use to-morrow after receiving TLC from Irene.

"Grandma told me."

"Well, if Casper Randall was half the cattleman your grandfather said he was, the first thing he would have done when he got some money was build up his stock by buying new bloodlines."

"Maybe he did both," Hannah offered to smooth over the moment. Dax wouldn't even accept a family story by proxy from his mother. Was she crazy to think she could help this situation? "We're about done here. Next we'll wash the dishes so they're ready for tomorrow. Then I'll be out of your hair."

"Did you have supper?"

"Yeah," Will answered Dax for both of them. "I made us sandwiches. Then Hannah showed me how to make 'em special. Open-faced sandwiches, with special cheese topping on 'em—Chalmers's Cheese Delight—it's great. And then she baked apples for dessert. With cinnamon and...what was the other thing, Hannah?"

"Vanilla."

"Vanilla. That was the smell."

Hannah wondered what could make Dax sound—and look—so grim over a little vanilla.

"Yeah. We saved some for you. A sandwich, too. All you gotta do is heat it up in the microwave. The cheese is separate and you wait till it's melted, then you pour—"

"I'll get some later. Will, you got homework?"

"Yeah, but I said I'd help Hannah."

"Go do your homework. I'll help her."

When Will had left the room, Hannah put down the soup ladle with a thud beside a stack of dessert plates from the china she and Will had taken out of the dusty cabinet. "I don't know if I want to be in the same kitchen with you, especially not when you'll be handling knives. You've been like a bear with a thorn in its paw since you walked in."

"Maybe it's the sight of all that strange paraphernalia in my kitchen and all this folderol spread over my dining room."

"I told you I was borrowing a few things from Irene in case you didn't have the equipment I'd need for cooking," she said a little defensively, then shifted to the attack. "And, if you'll recall, you *asked* me to do this. For Will."

He winced slightly. Good—if he felt contrite, she would press her advantage.

"As for this *folderol*," she went on, "it's part of your son's heritage. A piece of his family that he'll inherit eventually."

"If it doesn't get broken first," Dax said with a pseudomaniacal gleam in his eye. At least she hoped it was pseudo when he straightened from the doorjamb and took up the stack of dinner plates. "I'll wash."

"I think it would be a better idea if I wash."

"It's my house, my china—my family's china—I'll do the washing. You dry."

The twitch at the corner of his mouth gave him away just before he turned and headed for the kitchen. His mood had definitely turned, and it made no sense to be grumpy at him for being grumpy when he no longer was. She took up the dessert plates and followed. "Yes, sir!"

Working in companionable silence, they settled into a

rhythm of his washing and her drying that dispatched the bulk of the china quickly.

But she still wondered what had caused his unusual patch of surliness. "Does it really bother you, Dax?"

"What?"

"All this."

"Not so much bothers me, but…"

"But you don't like that there's something you can't give Will, even this little bit of knowledge."

He shifted his weight and plunged both hands into the soapy water in the sink. "You're a damned insightful woman, Hannah Chalmers. You're right."

"You're a damned honest man, Dax Randall." She smiled. First to last, he was an honest man.

He looked up, their eyes caught and the air in her lungs suddenly burned.

"It's just all this stuff—" He spread his big hands in the water.

"This stuff?"

"This woman stuff. It's like a different world."

"Mm-hmm," she agreed. "That's exactly how I feel about car engines. It's not that I couldn't learn about them if I wanted to, I just don't want to. I'll leave it to someone else, though I sure like it when it runs smoothly."

But Dax shook his head. "It's more than that. It's mysterious—all this stuff." She thought he mumbled something about vanilla, but she couldn't make sense of it. He drew in a breath and let it out slow. "Hannah, Will and I'll be competing come Friday in the local rodeo like he told you, but I'm only doing team roping with him, so it's not like I'm going to be tied up the whole time and I thought—if you'd like—we could go together. I mean, I'd take you."

"That sounds nice. Will said Theresa's coming. We can all sit together."

He frowned, but didn't argue. "I'll pick you up at five,

then. We can pick out a supper from church-group food booths and such.''

''Are you asking me out for rodeo and dinner, Dax?'' she teased.

''No.'' Both his answer and its brusqueness surprised her. ''I'm asking you out for the whole damned Shakespeare Days weekend. We can go see the pro cowboys rodeoing Saturday afternoon and there's a fair and fireworks Saturday evening.''

''But Will and Theresa will be off at the country club dinner Saturday night, so there's no need.''

''Nope, no need.'' He challenged her with a perfectly level look and the slightest emphasis on the final word.

He was asking her out for himself, not for Will's sake. If she said yes, it would be saying yes to Dax, not the agreement they'd followed the past week.

This would be her last weekend here. Her last opportunity to spend time with Dax. Ever.

What could it hurt?

''I'd be happy to go to the fair with you Friday and Saturday.''

He grinned his heart-thudding grin, and a sliver of what-have-I-let-myself-in-for edged into her thoughts.

She shook out the dish towel and gestured to the pile of silver still on the counter to the left of the sink. ''But in the meantime, we have silverware to wash tonight and I have a table to set in the morning.''

''Good Lord.''

His kitchen didn't usually see this much activity in a decade. He and Will were mostly one-skillet cooks, sometimes throwing in a pot—and that's when they advanced from sandwiches or the microwave. Now a skillet and three pots sat on the stove, two covered, but one with some clear liquid bubbling gently. Various bowls and pans and a rolling pin were spread across the usually bare counters. And in the middle of it stood Hannah. With her hair tangled, her cheeks flushed, her eyes bright and a dab of flour high on her cheek.

He nearly groaned out loud as his body shifted all attention to the vicinity of his jeans zipper. Next thing he knew he'd be getting hot over Betty Crocker.

It was bad enough that he'd trailed Hannah around while she set up the dining room first thing this morning. He'd told her he wanted to help, but he couldn't claim to have done much at all. He put the extra board into the table in the dining room he and Will rarely used. Maybe he could count holding the other end of the pale lacy tablecloth Hannah said was courtesy of Irene while she smoothed it out so carefully on the old table. But it would be pushing it to consider placing dishes or knives and forks where she told him to as helping. And when it came to folding napkins the way she wanted, he'd been no use at all.

Especially since when he held one of the frothy white squares in his awkward hands, he hadn't thought that the lace matched the tablecloth like she pointed out, but that it resembled the delicate lace of her bra. Felt like it, too. Soft, the way it had felt Saturday night, when they were sitting on the little couch in her cabin, with her pressed against him, and his hands finding her skin, even softer and more delicate beneath the white lace.

No, he hadn't been much good to her getting ready. Just like he hadn't been much good to himself lying in bed through the dark hours last night trying not to dream about her. And he wasn't much good to either one of them, staring at her now with his body getting harder and his senses getting softer every second.

"Hi, Dax." Hannah said absently. Clearly she wasn't thinking along the lines of wondering just how hard this tile floor would be.

That jolted him partly back to reality.

She had her flour-caked hands full of some dough that seemed to be falling off the edge of a sheet-covered table she'd set up in the middle of the kitchen floor. He stepped forward to help her scoop it back up.

"No! No, don't touch it."

He halted at her command. "It looks like it's falling."

"It's supposed to. It has to stretch."

He looked at the dough that appeared as thin as paper, then at strips of thicker dough lying off to the side. "Why?"

"It's strudel," she said, as if that explained everything.

"Oh."

"It's a good thing Irene had a recipe similar to the one I use. I know it pretty well, but—" She stretched the dough more and more. What happened if it broke? "I didn't have it memorized. And her preserves will be perfect for filling."

"What's it for?"

"Dessert." She didn't turn around. "Dax, I don't want to be rude, but could you go away? This takes concentration and everything has to happen fast."

"I was so near the house—" after fording two streams and driving forty minutes "—I thought I'd make a sandwich for lunch."

"Give me half an hour? Okay?"

She shifted her hands on the dough and his jeans got tighter. Her blouse gapped across her breasts, showing a sweet curve covered by white. It was his dream, waking and sleeping, come to warm, breathing life.

"It's all a matter of timing right now," she continued. "But by then, I'll be at a spot where I can get out of your way."

"Sure. Okay." But he didn't move.

"Something wrong, Dax?"

"You got a...there's a button open."

"Oh!" She looked down. The movement made the material gap more. He swallowed. She straightened, caught sight of his face and turned partly away.

She gently twisted the dough she held and placed it on the closest open spot on the table. But when she raised her hands toward the button, she stopped and stared at the coating of flour and tiny bits of dough.

"I, uh, I'll have to wash my hands."

"That'll mess up your timing, won't it?"

"I don't know." She took a step toward the sink.

"Wait. I'll do it. It'll be faster."

She shook her head. "I don't—"

"I wouldn't..." Meeting her eyes, he changed his promise to, "I won't." Because they both knew that under other circumstances he sure as hell would.

She hesitated.

That was all he needed. He pushed off from the counter and came around in front of her.

"Did this a million times when Will was little," he reassured her breezily. But he had to wipe his suddenly sweaty hands down the sides of his jeans.

The button was tiny. Delicate. And slippery as all getout. He took it between thumb and forefinger of his right hand. Then took hold of the scrap of material with a buttonhole about the size of a pinhole in the other hand, holding it carefully away from her body.

The first try was an abysmal failure. He felt like he was wearing boxing gloves to do brain surgery. A single drop of sweat slipped down his backbone, and felt just enough like the trace of a lover's finger to make his jaw clamp hard at the effort not to think of everything he felt.

His second attempt was no better. The button slipped out of his hand just as he tried to push it through the hole. When he tried to recapture it, his fingers missed button and fabric and fleetingly encountered skin.

They both jolted.

"Uh, maybe I should—"

"No." He clipped the word when he saw how she stared off to the left like a patient carefully not watching the doctor approaching with a long needle. It was awkward, but she didn't have to act like she'd rather have a dozen shots than the brush of his fingers.

He grabbed the fabric around the button in a fist, so it stuck out like a cherry on ice cream. With more force than finesse, he rammed it through the buttonhole, tugged to make sure it was secure, then snatched his hands away before they got any ideas.

"Thank you."

Her words were faint, and he realized why in the next second when she drew in a couple gallons of air. She'd been holding her breath.

He had a sudden image of her breasts rising and falling under his touch. Not just an image in his mind, but in his hands and his gut.

"Welcome." He got that out, then a mutter about remembering he had an errand in Bardville, so he'd catch lunch at the café. He hightailed it for the door. But once in his truck, he sat for a long time before switching on the key and putting more space between them.

Everything that could be done was done. The table set. The strudel made. The meat ready for the broiler. The other dishes ready for the table or a final warming.

That left only being nervous.

Other than those few moments when Dax had been in the kitchen with her, this day was a blur of quarter-of-a-cups and three-minutes-left and stirring-until-just-before-boiling. Those minutes with Dax were like an exotic oasis—hot, steamy, seductive and unhurried—in a vast desert of timers, temperature gauges and burner dials.

Spending most of these past twenty-four hours in Dax's house had been surprisingly easy.

The time she and Will had spent alone yesterday had let her see the wonderful kid she'd caught glimpses of before. Then Dax had come in, and her heart had taken on an entirely different rhythm. Still, she'd been at ease with Dax and they'd worked well together. And she'd been touched all over again by his willingness to do what made him so uncomfortable to try to ease his son's way.

Which made it all the sadder that he *was* so uncomfortable.

And that was why she'd done what she did. Not on impulse, precisely. But perhaps not with as much thought to the possible reactions that now ran through her mind in vivid, horrifying Technicolor.

If she'd asked him, he'd have said no. Maybe she should have warned him. Would he have stayed away? Maybe she should have risked it.

But when she'd left for her quick dash to her cabin to shower and change to a blue silk shirtdress and black blazer, Dax hadn't been back to the house yet. And when she returned, he was showering and changing. When he came out—looking so nice yet still so much like himself in new jeans, white shirt and a gray heathered sport jacket—Will was pacing the floor, waiting for Dax to drive him into Bardville to pick up Theresa.

And now that the three of them—Dax, Will and Theresa—were coming in the door, it was too late. Because the other guests—the surprise guests she'd invited without asking and without telling Dax—were already here.

"Will, after you take Theresa's jacket, why don't you two go into the living room," Hannah suggested, trying to keep nerves out of her voice. "I'd like a moment with your father."

"Sure. Theresa, may I take your jacket?" Will asked, as Hannah had coached him yesterday.

Dax, who'd trailed the two youngsters into the front hall, tried to catch Hannah's eye over their heads. She busied herself with shepherding Will and Theresa toward the living room, then squared her shoulders and faced Dax.

"Dax, there's something—"

But his focus had shifted to over her shoulder, toward the dining room doorway.

"June," he said, and Hannah spun around to see that his sister was, in fact, standing in the doorway. Alone. His tone tried for irritation but mostly sounded amused. "Should have figured you'd get yourself included in this shindig."

"I'll have you know, I was invited by someone with a sight more manners than you'll ever have." The older woman gave her brother's upper arm a light backhanded thump as she passed him. "And now I'm going to earn my keep by helping with the serving."

"Mind you don't spill anything on Irene's tablecloth." His grin was trying to get out as he faced Hannah. "Is June being here what you wanted to tell me, because—"

A sound from the dining room behind him stopped him. It was a small sound. A faint shuffle, as if someone not totally steady had stood, perhaps holding tightly onto the back of a chair that moved slightly under the pressure. Even before he turned to face the dining room, Dax flinched, then quickly took on a barrier of cold that made his dark eyes bleak.

He moved forward as if in slow motion.

"Dax." Sally Randall's voice was so soft Hannah barely heard it.

Dax stopped in the doorway to the dining room. Hannah held her breath, but her heart hit double speed. When he backed up, two slow strides, then pivoted toward the kitchen doorway where she and June stood, her stomach sank to her toes.

"June."

Hannah moved between his dark stare and his sister. "It wasn't June. It was me."

Vaguely, she knew that June stood behind her and Sally Randall stood behind Dax, but all of her focused on the man who remained at arm's length from her, but seemed to retreat with every heartbeat.

"I invited June and your mother for dinner. I shouldn't have without asking you, but I did it, and I gambled that you wouldn't hurt your son—or the rest of us. That you wouldn't ruin this for Will and Theresa or for June and

Sally or…'' She took another breath, gathering her gumption. "For me.''

"Dax—''

"Shut up, June.''

"One evening, Dax,'' Hannah said, trying to make it easier for him, when she'd known all along it couldn't be easy. She was asking him to give up a lifetime habit of self-protection. Even for one night, that was a lot to ask.

He looked into her eyes for an instant then, and she almost cried for him.

"For Will.'' He turned on his heel and strode into the living room, his boot heels striking sharp thuds against the carpeted floor.

Not for her.

Hannah turned to the dining room doorway, where Sally Randall stood, one hand to her pale cheek, her faded eyes moist.

"I'm sorry, Sally. I'd hoped—''

"It's all right, Hannah. I didn't hope, not with Dax. But to have dinner like this with my grandson is more than enough.''

June's brisk voice got Hannah moving again. "Well, c'mon now, we've got a dinner to get serving, don't we, Hannah?''

"Yes, we do. We most certainly do.''

The food was a success. Everyone said so.

The marinated London broil introduced Will to something new without being *too* different. The wild rice with mushroom sauce and the broccoli florets provided mild dining challenges that, successfully overcome, visibly built his confidence.

After one false start toward the dessert fork when they started their salads, Will's table manners were nearly flawless.

The conversation didn't come close to that, at least not to Hannah's ears.

June and Theresa sounded natural, but they were the only ones. Dax's only contributions had to do with passing dishes and praising Hannah's cooking in the fewest words possible. Will concentrated too fiercely on not making mistakes to allow much leeway for idle chatter. And Sally periodically seemed to get lost in the contemplation of a piece of china or a portion of the room or her son's stony profile.

Hannah did her best to keep up, but her attention kept wandering. Like Sally's, it tended to migrate to Dax.

His stubbornly cold response to his mother's presence provided the sharp reminder she needed, and needed badly. She'd made the same damned mistake, thinking she could change someone. And of all people, hardheaded Dax Randall.

It could have been worse. She might have really made a fool of herself over this man. In that way, it was a good thing this had happened. Dax wouldn't change his outlook—not about his mother and not about having a woman in his life.

She tried to ease the clench in the pit of her stomach at that thought with a sip of ice water.

No matter what, though, Hannah couldn't regret including Sally.

Despite an underlying sadness, Sally seemed so pleased to be here. And Will obviously enjoyed his grandmother and aunt. Hannah wondered how many teenage boys would like having their relatives along on what amounted to a date, no matter how much Will tried to deny it was. Probably only the ones who'd had so few family gatherings in their lives.

Now that they'd finished dessert and the adults were drinking coffee, Will relaxed enough to take a greater share of the conversation. He told Theresa the history of the family china and silverware. "In fact, it's a Randall table from floor up," he finished with pride.

"Tablecloth belongs to Irene Weston." Dax's flat correction was dampening and unexpected, since he hadn't said a word since joining the appreciation for the ice-cream-topped strudel.

"Uh, you might have misunderstood what I said, Dax." Hannah was talking too fast, and she knew it. She'd let him misunderstand, fearing one more piece of the Randall past might be too much for him. "I did bring it from the Westons, but that's because Irene volunteered to wash it and iron it for tonight. But it's not—"

"It's not Irene Weston's." Sally's declaration brought every eye to her, even her son's for a moment. "My mother made it for my wedding chest. I brought it with me here as a bride. I used it in the old house and I used it on this very table the first meal we ate in this house. Plastic covered the windows instead of glass and nothing was painted, but we had the lace tablecloth and the good dishes out for Sunday dinner."

Sally seemed to see things in the room not apparent to anyone else.

"Oh, I was happy enough here, especially as a young bride. When we were first married..." She looked at Dax, who didn't look back. "Your father had come home from the war—that was World War II. He'd been to Europe—fighting and struggling for his life, but I'd just graduated high school and all I could think about was he'd seen London and Paris and other places I'd read about. He was so dashing, so handsome and brave in his uniform, and I thought he was the most glamorous thing I had ever set eyes on." She laughed, and for an instant they could see the high school girl who had adored a victorious soldier-come-home. "He *was* the most glamorous thing I ever set eyes on. And I'm not certain to this day if he swept me off my feet or I did it to myself."

Hannah shifted so she could see the other faces at the table. June wore a small, reminiscent smile of someone who had heard this before, but Will's eyes were wide. All this was new to him. That didn't surprise her much, considering the way Dax kept his mother at arm's length. What did surprise her was that under his careful air of uncaring, she detected flickers of interest in Dax's lean face. *He* hadn't heard these family stories before, either.

"We had Juney almost right away. And then we had Andrew."

"Andrew?" Will turned his startled gaze from his grandmother to his father and back. "Who's Andrew?"

Neither answered him. Sally Randall looked intently at her son, who kept his eyes steadfastly aimed at his folded hands.

"He was your uncle, Will," said June. "My little brother. But Drew died before your dad was born."

"He died? How'd he die?"

"He ate some poison plants. We both did. Some plants we found in the hollow behind the barn. I was big enough that they made me real sick, but I survived. Drew was too small. He died before your grandmother and grandfather could get us into town."

"If we hadn't been so far out..." Sally's voice quavered. "The roads were so bad and we didn't have a county hospital. If we'd been nearer a doctor..."

June placed a comforting hand on her mother's arm. "Being in town might not have made any difference."

"Sure didn't for our grandfather, did it?" Dax's gruff voice startled Hannah. "Old Adam Randall sold the place his grandfather and father had loved and moved into town for the easy life, and then he drank himself to death."

"The easy life?" Sally echoed bleakly. "Oh, Dax, is that what your father told you?"

His silence was enough of an answer.

"Your grandfather didn't have a choice about selling this place. It was the Depression, and he lost it. He tried to make your father understand, but William was young, and even then he wasn't one to forgive. Especially not when it came to the ranch. He'd have died to keep it. He thought his father should have, too. In a way, Adam did die over this place."

"But…" Will's face folded into a tight frown, trying to take in all this new information, and lighting on the most easily understood. "But there's no hollow behind the barn. The pond's there."

"That's right," June said. "But it used to be a hollow and that's where we found the plants. Pa came back after Drew's funeral and burned off the grass and plants and then he diverted the irrigation ditch to flood it into a pond."

"He said I shouldn't have let you children go over there. He said I should have watched you better. He worked seventy-two hours straight," Sally, her voice, heavy with memories and sorrow, took up the story. "Digging in the dark, moving rocks, burning and reburning. When the hollow was flooded, he drove into town and enlisted to go to Korea."

"Grandfather fought in Korea, too?"

"Yes. And he stayed on there even after the war ended. He kept volunteering, and God knows, nobody else wanted that duty."

Hannah wondered if the others at the table heard the hurt in Sally's voice. A woman whose son had died in a tragic accident and whose husband had left her to raise their surviving child and to deal with her grief alone. Especially, Hannah wondered if Dax heard it.

"We leased out the ranch and June and I moved to town. Your grandfather didn't come back until '56. He wouldn't consider anything but returning to the ranch, though the old house had gotten so run-down by then that we mostly lived in tents that first summer back while William built the first part of this house whenever he had some time. He worked like a man possessed, but it took a couple years to get the place back in shape. Then your father was born, and your grandfather—"

"Will, why don't you take Theresa outside now."

Dax's low voice cut across the mood like a cannon boom.

"But, Dad—"

"Your guest doesn't want to hear these old family stories. Show her around the place."

For a second Hannah thought Theresa might disagree about what she wanted to hear. Instead, the girl gave Will a slight smile, and his mulish expression eased. He pulled out her chair with an awkward gallantry.

"You can have another helping of strudel when you come back in if you want," June called before the door closed behind them. "Well, that was subtle, Dax. As usual."

Without rising, he stacked dirty plates one on top of each other. His motions were sure, but slightly jerky.

"They don't have to hear the past dug up."

"I wanted to tell Will how happy his grandfather was when you were born," Sally said softly. Her eyes never left his face.

Dax added a salad plate to the stack before him with a clatter. "Yeah, right. The whole family danced for joy."

"Not me," June said easily. "I didn't want a whiny, snot-nosed kid running around stealing my thunder."

Dax shot a look at his sister from under his brows that she returned with a wicked smile. He glared back, but the lines around his eyes eased slightly. The exchange only emphasized to Hannah how seldom Dax made eye contact with his mother.

"Your father wanted a son..." Sally insisted.

"He wanted a ranch hand."

"He wanted an *heir*. Someone to know and love the land the way he did." She glanced at June, apologetically. "He didn't think a woman could do that. Maybe some of that was his upbringing, maybe some of it was me, because I didn't have that same feeling for the land he did. Never did. And especially not after Drew..."

Dax stood abruptly. Hannah glanced at his face, then away. The lines were sharp with the strain of control. He wouldn't need so much control if he didn't have so much hurt.

Hannah suddenly remembered the tree that had so fascinated her at Shell Canyon. And now she knew why. It had reminded her of Dax. A solitary tree that grew so straight and proud out of sheer rock. But there had to be sustenance somewhere in that rock bed, some soil for those roots to hold on to—even if the tree didn't acknowledge it.

"But you had that feeling for the ranch, Dax. Right from the start. Even as a baby you always wanted to be looking out the window, staring off toward the hills. Your first word was *outside* and your second word was *horse*. As soon as you could walk, you took to following your father everywhere you could. You were always—"

He picked up the stack of dishes and walked toward the kitchen without a word. The door swung closed on Sally's final words.

"—your father's son."

Chapter Twelve

While Dax drove Will and Theresa back into Bardville, Sally and June remained, helping her with the dishes. No one referred to the revelations or reactions at the dinner table. No one talked much at all. Hannah did notice Sally keeping a close eye on the clock.

"We'd better be leaving, Juncy. It's getting late." Hannah realized Sally had timed it so they would leave before Dax returned—for her own sake or his? "I'm sorry we can't help you with the last of these, Hannah."

"Don't even think about it. You and June have been wonderful to do so much—especially since I asked you as guests, not as kitchen help."

"Guests," Sally repeated so softly that Hannah doubted she knew she'd spoken aloud. Hannah winced that her off-hand remark had reminded Sally she was a guest now in what had once been her home.

"Nonsense," June said. "The one who does the cooking

shouldn't have to do the cleaning. And you tell that brother of mine I said that—leave all the pots for him to scrub.''

Hannah smiled. ''Maybe I will.''

She walked them to the car, accompanying Sally to the passenger side, staying close in case she had trouble on the uneven ground. When she reached out to help Sally into the car, the older woman took her hands between both of hers.

''Thank you, Hannah. I am grateful to you.''

Hannah's eyes filled with tears at the sorrow and resignation in the older woman's face. ''I hoped it would be different, Sally. I hoped...''

''I know you did, dear. You have a good heart. I just wish... Some hurts don't heal, you see.''

June snorted, but her eyes, too, looked suspiciously bright. ''Especially not since my brother is as rock-headed stubborn as a mountain.''

''He has reason,'' Sally softly. ''He hasn't had an easy time.''

June jerked her car door open. ''And he's made it even harder. His reasons are stubborn pride and being scared spitless of being hurt more. If I didn't love the idiot, I'd shoot him to put us out of his misery.''

Hannah didn't know whether to laugh or cry at June Reamer's sentiment.

Sally looked as if she was balancing the same choice as she eased into the car and June started down the road to the highway. Just then Dax's truck pulled in. The two vehicles met halfway, with Dax pulling to the side to let his sister's car past. By the floodlights used to brighten the barns and sheds, Hannah could see Dax facing straight ahead as the vehicles passed, while everyone else exchanged waves. She could also see Sally turned to watch Dax's truck as the two vehicles went in opposite directions.

She went inside before Dax and Will pulled to a stop. When they didn't come in right away, she realized they must be doing some of the never-ending chores that kept a ranch going.

She had just put away the last of the glasses and had the dishes and silverware stacked on the counter ready to be returned to the dining room next when she heard the back door open, followed by Will's voice and two sets of footsteps.

"—and Hannah's right, if I take it slow, it's not so hard. Theresa said the country club doesn't even have that many forks."

He entered the kitchen with a jaunty step, followed more slowly by his father.

"Hannah, this was great. Thanks! I owe you."

She smiled, probably her first genuine smile in several hours. "You're welcome, Will."

"We didn't mean for you to do all the cleanup," Dax said, frowning around at the kitchen.

"I didn't do it all. Your sister and mother—" She said it deliberately, probing a bit. He gave nothing away. "They helped a great deal before they left. And there's still some to do."

"Will, you get these things squared away back in the dining room—" Dax indicated the china and silver on the counter "—then you'd best finish that homework. It's still a school night, even if it's only a half day tomorrow."

"Okay." Will headed off, carefully carrying the family pieces, then could be heard whistling in the dining room as he put them away.

"What else needs doing?"

A spurt of irritation at Dax's matter-of-fact refusal to acknowledge how the breach with his mother hurt him—much less trying to heal it—heated Hannah's blood. June was right. It was stubborn pride and fear of being hurt more.

"Packing up Irene's things to take back and washing the pots and pans, June," she said, deliberately trying to provoke him, "suggested making you scrub all the pots to make up for your surly attitude."

He didn't rise to the bait. He simply started rolling up his sleeves. "I'll do the pots and pans, then."

"Dax—" she started in exasperation.

But her exasperation couldn't match his granite defenses. He offered a cool, reasoned response of "Makes sense. You know what's Irene's and I don't. Besides, you've done enough of the Randall dirty work for tonight."

Randall dirty work. That was probably as close as he would come to revealing his feelings about the evening.

He had the water running in the sink and retrieved a granular cleanser and a pad from beneath the sink. Hannah turned to her own chores, finding her frustration and irritation with him waning as they worked independently, sharing the space and silence.

She finished first, laying the folded pastry cloths across the top of the second big shopping bag filled with equipment and supplies Irene had let her use.

From the open portion of the U-shaped kitchen, Hannah watched Dax's efficient, concentrated scrubbing. His shirt tightened momentarily across his muscled back, then ripples showed across his broad shoulders. He shifted to rinse a pan, and she saw the dampened hair across his powerful forearms.

He put the last pan in the draining rack, pulled out the sink stopper and gave a swipe to the sink surface with the pad. He did the actions with more familiarity than most men she'd known would have. Ethan wouldn't have seen the need; Richard would have considered it beneath him. But Dax wasn't the sort to live in filth—even more, he wasn't the sort to bring up his son in filth—and with no one else to do kitchen cleanup, he'd had no choice. He was a man who did what needed doing without making a fuss.

Even growing up without a mother, then raising his son without a wife.

"I'm sorry, Dax. I shouldn't have done it. It's just that I thought if you and your mother could talk…"

At her first words, he'd hesitated for a moment, then he kept wiping the sink. He continued now, wiping the same section over and over. "Doesn't matter."

She moved beside him, into the corner formed by the turn of the counter, to try to get him to look at her. He didn't. "I think it does. I think it's what matters most in—"

"Let it go, Hannah."

"Dax…" She laid a hand on his forearm.

He jerked around so fast she automatically stepped back, but the counter was right there, cutting off retreat. But when she saw the harsh pain in his eyes, pain his pride tried so damned hard to hide, she didn't want to retreat.

She reached up to put her palm along the sharp turn of his jaw and let her fingers stroke his cheek. "Oh, Dax."

No warning. One second she was gentling him with a touch, the next he gathered her into his arms, crushed her against his hard chest and claimed her mouth with his.

She slid her arms around his tense shoulders, parted her lips to his tongue's insistence, curved her body to the demand of his circling arms and taut body. He was need and she was giving. Only the giving ignited a need in her, and as he brought one hand up to cup the back of her head and stroked his tongue into her mouth with a pulse that timed her heart's beat, he answered the need with giving of his own.

The counter was behind her, somewhere, but she didn't feel it, because she leaned into his strength. A strength as enduring as the land he lived on. A strength like the beauty of this valley and the mountains that backed it—quiet, soothing and reliable until the instant it caught you in the heart with an amazement so intense it burned into your blood.

Dax released her mouth, but only for a second, adjusting the angle and heightening the rhythm as their bodies moved together.

Oh, Dax...

Such a fine man. But with such pain in his life.

If only he could see how much he hurt himself. If only she could make him see—

She gasped and broke away. Dax released her immediately.

If only she could make him see... If only she could change him...

Oh, God. There it was. Hadn't she just had that lesson slapped in her face? When was she going to learn?

She risked a look at Dax's rigid profile, where he leaned back against the sink.

When he stops hurting.

She didn't realize she'd made a sound until Dax said, "Hannah? You okay? Did I... Are you hurt?"

"No, Dax, nothing you..." *Nothing you did. Just who you are. And who you can't become.* "I'm fine. Fine."

"I shouldn't have—"

"It's not—" *—you.* But it *was* him. Who he was and how he made her feel and what she feared she might want. "It's getting late. I better get going."

She slung her purse over her shoulder and started to reach for the shopping bags filled with Irene's things. He beat her to them.

"I'll take these to the car," he said in a voice that brooked no argument. In fact, she nearly had to wrestle him for the front door handle—she won that wordless battle only because he had to juggle the two bulky bags at the same time.

At least he let her hold the car door open so he could put them in the back seat.

"Thank you, Dax. Good night."

"Don't thank me. We're in your debt, Will and me, for all you did for this dinner. If I'd known it meant so much work..."

"I enjoyed it, Dax, and I was glad to do it—for all of you."

He didn't respond to that distinction other than to dip his head slightly. "Three o'clock okay to pick you up tomorrow for the rodeo? We'll have to get the horses settled and get some early supper before the competition."

She tried to sidestep. "About that... I think, uh, I think maybe I should be available to work with Boone tomorrow."

"Boone hasn't had you work these whole two weeks, he's not going to start now."

No, of course, Dax wouldn't let her sidestep. "I don't think it's—"

"You're backing out on me."

Oh, that wasn't fair. Five flat, emotionless words and he put her in the same category with his ex-wife and his mother. Women who'd let him down. Women who hadn't kept their word to him.

"I'm not backing out. I'm just sayi—"

"Good. And I won't break my word again."

"Break your word?"

"No more..." He seemed to search for a word. It must have eluded him because instead of a word, he brushed his fingertip across her lips.

Under that light touch she became stunningly aware that her lips were still swollen, still overly sensitive. Heat shot from the faint connection of his fingertip to her lips to the pit of her stomach, pooling there to taunt her. At that moment, she didn't want him to keep his word. She wanted him to kiss her again, to hold her again. She wanted him against her, inside her. She wanted him— period.

"I—I've got to go, Dax."

She dropped into the driver's seat with more speed than grace. Closing the car door gave her only an illusion of protection from her desires. An illusion that shattered when Dax leaned into the open window frame.

"Hannah, I'll be on my best behavior tomorrow. You won't have anything to worry about from me."

She mumbled something he must have taken as acceptance, and maybe that was how she'd meant it. All she knew for sure was what worried her wasn't his behavior, but hers.

If June hadn't been sitting on the Westons' screened porch talking with Irene when Hannah returned from a visit to Boone and Cambria's house Friday morning, she would have sought her out.

"Hi, June. How are you?"

"Doing fine, Hannah."

"Good. Irene, Cambria asked me to bring these—" Hannah put down a stack of place mats and napkins "—back to you. The new ones she ordered arrived yesterday."

"Thank you, dear. That's nice of you. You weren't up there long."

"I hoped to go over some things with Boone, get his decision on two projects before I leave. But he wants to finish some things on the house. He says they're running out of time before they head back to North Carolina. But I don't know, I just don't think he wants to work."

"Boone has loosened up a good bit since he first came to us," Irene said with a satisfied smile. "But maybe he thinks you're the best one to make the choices. He trusts your decisions, you should know that, Hannah."

"You sound like Boone, Irene." Hannah tried to sound peeved, but didn't succeed. She turned from Irene's knowing eyes. "So, what brings you out here, June?"

"I'm campaigning for Cully."

"I wouldn't think you'd need to stop here—it seems to me all the Westons are solidly behind him."

"That's true, but Irene makes the best coffee around, and I couldn't resist. Besides, I wanted to talk to you."

Hannah's smile faded.

Irene stood and exchanged goodbyes with June. "I'll leave you two alone, then. There's a cake waiting for me to make it for the hospital auxiliary's booth tonight."

Hannah took the chair across from June. "I'm so sorry about what happened last night. If I had known—"

She batted the air with one hand to wave off Hannah's apology. "Mama and I did know. Like she told you last night, we both had a good idea how Dax would react. Actually, he reacted better than I expected. That must be your influence."

A knot clenched in her diaphragm—disappointment that June wasn't right, hope that maybe she could be and fear that maybe she would be, all tied together with that dangerous notion of changing someone.

"Not my influence, June. I have no influence over Dax. If Dax acted any different, he did it for Will. Because he didn't want to make things awkward for Will in front of Theresa."

"Well, I won't argue with you about you being able to change his course—even though you're wrong—but it's sure he doesn't want to hurt Will. I wish the big ox gave half a thought to not hurting himself," she added under her breath. "There's an expression I remember my father using when I was a girl about being between grass and hay that pretty much describes where Will is."

"Between grass and hay," Hannah repeated. She shook her head. "I don't understand."

"Cattle feed on grass all summer and into the fall. But when the weather gets cold and the snow and ice is covering up the grass, a rancher switches his herd to hay. You don't want to do it too early, because hay's expensive and you don't know how long and how tough a winter's ahead. You don't want to use up your supply early and have nothing later. But you don't want to wait too long, either, because if the cows aren't getting enough grass, they'll get weak and be more likely to sicken and die.

"It's an awkward time—touchy, if you know what I mean. And how a rancher handles it has a lot to do with how his herd turns out. I've often thought it was a good way to describe when a boy's turning into a man, or a girl turning into a woman. You don't want to push it too early, but holding it back too long's a promise of trouble, too. And each one's different, like every fall's different.

"I figure Will's stepping into that range between grass and hay."

"I think you're right. He's so grown-up in some ways and—"

"Grass green in others," June finished with a wry smile. "But you've helped."

"I haven't done much."

"You've done a lot, though I'll give you that some of what's helped Will is you just *being* here. Or more like, you being here for Dax to be interested in."

"To pretend to be interested in."

June snorted. "He's interested all right. He just doesn't know what to do with the notion."

He knew what to do. He knew much too well for Hannah's peace of mind. The problem was, he didn't want the same thing Hannah wanted—or would want if things were different.

She wanted someone to be her partner. Someone to share the concerns and joys. Someone to rely on and be relied on by. Someone to watch the stars with. It should have made her laugh—she wanted what Mandy always talked about.

Dax didn't.

Dax didn't? Why didn't that sound right? He *said* he didn't. And most times he *acted* as if he didn't.

He never pretended he wanted the emotional closeness she craved when it would have gotten him something he clearly did want—such as her in bed. She'd known a lot of men who would have done that in a heartbeat. Not Dax. He was always scrupulously honest. So, when that longing she saw in him surfaced at odd little times, there must be some reason he kept pushing it down.

Why would someone do that? Because they thought that what they wanted would be denied them? So they avoided the disappointment and pain by not trying? Maybe. Or maybe this was all wishful thinking on her part.

The realizations that she had been silent for a long time and that June was watching her closely hit simultaneously.

"Sorry, I...I lost track."

"Uh-huh." June sounded oddly satisfied. "I should be on my way anyhow, rounding up a few more votes for Cully before I call it quits today. But before I go, there's another side to that saying."

"Saying? Oh, the one about Will—between grass and hay."

"Yep. The other side's between hay and grass. It means the hard times. The times when a real hard winter's used up every bit of hay you put up and before nature's brought along the grass to where the cattle can graze. It's a scary time. Everything can go, all your work, all your planning, all your heart. Those times between hay and grass are when you try to get by and hope for the best. You have to hold on, be patient and believe. Yeah, mostly, you have to believe."

For no reason she could express, Hannah felt the hot press of unshed tears in her eyes.

June nodded, as if Hannah had said something. "That's right. That's where Dax is. Been there a long time. He's still holding on, but that's about it. He's never been much of one to believe, and believing's the hardest part."

Long after June continued on her way, Hannah sat on the porch, staring toward the mountains, thinking.

And believing's the hardest part.

"Howya doin', Dax?"

The greeting stopped Dax and Hannah as they strolled among the booths selling baked goods, trying to decide whether to have cupcakes offered by the First United Church of Bardville or cookies made by the high school athletic boosters or a slice of cake baked by a certain volunteer for the hospital auxiliary. The decision on dessert had lost a great deal of urgency since they'd filled up on the 4H Club's chili.

Hannah saw a man in a brown law enforcement uniform with gray hair showing beneath his hat and a comfortable paunch showing above his belt. The woman at his side had short, graying curls and a warm smile amid a fan of lines.

"Hello, Sheriff, Rita. Hannah, this is Tom Milano, Sheriff of Shakespeare County, and Rita Campbell."

"It's a pleasure, Hannah. I work at Jessa's shop, and I've heard so much about you."

"And I'm the man Cully Grainger's going to replace, soon as he gets himself elected, so I can retire in peace and Rita and I can get married and go have some fun."

Hannah offered congratulations on his impending retirement and their upcoming wedding. Rita talked a little of the wedding, while the sheriff and Dax discussed the election. Then, as the conversation wrapped up and the other couple prepared to move on, Sheriff Milano gave Hannah a friendly wink as they shook hands farewell.

"Sure is nice to meet the woman who got Dax Randall into the corral."

Hannah's hand, suddenly numb, slid out of his meaty grip. "No. You don't understand—"

The sheriff didn't seem to notice her protest. Dax must have heard what he'd said—he had a sort of frozen expression on his face, like someone listening to important news being broadcast on the radio, still uncertain how it would turn out.

"And don't forget the fifty-fifty drawing," the unheeding sheriff continued. "I'm banking on being lucky in love carrying over to all kinds of luck, no matter what that old saying is—and so should you, Dax."

The gray-haired sheriff chuckled and squeezed Rita's shoulders. But still, Dax didn't correct the older man. Instead, he gave a casual wave as they walked off with smiles.

"Dax, I think your friends have the wrong impression."

"Hmm?" He sounded distracted.

"About... They seem to think... They don't know I'm leaving."

"Yeah." He looped his arm casually across her back, curving his hand around her waist. "Well, they'll figure out soon enough they were wrong. No sense making 'em uncomfortable now."

He was absolutely right. When she left and didn't return, anyone who thought that something special was going on between her and Dax would eventually figure out they were wrong. That could lead to some awkward questions down the line. But since Dax—the one who'd get those questions, while she was back home in North Carolina with no one asking questions—appeared unfazed by the prospect, why should she be?

"I'd almost forgotten about the fifty-fifty," he said. "You know what that is?"

"No."

"People buy chances and half the money goes into a pot. Winner of the drawing gets the pot, and the other half of the money goes to whoever's running the fifty-fifty. C'mon, let's go get some chances before they call Will and me to rope. I'm feeling lucky."

And he put his arm around her shoulders for all the world like the sheriff had done with his fiancée.

That set the tone for the evening. It was as if Dax had decided to ignore anything but this moment. And she gladly went along.

Watching him and Will compete against other amateurs in the local rodeo challenged her nerves to the maximum. It was thrilling and exhilarating. She thanked God that Dax didn't compete in what he called the rough stock events. Watching Will get jounced, jolted and rattled on the backs of horses and bulls had her wishing she hadn't eaten that spicy chili. But at least he was young and limber and likely to heal fast.

Of course, she didn't tell Dax that. Especially not when

she caught a glint of longing in his eyes as he stood on the fence rails helping Will get settled on one or another peevish animal.

But to see Dax and Will roping together...that was a basketball slam dunk, a tennis ace, a golf hole-in-one and a football touchdown bomb all rolled into one. Fluid motion. Control. Timing.

The chute would open, releasing a hard-charging steer, and the horses on each side would spring forward. Dax would swing his rope first, looping it over the head of the steer, and when Strider pulled up, Dax would tighten the rope and swing the steer's hindquarters around. Will, already swinging his rope, would let loose with a loop that somehow went under the animal and caught its hind feet.

They were a team. First, last and always. Her heart seemed to swell as they accepted the award for second place, standing side by side looking so much alike. She and Theresa clapped so hard their palms turned red.

"You should have gotten first place," Hannah said, as they came up the final bleacher steps to where she and Theresa sat. "You two were much more fluid and you worked together better than that other team."

"No style points given in team roping," Dax said, but he looked pleased. "The header from that team was on the pro circuit until year before last."

"I spent way too much time building a loop on the first go-round," Will said.

Dax shook his head. "Better to take your time there, than waste a loop and risk going out."

"Especially with that steer hornswoggling like that," said Theresa. "And when you threw it, I could hear that rope sing all the way up here."

"What's the matter, Hannah?" Dax grinned at her, and for that moment nothing was the matter in the entire world. "You look confused."

"Most of the time y'all speak English, but this is not one of those times."

"*Y'all*," Dax murmured, and their eyes locked in another smile.

"Sorry, Hannah. But I did try to explain it to you," Theresa reminded her.

"Yes, but that wasn't English, either. Header, heeler, loops, rodeo as a verb and hornswoggling. My head's spinning."

"Hornswoggling's when a steer gets dodgy, tries to throw off the rope after it's been put on him."

"Dodgy? What does that mean?"

"Tell you what, Will," Dax proposed as he stood. "You stay here and answer Hannah's question, and Theresa and I'll go down and get us all something to drink."

Will didn't argue, which didn't surprise Hannah, but did please her.

"It's okay, Will, you don't have to explain it all to me," she reassured him as they watched the crowd around the concession stand absorb Dax and Theresa. "I understood enough to enjoy what I saw—and to yell like crazy."

He looked at her from under the brim of his hat. "It was kind of nice having somebody cheering for us."

"I enjoyed cheering for the two best ropers out there." The best looking, too, but she kept that to herself. "Theresa cheered, too."

"I know, but..." He lowered his head so nothing was visible of his face except the jaw so like his father's. It tightened before he spoke again. "I never had like a mom to cheer for me before."

Fragments of phrases piled up at the tip of her tongue. *Oh, Will, you sweet boy...any woman with an ounce of sense would be proud to be your mother... I am so honored.... You really like me?* She rejected them all in the second of silence before he spoke again.

"You know she left when I was a baby."

"Yes."

"She didn't even wait until I was weaned. Cows do better than that with their calves."

Oh, Will. Her heart constricted painfully, bringing hot tears to her eyes.

"Dad doesn't think I know about that. But I do. And I know she went off with some guy from Texas. Guess she didn't want to stick around and take care of a kid when she could go back to the city."

"Will," she said as gently as she could, "that was her problem, and her loss. You're a terrific kid—a terrific person."

He shrugged and gave a bob of his head that she translated as skepticism. He found something of great interest in the direction of the mountains visible above the top of the grandstand as he asked, "You're really leaving Monday?"

"Yes." *What choice did she have?*

"He likes you." No doubt who *he* was.

"I like him, too." She swallowed the understatement. "We've had a good time."

"No, I mean he *really* likes you. He watches you when he doesn't think anybody's noticing and—and he smiles more when you're around."

"Does he?" She heard the wistfulness in her voice and had to blink to keep it from being joined by tears. "Knowing you and your father has made this trip truly special for me. But now it's time for me to leave."

"I guess that's what women do—they leave."

If he'd put all the power of his broadening shoulders and work-muscled arm behind a punch to her stomach it wouldn't have hit her as hard.

"Oh, Will."

He shrugged. "My mother did it. Grandma did it when Dad was a kid. And now you are, too. Guess that's just what happens."

"No, Will, that isn't *just what happens*. I don't know why your mother left, except it had to be something inside her, not anything to do with you or your dad. And with your grandmother, I'm sure it's not because she didn't love him—or doesn't love him now. It's much more complex than that, and it's something I hope they'll work out soon—for both their sakes. As for me…your father and I have known from the start that I'd be leaving this Monday. Sometimes, with grown-ups, that's the way it's meant to be. That's the way they want it.''

He leveled at her a devastatingly disbelieving look.

''Sure.''

He might have said more if Dax and Theresa hadn't returned then, but he'd said enough. He thought she'd handed him a line of bull.

And he was right. She was lying. She didn't want to leave.

Saturday afternoon, she, Dax and Will watched the pro rodeo. Will left before the last events to walk to June's house where he would change into the good clothes he'd left there earlier in the day.

Hannah and Dax stayed at the fairgrounds, with plans first to see off Will on his big evening and then to meet up with the Westons, Jessa and Cully for dinner and the fireworks.

They had continued the attitude started yesterday. By tacit agreement, they didn't refer to departure or their agreement to keep things platonic or the decidedly unplatonic end of their date a week ago. Though the same heat hummed along through her blood at every touch, accidental or not.

He'd driven her home last night and walked her to the door, leaving Will in the truck. She wouldn't have kissed Dax even if Will hadn't been there, she told herself. But a handshake to thank him for the wonderful evening seemed so cold. So she reached up and gave him a quick brush of a kiss on the cheek, then went inside before she could see his reaction.

This was their special time. Time out of time.

Time to enjoy to the fullest, without thinking how soon it would end.

"This country club dinner's probably the closest thing Shakespeare County has to high living."

Dax made the announcement as they strolled along in front of the booths displaying handicrafts and information that formed an entryway to a trio of carnival rides. Strings of small white lights dazzled against the western glow.

"Mmm." She preferred the stars to the electric lights, but she supposed that wasn't practical for a festival.

"You could've gone with someone else."

That brought her eyes around to him, trying to see if he was serious. He was. *Oh, Dax, you idiot.* The well of emotion in her was so strong for this man who had more to offer than he allowed himself to know that she had to fight back tears. That would never do. Especially not today.

She moved in front of him, forcing him to stop, then faced him head on and said with great seriousness, "If you give me a ride on the Ferris wheel, all is forgiven."

He stared at her a long, anxious moment before that twitch at the side of his mouth gave him away.

"You drive a hard bargain, Hannah Chalmers."

Her long pent-up breath eased out of her in relief when Dax put his head back and laughed out loud.

People passing by smiled at them, as he laughed and she stood there chuckling. From the corner of her eye, she noticed several people shift to openmouthed surprise when they recognized the laugher, but that quickly changed to grins of delight.

Apparently oblivious to anyone else—and to the pleasure seeing him laugh provided some others—Dax finally pulled her to his side and slung his arm around her shoulders.

"Hannah, you are good for me."

Before she recovered from that shock, he kissed her. His hat shielded them partly from view. But that didn't change that he kissed her in front of God and everybody. It didn't change that his mouth was on hers, in a kiss that proclaimed familiarity, hinted at passion and held out the lure of more.

She hadn't recovered from the kiss when he raised his head, returned his arm to her shoulders, started them walking again and said, "Let's go get that Ferris wheel ride. And any other ride you might be interested in taking before we meet up with Will."

So she sat next to him on the gently rocking seat as it circled high enough for them to see the lights of Bardville stretch into isolated dots in the valley, then give way to the dark bulk of the Big Horns. Next, given a choice of bumper cars or the merry-go-round, she decided she'd skip the jolts right now. But the merry-go-round filled her with a strange melancholy. Perhaps it was the sight of Dax's steed going down while hers went up and they both went around and around.

Dax seemed to sense her mood, and insisted on a final ride on the Ferris wheel. This time, she focused on nothing except Dax's warmth surrounding her and the sky above them.

They'd barely arrived at the truck to meet Will when June brought her battered car to a stop, with Sally in the passenger seat and Will already piling out. While Dax gave a general wave toward the car, then concentrated on helping Will get his duffel stowed in the truck without contracting any of its dust, Hannah exchanged hellos with the two women as well as exclamations at how handsome Will looked.

As they drove off, she turned back to father and son standing face-to-face under the parking lot lights' glare. *Will does look handsome. He looks just like his father.*

Dax adjusted the shoulder line of Will's suit jacket, an excuse to touch his son, Hannah suspected. When he shifted the knot of the boy's tie about an eighth of an inch to the right, she was sure of it.

"You did a fine job with that tie."

"Grandma helped me with it."

Dax's hand stilled an instant. Then he stepped back, narrowing his eyes as if judging the entire effect of Will's outfit. "It looks good. Better than the bolo tie would've."

A horn tooted a greeting and a big, new four-wheel drive pulled up with a smiling couple in the front seat and Theresa in back.

"Hey there, Will, you ready?" asked the sandy-haired balding man with a smile.

"Yes, sir, Mr. Wendlow."

Will glanced back, and Hannah gave him an encouraging smile. "Have fun, Will."

Dax took a couple steps with him, then let Will go on by himself. "What time should I pick him up, Harry?"

"No need for that, Dax. We'll see that he gets home." Harry Wendlow twisted around to confer with his wife, before adding. "Say by eleven? If that's okay with you. They'll be with us the whole time."

"Sure. But that's a long drive out for you—"

"Uh, Dad?" Will stood with the door open. "I thought I'd stay with Grandma and Aunt June tonight and tomorrow. Grandma said you might not like it, but Aunt June thought, uh…" His eyes darted from his father to Hannah and back. "You might not want to drive back to get me, and this way the Wendlows wouldn't have as far to drive and there's stuff going on tomorrow…"

"Okay, Will. That'll be fine. If you don't mind taking him to my sister's, Harry?"

"Not at all. See you folks later, then."

Will gave his father a dazzling smile before disappearing into the big vehicle. Dax remained there, watching it pull away.

"Hard to watch them grow up, isn't it," Hannah said softly, moving next to him. "When Ethan got ready for the prom and I tried to tie his bow tie, I had so many tears in my eyes I could hardly see the thing."

Dax put his hand to his open collar for a moment, then let it drop. "My mother never tied my tie in my entire life."

For a moment she froze. It was so unexpected. Not only that he'd talk about his mother, but in such a way—not bitter, but still revealing.

"Dax, that's—"

He jerked, as if a muscle had spasmed, then took her arm. As quickly as it had come, the moment was gone. "Doesn't matter. We'd better get going. The Westons and everybody's waiting for us for dinner and then there's dancing and fireworks."

"But, Dax—"

"We'll be late."

Hannah flopped into a corner of the cabin's couch. "What a wonderful, exhausting evening. Those fireworks were amazing against the sky. And the rodeo, I love it. I must smell like a cowboy."

With his hat still on he sat a respectable distance away from her on the couch. "You sure ate like one."

"Thanks a lot."

"You're welcome. I like to see a woman with a healthy appetite. And you worked off every bit you ate with the dancing."

"Good recovery." Without raising her head from the back of the couch, she toed off her shoes, drew up one leg and started to massage her arch, groaning. "That's not dancing, it's aerobic torture."

He reached out to cradle her foot in one big hand and used the other to take over the massage. "You had a good time?"

Lulled by the magical kneading that sent warmth and tingling up her tired leg muscles and even more by the husky tone of his voice, she smiled at him from under lowered eyelids. "I had a time I'll always remember, Dax. Thank you."

He leaned closer, perhaps to read the expression on her face. His massaging hand slowed; the other one slid up to the back of her calf.

"You're welcome."

They stayed like that while her heart beat heavy and slow. She'd tried to deny what she felt. Tried and failed. Desire had hummed between them from even before the first time they kissed. It had only grown stronger over this past week of not acting on it.

She leaned forward. Not much. Just enough to strike a spark, stir a conflagration, end self-delusion. Just enough to brush her lips against his.

He met her kiss. Not with the desperate power of pain of two nights ago in his kitchen, but with the strength of passion held in check by restraint.

The hell with restraint.

She traced the hard line of his lips and they parted. She stroked her tongue inside and his responded, touching hers, then stroking past, to claim its own heated spot in her mouth.

His hand slid higher, under her denim skirt, above her knee, over the curve of her thigh. No barrier between the slight roughness of his hand and her skin.

That's what she wanted. No barrier. No restraint. Just Dax.

She spread her hands across his shoulders, drawing closer to him. Their bodies absorbed the rhythm of the kiss, rocking together, pressing in search of what their mouths promised. His hands cupped her bottom, drawing her partly into his lap, against the hard ridge under his zipper.

He slid her blouse over her shoulder, exposing her skin to his kiss. He drew lower and lower. She shifted, giving him greater access, wanting his mouth on her, wanting... His tongue touched her through the fabric, hardening the tip to an exquisite, tightening ache that both eased and accelerated when his mouth covered her nipple.

"Dax..." *I want you. I want to make love with you.* Those were the words in her mind.

But he must not have heard them. Or maybe he heard the words in her mind but didn't share them. He stilled;

restraint returned. When he raised his head, tendons stood out in stark lines on his neck. A rivulet of sweat gathered between them.

He eased back, putting space between them. "I promised you this wouldn't happen."

"You weren't alone."

"I made the promise."

"I asked you to." To make the promise and to break it.

"I better go, or..."

He stood and drew her up, then held on to her hand as he started toward the door. She slipped free and stopped where the wall turned toward the bedroom alcove.

Without turning toward her, he said, "Good night, Hannah."

Did she hear goodbye in that? "Good night, Dax."

At the door, Dax turned back. She could see the words of a final good-night forming on his lips.

And she knew she didn't want him to leave. Not tonight. Not ever.

Chapter Thirteen

He would have kept his promise if he hadn't turned back.

She stood where he'd left her, watching him go. And he couldn't do it. He couldn't leave, not on his own. Not unless she told him to go.

She didn't.

Two strides closed the distance between them. His arms around her brought their bodies together. She wrapped her arms around his neck and tipped her head back, opening to his kiss. A kiss as hungry for her as if they'd been apart for years instead of minutes. He'd been a fool to think he could walk away.

He crowded her against the wall, using it to press her more firmly against his rigid need. With the wall supporting her back, he lowered his hips and nudged her knees wider to fit more firmly into the cradle of her body. Then he straightened and felt the heat and softness of her even through the layers of clothes. She moaned, a soft sound against his lips that traveled down his backbone and into his groin.

He pulled at the buttons of her blouse. The need to touch her again rushed his awkward hands. More efficiently, her soft hands opened his buttons, then spread wide and warm on his chest.

He pushed the covering material off her shoulders, even with the bottom buttons still in place. Kissing her lips, her chin, her ear, her throat, he overcame the barrier of her bra by slipping his hands inside it to cup a breast in each hand. She gasped, and arched her back, pressing into his hands. Her nipple was hard and still slightly damp. He stroked a thumb across each tip and she gasped again, rocking her pelvis against him, and he groaned.

"Hannah…"

Her hands skimmed over his chest. In tempting, tormenting turnabout, she drew a fingernail over his nipple and his hips pressed into her. She followed the touch with her mouth and he felt the flick of her tongue clear to the toes of his boots.

"Hannah, look at me."

She slowly raised her head, but her mouth didn't leave his skin, leaving a path of shimmering heat across his chest, to the base of his neck, over his Adam's apple swallowing hard in a grab at fast-fading control, along his jaw and finally to the corner of his mouth. If he turned his head, no more than an inch, they'd be mouth to mouth and he'd never get this said. He had to…

"Hannah, look at me."

She did. But he couldn't see what he needed to know. He couldn't read the clouds in her eyes the way he read the sky. Did the haze of passion cover doubt? If she had doubts, he'd keep his promise if it killed him. And it might.

"It's gotta be clear. You gotta know—"

"Dax—" She put her fingers to his mouth. "I know. You've always been clear—no commitment."

Why didn't that satisfy him? Why didn't that release the leash he'd put on his passion?

She touched the lines beside his mouth and the desire in her eyes flared. "I want you, Dax."

Prepared to deny himself, he couldn't deny her.

Balancing her against the wall, he drew her legs up. She wrapped them around his waist and her arms around his neck. He brought her to the bed, dragged down the spread and lowered her gently. Still poised over her, he deliberately held her eyes as he pulled a condom packet from his pocket.

Solemnly, Hannah watched his every move as he placed the packet on the nightstand, then her gaze came back to his face. She put both hands to the center of his chest, then skimmed them down, past his waist. Holding his eyes with hers, she unsnapped the waistband and drew the zipper down with a quick hiss.

That galvanized him. Jerking his boots off with more speed than care, he dumped them on the floor, a blatant noise of heel on wood that might have undercut his promise of "We'll take this slow, Hannah."

"Do we have to?"

Her sweet question brought his head around.

She had nearly finished shimmying out of her denim skirt, and she was smiling at him. A little shy, but with no clouds.

He grinned, but only for a moment. He shucked the rest of his clothes and helped with hers. She didn't help a bit—not with his promise to go slow. She did a lot more than help in pushing his body to aching, pulsing readiness and beyond as he drew on the condom.

Kissing him, openmouthed and deep, she cradled him between her legs, shifting and opening when he stroked a gentle hand to the incredible softness of her upper thigh, and higher to where moist heat met his fingers.

"Yes..." she breathed.

Positioning himself, he entered her in one, long stroke.

She cried out and he froze to absolute stillness, cold over-laying the heat consuming him. After an instant, he raised his torso on straightened forearms.

"I hurt you."

"No. No, Dax." She touched the side of his neck, where he could feel a trickle of sweat. "It's okay."

She rocked her hips slightly, then bit her lips on a gasp.

"Hannah—"

"It's not pain, Dax." She pulled in a breath. "Not pain. Truly."

He looked at her another moment, then bowed his back and dropped his head to take her hardened nipple between his lips. He drew on it, rimmed it with his tongue, then drew on it again. And again.

He felt the shudders welling up from her center, breaking over her—and him—in long, rocking waves. He courted those shudders, tended them, enticed them until Hannah called out again. And he took that sound inside himself and poured it out in return as his body stroked into hers.

Dax held her and breathed in her scent and their scent.

She'd be leaving Monday.

He'd known passion before. His body had ached before. But Hannah brought him more, and demanded more.

He'd always believed in dealing with what was, and not wasting time wishing for what he couldn't have. But now he did indulge in a wish. He wished he was the man who could give her what she deserved.

Repositioning her slightly, he freed himself. When he came back from the bathroom, she had a pillow behind her head and the spread drawn up over her breasts. He sat be-side her, and drew the spread over his legs, too.

"Are you okay, Hannah?"

"I'm fine. I—oh!" She jolted as he stroked the damp cloth he'd brought over her.

"Sore?"

"No. I didn't expect—" She tried to shift away from his caress.

"No sense being shy now, Hannah." His movements showed as ripples in the spread.

Her hold on the material over her breast eased and she met his eyes fully for the first time. "No, I suppose not."

"So what's bothering you?"

"I don't usually… I mean, I've never…" She ground to a halt, then started again in a small voice. "I was awfully, uh, vocal."

"I like it."

"You do? Do you mean that?"

Her gaze followed his as he looked down at a new development disturbing the smooth flow of the spread. "Safe to say I mean it, as long as I'm not hurting you."

"I told you, it wasn't pain." She smiled—slow, heated and private—and he reached for her.

She'd be leaving Monday….

She pretended to be asleep when he got up and dressed in the diffused gray light before full dawn. His quiet movements paused a moment, then a warm, moist imprint touched her temple. She listened to him cross the floor in his stocking feet and quietly open the door. She heard it squeeze closed, then the thud of feet sliding home in boots on the wooden porch floor. In another moment, a truck engine turned over. And he was gone.

Then the tears came. One slid from the corner of her eye to the rumpled pillowcase, then another. She didn't move. She didn't try to stop them.

She wasn't crying because he'd left. She wasn't crying because he'd stayed at all.

She could have stopped that. If she'd said no—not even that; a look would have done—he would have stopped. He'd given her every opportunity. She hadn't, because she'd wanted his kiss, his touch, his lovemaking, more than she'd wanted her next breath.

She'd fallen in love with Dax Randall.

She was crying because she'd been fooling herself. She thought she'd been so smart, with this reintroduction to romance. They'd agreed to a no-ties, no-future flirtation. The physical desire had been stronger than either of them had counted on, but when it came to the basic premise of their agreement, he'd stuck to the bargain. She hadn't.

She hadn't and he had.

He should have been so safe—because he'd made it so clear he didn't want any commitment. But it didn't matter. She'd lost her heart and, deep down, she'd been hoping he would lose his, too. He hadn't.

He hadn't and she had.

And that was the long and short of it. She couldn't change his feelings—or him. He'd told her from the start how it was. It was no fault of his that her heart hadn't listened.

She rolled to her back, and the lingering tears slid down the indentation above each cheekbone.

But she knew Dax—and if he knew she'd fallen for him, he would take on the fault, take on the guilt. That was the man he was—and part of why she loved him. She couldn't do that to him. She wouldn't lay that guilt at his door. No matter what.

She would finish her stay in Wyoming without putting either one of them through the heartache of letting Dax know her true feelings. Then she'd go home to North Carolina and get down to the serious business of getting over one laconic Wyoming rancher. It shouldn't take any more than a lifetime.

But first, she had to face the time until her flight on Monday.

Less than two days. Less than two days with the man she loved.

Dax took her riding Sunday afternoon. Maybe it was selfish. He had a task that needed doing before they showed up at the café tonight for the annual shindig to close Shake-speare Days and he wanted Hannah with him this last day.

Last day.

The knowledge of it hung heavy over him, though nei-ther of them talked about it as he showed her another area of the ranch on a day that was a pure throwback to summer, with a bright blue sky and July breezes.

They talked as they rode. About the ranch, about the scenery, about his friends and neighbors she'd met. Most times talking was more chore than pleasure for him. Maybe because he'd spent so much time alone. He'd never known talking could be this easy. Even when the talk shifted to Will.

"He says he wants to ranch with me," he heard himself saying. "But I don't want him saying that because it's the only thing he knows. That's why I want him to go to col-lege—so he sees what his choices are. I had to break with my father to have any choices. I don't want him having to break from me to have them."

"That's wise of you, Dax. No matter what he does, he'll be happier doing it because he loves it and not just because he couldn't see any other possibilities."

"Yeah, but sometimes… It's selfish, but part of me was real worried when he showed so much interest in space and astronauts and such." He'd never admitted that to another soul. "And when he stopped being interested in space, I worried about that, because he was unhappy."

"You're a good father, Dax. I know you'd do anything for Will." The topic of what he'd do for Will edged close to their situation, so when she turned the conversation by asking, "What was your father like?" he was relieved enough to answer.

He told her. A lot. Not everything. Not about the day he left for good and his father looked him full in the face—one of the rare times he did—and the expression of surprise on his father's stern face. As if he didn't recognize his own son who'd lived and worked beside him his whole life.

"He must have cared for you to teach you so much."

"He cared about the land. He didn't want anybody running the Circle CR who didn't care for it right. He taught me because I'd be the next caretaker."

When he shot a glance at Hannah she regarded him with neither disgust nor pity. She simply seemed to *understand*. Still, he stretched in the saddle, suddenly uncomfortable.

"What were your parents like, Hannah?"

She talked lovingly of a laughter-filled, busy household in a close-knit community. She answered questions so readily about her growing up, and the past few years of raising the twins, that when the conversation circled back to his ex-wife, it didn't seem right to sidestep her questions.

"You never heard from her again?"

"Only divorce papers to sign. Kind of surprised she bothered. It didn't matter for me, but it was good it was settled for Will."

"Maybe she wanted to remarry. Or maybe she thought you would want to."

His sandpaper laugh held no humor. "Probably did it because she was sure I wouldn't want to get married again. As for her, well, the papers came from a lawyer and I figured she was tied up with him. Quite a step up from a small-time rancher to a lawyer in Dallas."

"Not everyone would think so."

"Most women."

She didn't argue that, and he called himself a fool for letting that get under his skin. He shifted around in the saddle, trying to find a cure for that and succeeding only in making Strider edgy, when Hannah abruptly spoke again.

"Dax, I'm sorry."

"What for?" he said absently. On second thought, maybe his movements hadn't made Strider edgy. Maybe it was the whirl and whoosh of the rising wind. It still blew warm, but the gray-edged clouds looked like winter to him.

"Clouds on the horizon."

But Hannah pursued her own thoughts. "I'm sorry for not being honest about the tablecloth."

He blinked away from surveying the sky. "The tablecloth?" The damned tablecloth hardly figured into what had dogged him these past days.

"I've appreciated your honesty. I should have given you the same sort of honesty about the tablecloth instead of misleading you, or letting you mislead yourself. But as for inviting Sally—I'm not sorry for that. For one thing, I'm sure you don't tell me everything, either."

Now that was a hit. He deserved it, and he didn't like it. And she saw it. She put a soft hand on his arm as she went on.

"I'm not saying that's wrong. Not the way things are between us. After all…"

Now she would talk about her leaving. He tensed.

"It's not as if we have to tell each other everything."

He relaxed, but not all the way. He still didn't like the trail this talk followed. When she continued, he liked it even less.

"Besides, I'm glad Sally came to the dinner. For Will's sake and for hers." Her wistful tone seemed to lodge under his ribs. He ignored it. "I'd hoped it might help things between the two of you, too, but that's my failing, not yours."

"Failing?"

She sighed deep enough to stir the remaining leaves on the trees. "Failing. Fatal flaw. Call it whatever you want. It gets me into trouble, this thought that I might be able to change somebody."

"That guy you married." From what she'd said about him, that ex-husband of hers needed a damn sight of changing.

"Yes. I thought I could change him and make him a happier person, but he *liked* the way he was. But I was unhappy when I couldn't change him because I didn't really like the person he was."

"And you see me the same."

"Oh, no, Dax. I'm not saying that at all. You're a wonderful man, it's just..."

The melting warmth of her voice calling him a wonderful man chilled beneath the reservation of her next words. Part of him didn't want to know, but he'd never run from painful truths. "What, Hannah?"

"I hate to see this rift with your mother. I hate to see you sad."

"You thought inviting her to my house would fix that?" He didn't temper the harshness in his voice.

"I thought it might be a start. You need to start somehow."

He said nothing, because he had nothing to say.

"Remember you told me how people built over the original homestead on the Circle CR?"

He saw no connection, but she had the reins. "Yeah."

"How building over the old meant the people didn't have to make a new design and how sometimes those old walls got more and more rotten until they dragged down what had been built around them? And then there was nothing left at all."

He didn't recall being that dramatic, but he wouldn't split hairs. "Yeah."

"I've thought about that. A lot. And I don't think you can build something new and strong around the walls of something that's not strong in the first place. It only gives the new walls a weak core."

"People have been doing it for years. Works well enough."

"Maybe with buildings, but not people—oh, I know they do that, too, but it doesn't work, especially if you want more than *well enough*."

He stared at her, and she looked right back. "What're you saying, Hannah?"

She drew in a breath, as if she might be nervous, but her words came calm and steady. "I'm saying you haven't had good relationships with women because they're based on your relationship with your mother. You blame her for leaving, and you think every woman will do that.'' He opened his mouth and she rushed on. ''But it's what's going on with your mother that's important now. You need to tear down the wall you've set up between you.''

He said nothing.

''You know what you're doing?'' She didn't wait for an answer. ''You're doing what your father did. He blamed your mother for Drew's death and he never forgave. He shut himself off from everybody and hurt her and June and you. Now you're blaming your mother and shutting her out and that's hurting her and June and Will and yourself.

''I'm not saying you don't have good reason to be angry and terribly, terribly hurt. Nothing can take away the pain of having your mother leave you like that, but you've got a chance to make the present and future so much better than the past. Give your mother that chance. Give yourself that chance. You deserve it. Not forgiving her is hurting you, Dax. It's even hurting Will. And— Why are you stopping?''

He didn't say a word. Just got off Strider and came over to help her off Spock. She held back.

''Are you angry at me for sticking my nose in your business?''

''No.''

''Good, because I don't regret anything I said. And I don't regret inviting Sally.''

''Hannah—''

But she swung her far leg over Spock's wide rump and he caught her by the waist, forgetting whatever he'd meant to say.

''Why are we stopping here? Oh, that's the path we took into Kearny Canyon, isn't it?''

''Yeah. This is where the irrigation ditch cuts out from the stream. I'm ditch boss, and it's time to cut off the water for winter.''

"Ditch boss? What's that?"

"People on a ditch line get together to share costs and work. One person's voted boss to open it in spring and close it come winter, keep track of repairs and such."

"They all must trust you."

He shrugged, "It's on my land and I'm closest."

"Is the ditch boss always the one who's closest?"

"No, but—"

"Dax, just take the compliment of people trusting you, and do what you have to do."

He didn't argue anymore, but he didn't agree, either. Hannah watched him climb down a slight embankment, before disappearing around the side of a big boulder.

He is one stubborn man.

She leaned against the slim trunk of a young cottonwood tree and squeezed her eyes shut against threatening tears. *I have fallen in love with one stubborn man.*

A sound alerted her to his quick return. She straightened and forced a smile as he went to the pouch tied behind Strider's saddle. He gave her a sharp look, but said only, "It's sticking." He pulled out a pair of pliers.

"Can I help?"

"No. Thanks." He took two steps, then slowly faced her. "Am I like him?"

"Like him," she repeated, trying to understand.

"Do I look like him?" His jaw was tight, making him sound fierce.

"What?" Dazed by this sudden intensity, she couldn't imagine what he was talking about. "Like who?"

"Like that other man. The one you were married to. The one you want to forget. The one you wanted to change."

Like Richard? Two men could not be less alike.

"No. You don't look like him at all." Though maybe that wasn't the whole truth, because at the moment she couldn't recall Richard's face. But she knew the broader answer was absolutely true. "You're not like him at all."

"Good." He made it more a growl than a word. Before she could react, he'd disappeared again.

She tried not to think, but simply to absorb the sun's heat, the sharp, dry tang of sagebrush, the regular breathing sounds from the horses, punctuated by the creak of leather. All this she would take back with her. All this would be part of her forever. As loving Dax would be.

Had she said the right things to him about his mother? Should she have said more? Less? Was there any hope that someday he would— No, no, she wouldn't hope. She'd learned the foolishness of that.

A grumbled curse word announced Dax's return.

One side of his shirt had come out of his pants and two more snaps had come open at the top, revealing a sheen of moisture down the center of his chest.

"Damned thing stuck like a—" He swallowed the last word as he stowed the pliers and retied the pack. "Next time I'll bring the big pliers and lubricant. Or send Will. He can— What?"

He'd come to stand just in front of her.

She didn't answer. With two fingers she brushed away the beads of sweat between the cords at the base of his neck, then kissed the spot. With her tongue she placed a new moisture there, and felt a surge in his pulse. Reaching up, she flicked her tongue over the single droplet in the hollow beneath his bottom lip.

He stood absolutely still, except for the tumult she could feel under the surface, the blood pounding, the breath rasping, the muscles tightening.

She unsnapped the rest of his shirt, and the hot breeze caught one side, billowing it away from him and against her, fluttering and tickling against her breast and arm. Like that first walk along the stream. Only this time it really did reach for her, touch her. She wanted him to do the same.

As if he'd heard her thoughts, he traced the rise and peak of her breast with the back of one gentle finger. "I want you, Hannah."

The gruff rumble of his voice rubbed against her nerve endings as strongly as his touch. "I want you, too, Dax."

"Now?" he asked, but already reaching for a rolled blanket from behind Strider's saddle.

"Now."

"It'll be hard and scratchy." He kissed her hard and long.

She had the sun's heat, the sharp scent of sagebrush, the shifting, creaking leather sounds from the horses, and Dax, always Dax, to add to her memories.

Even making love, and being as close as two human bodies could be didn't settle Dax's uneasiness.

At the party at the café Hannah stayed by his side, talking to him and smiling at him...and yet part of her wasn't there at all. He could stretch out his hand, feel her skin against his, wrap her in his arms...and yet he couldn't hold her. He'd have walked barefoot over the Big Horns before he told any of this to the dozen people who asked him if he felt okay during the course of the evening. But he knew in his gut it was true.

He couldn't reach her because she was leaving in the morning and he was staying. No way around that.

By the time they left the café—long before the others—the wind had done its job, blowing out the day's warmth and ushering in the cold. In one day, summer had gone and fall had dropped to its knees before the power of winter.

He cranked up the heat in the truck and brought Hannah close to his side, but he felt her shiver before he stopped in front of her cabin. He turned off the engine, but neither moved.

The silencing of the engine opened the way for the sounds of the night—the nearly bare branches of nearby trees sighing and clicking, the wind's raspy breath as it encountered the truck, parted resentfully around it, then rushed to rejoin and continue on its hurried way.

"Can I come in?"

"Yes."

He put his hand on the key, but paused before pulling it out. "If I come in, I won't be leaving till morning."

"Yes."

"Hannah—"

"Yes."

She gave up sleep that night with no regret. They made love. Once or many times. It didn't matter. It was one act of love with many scenes.

She'd never known she could be so happy, so at peace, so right while her heart ached.

This was what she had of Dax, this was what she would carry with her forever. So she wasted none of it in sleeping.

She experienced every second of his holding her, touching her, loving her. Every second as the seconds dwindled.

Twice, when she thought Dax had drifted into sleep, she watched his face. None of its formidable strength softened in sleep—if anything, he appeared less vulnerable. That was what he presented to the world—rock-hard bone and sinew. His eyes were what gave him away.

Both times, as she watched him, his dark lashes lifted and she looked directly into those dark eyes already burning. For her.

She didn't know if he really was asleep when she finally slipped from his arms with the first hint of dawn easing light into the reluctant world.

With her mind carefully blank, she stood in the shower for long, still moments. When she came out, she put on her underwear and the two-piece knit dress she'd chosen for the long day of traveling ahead of her.

Usually by this point in a trip, no matter how wonderful it had been, her thoughts were turning to home. To what awaited her at work. To what event was coming up next week. Or whose birthday would be celebrated in the family or neighborhood.

Not today. Nothing beyond this cabin seemed real at the moment.

She didn't bother with panty hose or shoes. She had plenty of time for that. But the dress reminded her she was truly leaving; she needed that reminder before she faced saying goodbye to Dax.

Even without looking at him, she knew he was awake as soon as she entered the bedroom.

She was brushing her hair in front of the small mirror over the tall dresser when Dax rose from the bed with slow, deliberate intent. Still facing the mirror but no longer focused on her image, she froze with her brush in midair as he came to her side. He laid his hand at the base of her throat, but meeting her bare skin above the top's scoop neckline. She couldn't see him in the mirror, only his hand Large. Scarred. Dark. Powerful.

And then he drew his hand slowly—oh, so slowly— down. Not hurting, but not gentle, either. A solid contact. A sensation that allowed no doubt that he was touching her, absorbing the sensation, as his hand lowered over her chest, following the outward curve of her breast, tipping to cup beneath it.

Was he memorizing her the way she had tried to memorize him? Storing each scrap of touch or smell or sound so that later it could be rewoven into a fragment of memory?

His hand continued down to her waist as he moved directly behind her. She felt the pressure of his fingers at the waistband of her skirt as he found the button there, then eased the zipper down. She didn't move. Not even when he slid the skirt over her hips—a hand at each hip—and let it fall around her bare feet.

Then he started on the back buttons of her top. A fragment of thought pierced the sensuous fog swirling through her that Dax Randall was considerably more sure-fingered at unbuttoning than at buttoning. Then she felt the final button give way, the material swing open and the mingled cool touch of air and warm breath of Dax's sigh on her nape.

Only when he reached up with one hand to take the brush from her numb fingers did she realize she still held her hands to her hair. He dropped the brush to the floor, then spread his hands wide at the back of her waist, thumbs meeting in the valley of her spine. When he started sliding his hands up, her hands dropped to grasp the edge of the high chest.

His hands reached her bra strap, and for an instant she thought he might stop. She knew she'd beg him not to. But he didn't. He unhooked the closure, letting the material hang loose, then slid his hands underneath, next to her skin, and brought them around to her breasts, surrounding them with his warmth.

His tongue touched the spot where her neck met her shoulder. She turned her head slightly, then repeated the motion to again feel the soft brush of his hair against her cheek. When his mouth opened over the spot he had dampened and drew on her skin, she sagged back against him, absorbing the reality of his arousal pressing against her.

He used his forearms and mouth to push the material of her top down. She lowered her hands, and top and bra slid off. She stood naked except for her panties and Dax's hands covering her breasts.

"Dax." *I love you.* "Please, make love to me." *One last time.*

He stroked his right hand across her abdomen and belly, under the waistline of her panties and lower still, cupping her, then parting her gently. She gasped as one finger entered, measuring her moist heat.

Her knees barely held her as he pushed down her panties and guided her to the bed. She would have moved beneath him as he put on a condom, but he held her off slightly, shifting to his side and drawing her to lie the same way, face-to-face, heart to heart, body to body.

He stroked his left hand from her waist, over her hip,

and reached down to her knee. Hooking his hand under her knee, he drew her leg up over his thigh, then higher, over his hip.

"I want to see you."

Eyes locked on hers, he cupped her bottom, drawing her against him as he slowly entered her.

"Hannah."

She opened the bathroom door to him, holding the towel wrapped around her.

"You took another shower."

"Yes." She said it a little hesitantly, as if she couldn't figure what he meant.

He couldn't blame her. It made no sense for him to wish she hadn't washed off the scent of their lovemaking. What sort of fool thought was that?

"I've got to go. Westons will be stirring soon. And I've got morning chores, but I'll be back to take you to the airport."

"Dax, there's no need—"

"—for you to take me to the airport. I keep telling you—"

"And I keep telling you— I'm taking you to the airport."

Dax stood in front of her as solid and stubborn as the mountain range behind him.

All the time she'd finished packing, she'd been torn between hoping he wouldn't come back at all, and the dream that he'd take her in his arms and beg her not to leave.

He drove up as she said her goodbyes to the Westons and Smiths, and it was obvious he wouldn't give her either wish. She tried to talk him out of it by pointing out she needed to return the rental car. Fine, he countered, they'd take her rental car and June would give him a ride back.

He thought it his duty to take her to the airport, and he would do his duty, come hell or high water. She just prayed the high water didn't come from the tears that kept threatening.

She would not cry. She would not cry.

The effort left no energy to protest when Dax decided he'd drive her car, but she made it through the silent drive to the Bardville airport, even when Dax tugged at her arm to draw her closer on the seat as soon as they were on the main highway. She did tear up when June came out from behind the counter at the airport to give her a hard hug complete with thumps on her back.

"You take care of yourself now, Hannah."

"I will. You, too, June. And give my best to your mother. And take care of—" she risked a glance to where Dax was handing in her luggage to the airline clerk, and nearly broke her vow "—of everything."

June muttered something that included the phrase "damned fool," thumped Hannah on the back a final time and assured her, "I'll take care of him all right."

And then it was only Dax and her.

The ticket-taker told Dax he had to stay inside the one-room terminal, but Dax ignored him, taking Hannah's elbow as they moved out to the tarmac. Once the ticket-taker stopped sputtering, Hannah could hear the airline clerk and June telling him not to bother to call security or the sheriff's department.

They stopped a couple yards short of the portable stairway that led into the commuter plane.

"Hannah..."

Only then did she face him. She could see his painful struggle to come up with some words to make this all right. No such words existed. And because she loved him and didn't want him to hurt, but also because she didn't think she could bear right now to hear inadequate words, she ended his struggle.

"Thank you, Dax. For everything. For showing me your Wyoming. I'll never forget it, and I'll never forget you. I hope your horizons never have clouds. Goodbye."

With a palm on his chest to steady herself, she reached up to kiss him, hard and fast. But as she started to pull away, his arms came around her, one hand cradling the back of her head, and he slid his tongue into her mouth, drawing hers back into his mouth. He drew her lower body tight against him, between his slightly spread legs, to feel the imprint of his arousal, and he kept on kissing her. An earthy, complete, devastating kiss.

A kiss that should have led to naked, sweaty bodies and hot, fast union, followed by slow, soul-slaking lovemaking.

But all this kiss could lead to was goodbye, and the heartache that waited beyond it.

"Final boarding call!"

The faintly amused shout from behind Hannah made Dax jolt, and she stepped back, away from him. He stood with his arms still slightly extended toward her, his eyes hot and his body hard. She put a hand to her mouth to keep from crying out, then turned on her heel and started up the stairs to the small plane.

She passed the solitary flight attendant and took the first empty spot. Tears coursed down her cheeks. The attendant, passing down the aisle to check on seat belts, stopped a moment beside her.

"Oh, honey, is there anything I can do? What—" The attendant looked out Hannah's window to the tarmac where Dax stood. "I see what. Here." She pressed a packet of tissues into Hannah's hand. "There's plenty more when those run out."

Hannah stuttered out some thanks, but couldn't take her eyes off Dax, standing so still and solitary.

He remained there as the plane took off. Distance and tears finally blurred his image.

Chapter Fourteen

"What a shame," came a whispered female voice from somewhere behind him.

"Yes, indeed," agreed another from the depths of Jessa Tarrant's sundries store. "A real shame. I thought it would work out for Dax Randall at last. Thought he'd found love. What a sad life. Poor boy."

Dax dug in his pocket for money to pay for his purchases and slapped it on the counter. His skin felt tight and hot over his jaw. Not embarrassment. It was from clamping his jaw tight. *Poor boy, his ass.* His life was fine.

"Sorry, Dax," Cully Grainger said. He leaned against the wall behind the register, making no move to pick up Dax's money. "You'll have to wait for Jessa to come back. Jessa made me swear I wouldn't mess with her cash register."

"That," said Jessa as she came down the aisle toward them, "is because I know you're fully capable of setting it up so I can't get into the computer without going through you."

"Just because I said I thought you work too much…"

Jessa grinned at Dax, inviting him to join the banter. "This from the man who's been campaigning nonstop."

"Uh, yeah, how's that going?" Dax asked, not from any real wish to know. He'd vote for Grainger himself after seeing how he'd handled the trouble Jessa had had early in the summer, but he wasn't in the mood for making conversation.

"Seems to be going okay."

"It's going great," Jessa amended.

"Good. Would hate to see a good man like you have to go back to North Carolina."

North Carolina…Hannah.

"We're here to stay, Travis and me. Win or lose. I've found what I've been looking for here."

Dax stared toward the storefront window, seeing only the glare of the sun bouncing off it. When he looked back, Jessa and Cully were smiling at each other.

Hannah's smile put that dimple alongside the left corner of her mouth. She'd smiled when he'd taken her riding in Kearny Canyon and when he'd shared his star spot with her and when they'd made love. But there'd been no smile that last morning. Tears stood in her eyes the last time he had seen her. The last time he would see her.

"Dax?" Jessa's voice drew him back from watching a speck of silver disappear. "Have you heard from Hannah?"

"No reason I would." He sounded harsh after Jessa's soft question. "People made too much of this. Two weeks. That was all it was ever going to be."

"Sometimes things don't go the way you plan, Dax."

"Yeah. Well, I gotta go. Got a ranch to run." He pushed the money forward on the counter.

After giving him a look he avoided, Jessa sighed and took his money, punching in numbers and handing over his change. He felt Cully watching him behind the sunglasses he wore. He didn't return that look, either.

Jessa put his lightbulbs in a bag, then paused with a small box in her hand before she put that in, too. "Vanilla? Are you baking?"

"No." He pushed the words out. "It's for June."

"I see. Take care of yourself, Dax," Jessa said.

"See you." Keeping his head down, he gave them both a wave.

Yanking the door open started the bell clanging over his head.

"Whoa! Don't run over the pregnant lady!"

Dax jerked back to avoid bumping into Cambria. "Sorry."

"No problem. You look like a man with something else on his mind."

"Got work to do. See you later."

"Hey, wait a minute, Dax. I wanted to ask if you've talked to Hannah since she went back to North Carolina. It's been three weeks. Boone is—"

He didn't believe in being rude. Specially not to friends. Not usually. But this wasn't usual. A man could take only so much. He walked past Cambria without another word.

At least once he got out of Bardville, he wouldn't have people yapping at him all the time about something they didn't know anything about. You'd think people would have better things to do with a Friday morning than try to tell him how to live his life.

He'd get back to the Circle CR where it was quiet. Very quiet. Will had a party at Theresa Wendlow's tonight and then would stay with June overnight. June would drive him out in the morning when she brought the dried apples she'd put up. More than once Will had said it was just a bunch of kids getting together. Not a date. *Why not, Will? Why not a date? The girl likes you and you like her, so why not?* He'd come close to asking, but he hadn't.

He gunned the truck's engine.

Just before he reached the back side of the Welcome To Bardville sign, strobing lights showed up in his rearview mirror.

Sheriff Milano hoisted himself out his car and strolled up to the side of his truck.

"Hey there, Dax. I was hoping to catch up with you, but I didn't 'xpect you to make it so hard—wanted to ask if you've heard from that nice Hannah Chalmers lately."

Dax's response was profane and succinct.

Coming in the back door in search of his own Saturday breakfast after doing the early feeding chores, Dax heard the voices right away.

He knew—absolutely—that it was his sister with Will. It had to be. But for a time he couldn't measure, he stood with his hand on the knob and the Wyoming wind gusting cold through the open door and thought he heard another woman's voice. A good portion of Southern mixed into a natural warmth and simmered with laughter. The laughter would turn up that generous mouth of hers and the warmth would glow from hazel eyes. He'd walk in, and she'd be smiling at Will, and turn that smile to him. And her eyes would understand, and he'd feel the peace she'd—

"Dax! That you headin' the outdoors? Or has somebody punched a hole in the side of your house?"

June's voice jolted him out of his nonsensical dreaming and into action. He slammed the door, but tried for a smile as he walked past Will's duffel bag dumped by the doorway.

"Morning."

Will repeated his greeting, but didn't pause in dropping bread slices into the toaster.

June considered him over the rim of the coffee cup she'd filled from his early-morning pot. "Doesn't look like a good morning for you, Dax. What's the matter with your face? You look like a gargoyle."

He gave up on the smile, but otherwise ignored his sister. "Have a good time, Will?"

"Yeah, it was great." Will rummaged in the refrigerator.

"You'd think he hadn't already eaten a stack of pancakes a foot high this morning," June grumbled indulgently.

"Pancakes, huh?" Dax had a weakness for those himself. Wasn't half-bad making them, either. But it was hard to cut the time out of a morning.

"They were great. Grandma made blueberry."

Dax grunted, an odd hitch catching him in the chest. Over missing out on his mother making him blueberry pancakes? Nonsense. He made out fine on his own. "So tell me about the party."

The toast popped up and Will started slathering on butter. "I told you, it was fun."

And that, apparently, was all the detail forthcoming. He cocked a brow at June, who shrugged. "So," he said, as casual as he could, "I guess the next big thing is Homecoming, right?"

Will mumbled an affirmative around a swallow of milk from the carton.

"I know it's not for a few weeks yet, but I suppose a lot of people are already doing the asking."

"I guess. Do you want a piece of this toast, Dad?"

"No, go ahead, finish it up yourself. But how about you, Will? Have you thought about Homecoming?"

"You mean the dance and stuff? That's a real date. Where's the grape jelly?"

"Fridge door," Dax answered absently. So Will still held off from the idea of going on "a real date." He was considering that when his sister changed the subject.

"I hear you were in town yesterday." June's tone was as innocuous as her comment. Dax immediately went on guard.

"Yeah. Needed lightbulbs."

"You could have waited a day and I'd have brought them out. Along with the vanilla."

He ignored the second part. "I didn't want to spend another night with this house as dark as a cave."

"A man in a hurry, huh? Heard you were in such a hurry to leave Jessa's shop you almost bowled over Cambria. And even more of a hurry to leave town. Sheriff says it gave him a real start to see your old truck moving like it was in the Indy 500."

"It's a damned good thing that old coot is retiring. It's high time Milano got put out to pasture. He's getting too old for the job."

"He caught you, didn't he?"

"A speeding ticket—that's all."

"That's not what I heard. I heard something about failure to obey a law enforcement officer's orders."

"The old fool had already given me a damned ticket. When I got fed up listening to his lectures on matters that are none of his concern and pulled away, he stopped me again and cited me."

June harrumphed. "All in all, you made yourself a real popular fella, huh?"

"Geez, Dad," Will said around a mouthful of toast, "you've got to start being nicer to people. You know, I won't be around here forever."

Stunned by the unexpected criticism from his son, Dax growled, "You announcing a plan to run away from home?"

"Don't tempt the boy," June contributed.

Dax glared at his sister, who appeared totally unaffected as she leaned comfortably against the counter. He made an effort to keep his tone reasonable when he asked, "What are you talking about, Will?"

"I'm talking about when I go to college."

"That's not for years yet."

"Less than three," June said.

"Fine," Dax snapped. "Less than three years. So what?"

He'd meant it for June, but Will answered, and sounded

a bit agitated. "So what are you going to do then? You'll be all alone."

"I can handle the ranch."

"That's not what I mean. What about…" Will gave a wave of his hand, obviously trying to find words. "What about *people?*"

"I see people," Dax protested.

"Not if they see you first," June said.

"June—"

Dax's warning died abruptly as Will cut across his words. "Aunt June's right. And you keep making it worse. Getting on the wrong side of Sheriff Milano, and Jessa and Cambria yesterday… You already snap at Aunt June, you won't talk to Grandma and you drove Hannah off—"

"I didn't drive Hannah off."

"Yeah, you did. She told me. She said women don't always want to leave, but sometimes it's what's decided between the man and the woman. I know she didn't want to leave—everybody says so—so it was you who decided. You drove her off."

"I didn't—"

"The hell you didn't!"

"*Will!* Don't you talk to me that way."

"Fine. Then I won't talk to you at all." He jammed the remnants of jelly-slathered toast in his mouth, leaving a smear beside his mouth. But Dax felt no urge to chuckle at his man-child, especially when the slam of the back door reverberated into silence.

Dax threw up his hands, then slapped them back to his thighs. "What is the matter with everyone?"

June brought her cup down to the counter with a thud. "Not everyone—*you*. You're an infectious black cloud. And you have been ever since—"

"Don't say it."

"—Hannah left," June finished grimly over his warning. "Where are you going?"

"I've got a ranch to run. I've got haying to finish and

cattle to move.'' He grabbed his jacket and kept going. June's voice dogged him, anyway.

''Well, I hope it helps you get yourself straightened out. In case you didn't notice, now you don't have your son talking to you, either. The way you're going, pretty soon the *cows* won't put up with you!''

The trouble with haying was it left a man on a tractor using only the little bit of his brain needed to keep the thing moving straight and the hayer from fouling. And that left entirely too much time to think.

The trouble with moving cattle was it left a man on a horse who knew its business so well that it could spot a heifer about to bolt, ease her back into the herd and keep plodding away without the man having to do any more than not fall off. And that left entirely too much time to think.

The trouble with both haying and moving cattle was Hannah rode along with him. He saw her face, felt her touch, smelled her skin and heard her voice. Especially he heard her voice.

If you and your mother could talk... I think it's what matters most....

I'm glad Sally came to the dinner. For Will's sake and for hers.

Will's sake?

Was he hurting Will?

Hannah thought so.

Not forgiving her is hurting you, Dax. It's even hurting Will. You've got a chance to make the present and future so much better than the past. Give your mother that chance. Give yourself that chance. You deserve it.

He deserved it? Hannah said he did.

But with Will there was no question. Will deserved everything in his life being as good as Dax could make it.

Why was Will having such trouble making the step of asking Theresa for a real date? Dax had done that—he'd asked Hannah out. That had been the whole idea, to let

Will see his father showing interest in a woman, asking her out, going on dates with her. He'd done all that. And more...

Ah, maybe seeing what followed had Will holding back. Maybe Hannah's leaving...

I know she didn't want to leave—everybody says so—so it was you who decided.

Was it his fault she'd left? Did that mean she might come back?

His mother had tried.

The thought hit him so hard he hauled back on Strider's reins, and the horse shook his head indignantly.

You need to tear down the wall you've set up between you....

You need to start somehow.

"Oh, Dax!" Sally Randall's eyes widened when she saw who stood outside the back door. She opened it quickly. "Come in, come in. It's a snow's-coming wind blowing out there."

"I know. I've got that replacement storm window in the truck. It finally came." He stepped in, then hesitated as if he'd never been in his sister's house before.

"June's not here, Dax. She's got a flight coming in."

"I know." He cleared his throat. And again. It still felt tight. "I came to see you."

"Oh. Oh." Her hands fluttered to her chest. "Then you better sit down. Would you like some coffee?"

"Yeah. Thanks."

He took one of the chairs and deliberately didn't watch his mother's movements, concentrating solely on the mug as it was placed before him. When she sat on the bench at right angles to him instead of on the chair across the table, his muscles twitched as if urging him to get up and move from her nearness.

But he'd come this far. He wasn't a quitter.

"Why'd you leave me when you left the ranch?"

She sucked in a quick breath, but she spoke slow and calm, as if she'd been practicing the words for a long time. "I thought it was best."

He snorted in disgust. "That's what you tell a seven-year-old and maybe he tries to believe it. But not anymore. I'm a man, and I want the truth."

"I've told you the truth before, Dax, but you've never listened. Not when you were seven, not when you were sixteen, not when you were twenty-one and had a baby to raise on your own and I wanted to help you more than anything in the world. Leaving you at the ranch was the hardest thing I have done in this life. Harder than leaving my husband. Harder than burying my first son. But I searched my heart and as much as I wanted you with June and me, I knew that doing that wouldn't make any of us happy. Because you would have hated it, and that would have made me miserable in the end, too."

He held his disbelief in silence, but she seemed to hear it.

"Do you remember before June and I left for good? Do you remember the summer we stayed with my sister in Denver? I brought you with me then. I thought maybe by getting away for a spell your father and I could... We stayed more than two months. You hated it. I thought you'd get used to it. I thought you wouldn't miss the space and the animals and the land. You were only six. I thought it couldn't be that deep in you already."

He had a memory, faint and drifting, of white curtains blowing in the breeze, of strange smells, of a loneliness that seemed to come from his bones, of deep, racking sobs that shook his soul.

"I couldn't bear to see you so unhappy. So we went back. But your father and I couldn't get back to where we'd once been. I knew we never would. That time when I left, I knew I couldn't take you away from the ranch. I couldn't do that to you."

"So you left me with a man you hated."

"Oh, Dax, I never hated your father." Her distress was too real to be disbelieved. "Never. I couldn't live with him anymore. But I still loved him too much to take you away from him, when you wanted that life, too. If you hadn't loved the ranch so much, if you hadn't idolized him so much… But how could I separate you from the two things you loved the most? How could I take away from him the one person he loved more than anyone else on this earth? You and the land were the only things that brought him any peace. I know in my heart he hoped he'd get killed when he reenlisted after Drew died."

Had his father loved him? He'd been so sure for so long that he hadn't. And he'd always known his father loved Drew, so with a child's logic, he'd known it was his fault he wasn't loved. He'd grown to a man and discarded the logic, but the pain and the doubt hadn't gone. And he'd never considered it might have been his father's pain that kept him from loving too deep, or maybe just from showing it.

"He called me that a lot." Odd, saying it now didn't hurt.

"What?"

"Drew."

"Oh, Dax."

She reached out. He felt the old urge to pull away. He didn't. Her touch fluttered against his temple and he realized her hand was shaking.

He looked down at her and was shocked to see how wrinkled her skin was, how faded her eyes had become. He hadn't really looked at her in years. She no longer was the dark-haired woman with the smiling eyes of the photograph he'd kept deep in his bottom drawer, the woman sitting on a porch step with both arms around a little boy and her check pressed lovingly to the top of his head.

She was crying.

"You haven't let me touch you for a long, long time."

He hadn't ever known if he was the boy in the picture or if it was Drew. Now it didn't matter.

He slid onto the bench beside her, put his arms around the frail shoulders, and when she put her head against his shoulder, he rested his cheek lightly against the gray hair. A burning in his eyes made him blink twice, three times. A tear slid down, and then a second.

Later, still sitting side by side, she asked, "What are you going to do about Hannah?"

"What's there to do? She left."

"Like Elaine? Like me? Is that what you're thinking, Dax? Because you're wrong."

"I don't..." The denial faded under his mother's gaze.

"There's a world's worth of difference between leaving and not being asked to stay."

He hadn't asked Hannah to stay. The knowledge hung there between them.

"Will said I drove her off. But that's not true. I didn't make her leave."

"Are you sure of that? Did you give her a choice?"

Had he?

"Would you have still left if he'd asked you to stay?"

His mother put her hand over his where it rested on his thigh. "If William could have asked me to stay, I wouldn't have had to leave."

Dax walked over to the four-wheel drive that pulled to a stop by the open barn door. Boone sat behind the wheel, with Cambria in the passenger seat, the seat belt across the mound of her pregnancy. After greetings, Boone got right to business.

"Dax, I've got a proposition for you if you can get away from the ranch for a while. Can you?"

"Depends." Fall was the quietest time on the ranch, with the cattle down in the home meadows, but the grazing still good enough that he didn't have to worry about feeding them.

"On what I have to offer?" Boone grinned. "I think you might be interested. Cambria and I are heading back to North Carolina. Trouble is, we've got the two vehicles to get back there, and I don't want Cambria driving alone so close to her due date."

"No reason I couldn't drive," Cambria grumbled. Then she seemed to catch herself. "Not that I don't think Boone has a good idea where it concerns you, Dax."

"Too close," Boone said firmly. "So we're going to drive back in the four-wheel drive, and that leaves the truck. If you'd be willing to drive the truck to North Carolina, we'll pay for your expenses during the trip, put you up a few days at the other end and give you a first-class ticket to fly back."

North Carolina...Hannah.

Their ploy was as obvious as a thunderstorm boiling across the sky.

Hannah.

"When?"

"Up to you, as long as the truck's there after the baby comes."

"And what are you going to do without wheels until then, Boone?" Cambria's question was sugar over steel.

"Cambria, I don't think you should be driving—"

"Too bad. The doctor says it's fine. I'm indulging you on this trip back to North Carolina, but if you think I'm going to let you wrap me up like an invalid—" She caught herself. "But we can talk about that later. It's Dax we should be talking to now."

Boone turned to him. "So, what about it, Dax?"

Dax had heard their wrangling, but his mind had been caught on one image. Hannah. Trying to smile as she said goodbye. Then a wavery image of her face framed in the airplane window, growing smaller and smaller.

If William could have asked me to stay, I wouldn't have had to leave.

"I'll think about it." He extended his hand. "Thanks for the offer."

"But—"

Boone overrode his wife's objection. "Good enough." Boone shook his hand as his mouth twisted in a wry smile. "One last thing."

"Yeah?"

"There's one expense we won't cover."

"What's that?"

"Speeding tickets."

Hannah shifted the phone to her shoulder so she could transfer clean glasses from the dishwasher to the cabinet and repeated, "Mandy, I am fine. A little post-vacation letdown is natural."

"You don't sound fine. Ever since you came back from Wyoming you've sounded strange. I thought that trip would do you good. Now I regret encouraging you to go. I mean, you sound worse than when you and Richard broke up. You sound like—"

"Mandy." The warning went unheeded.

"Like your heart's broken."

Hannah squeezed her eyes shut. Mandy had one thing right. This pain was worse than when she had separated from Richard. She'd been *married* to Richard, yet two weeks with Dax had brought her richer happiness, deeper change and, yes, sharper pain.

She'd made the same mistake with both men, though— thinking she could change them. She'd tried to change Richard into the person she'd thought he *could* be because that was the phantom she thought she loved. But Dax was no phantom. She'd fallen in love with the true man—flawed and magnificent. And so very wary of trusting love.

If he could have changed, maybe he could have believed in her love. Maybe he could have loved her. And maybe they could have been happy together for a lifetime instead of two weeks. If...

Mandy's monologue wound to a halt, but all Hannah retained were the final words. "...coming home this weekend."

"Oh, no, you aren't. I won't have you missing your first Homecoming weekend. You go to the parties and football game and have a wonderful time."

"How can I when my dear sister is so unhappy?"

Hannah put plenty of pretend exasperation behind a sigh. "Are you sure you didn't switch your major to theater and forget to tell me? This is way overboard on the dramatics, even for you, Bernie."

A faint chuckle at the nickname rewarded her, but then Mandy hit her with a solemn, "Hannah, tell me the truth. Tell me about this guy Dax that Ethan said you were dating."

Hannah opened her mouth to offer her sister more vague reassurances, then closed it. *Tell me the truth.* The truth was how you built trust. She'd respected that in Dax; how could she not give the same to her sister? So she told Mandy the truth. She told her about Dax and how she'd fallen in love with him.

"Oh, Hannah, I'm so sorry he broke your heart. You must wish you'd never gone out there."

"Mandy, *he* didn't break my heart. If it's broken, it's my responsibility. He told me how things were from the start. And do you know, I have absolutely no regrets." She surprised herself as well as Mandy, discovering the truth of the words as she said them. "Not about meeting him and not about loving him. I learned a lot from Dax. Including how valuable a family's love is."

"I wish I could meet him."

"I'm afraid that won't happen."

"Do you have a picture at least?"

"I haven't had my film developed yet." She hadn't been ready to see that picture of Dax at Shell Canyon. Fuzzy blur or perfect depiction, either would have reminded her it was all she had left of the original. But maybe not. Maybe what had happened with Mandy showed she also had an element of Dax inside her. "I'll show you at Thanksgiving."

"We could come sooner, if you need us."

Eventually Hannah persuaded her softhearted and hardheaded sister that having her here would not help. She just wished, Hannah thought as she hung up, that she could shake the feeling that this post-vacation letdown would last a long, long time.

Hannah tucked one pumpkin against her hip and balanced the other awkwardly across her forearm to free a hand to open the front door. The pumpkins would join the pot of chrysanthemums. Seasonal decorations had always perked her up in the past. Maybe she'd add some Indian corn on the front—

Dax.

One pumpkin hit the porch floor with a dull cracking sound. The other rolled away from her toward the steps.

Dax Randall stood on the bottom step, looking up at her. She was too stunned to do anything more than stare and too fearful that if she moved it would be to throw herself in his arms.

He righted the pumpkin, then came up the final steps to stand two feet away from her. Close enough to touch. But never close enough to hold on to if he wanted to walk away.

"Hello, Hannah."

"Dax…? How did you get here?"

"Drove." For an instant the quirk at the side of his mouth flickered to life, then it died. "Brought Boone's truck so Boone and Cambria could drive together."

"I see."

Dax filled the strained silence by saying, "Interesting country."

She smiled wryly. "I think that qualifies as damning with faint praise, Dax. You don't like the Blue Ridge Mountains."

"I didn't say that. It's pretty country. Lots of trees." He glanced up, as if expecting the dark shadows of the arching branches to have moved closer to his head. "Trees are sort of an event in parts of Wyoming."

"You don't look comfortable here, Dax."

"Guess not. Driving in under all these trees, it felt like the sky got closed out."

"You should see it when all the leaves are on the trees."

"Kind of closed-in feeling, isn't it?"

All her humor faded. He wasn't talking about trees now. He was talking about emotions. "You can fix that real easily, Dax. Go back to Wyoming. Go back to the Circle CR, where it's open—wide-open. Nothing to get in your way. That's how you like it, how you've always wanted it to be. So why did you come here?"

Dax pushed at the splintered pumpkin with the toe of his boot. "I came to show you something."

Drove eighteen hundred miles to show her something? "What?"

He slid his hand inside his jacket and under the flap over his chest pocket to pull out a small black and white photograph. "This." He held it out.

She studied his face for a moment, but found no answers there, and took the picture, hoping for more.

"Is this…?"

"My mother."

Did she hear something in his voice because it really existed or because she hoped so badly to hear it? She flashed him a look, but with his focus on the photo, his eyes were hidden. "And this is you."

"Yeah. But I didn't know that for a long time. It could have been me, could have been Drew. Hard to tell us apart in the few old pictures I'd seen."

"But now you know it's you? How did you find out?"

"My mother. Sally said it was me right off. Said she never mistook us."

Under the gruff evenness of his voice, she heard a deep, core of pleasure.

"You...you talked to your mother?"

"Yeah."

"How'd that happen?" she asked carefully.

"I went to the house. Asked her about when I was a kid."

"Oh, Dax."

"Hannah, don't cry." Dismayed, he looked around as if for help, and found none. "Lord, that's what Sally did, too. I never know—I don't have a handkerchief." He used the tip of two roughened fingers to wipe at the moisture under one eye, then the other. "I hate seeing you cry, Hannah. I thought you were crying when that damned airplane took off. I nearly ran after it and held on to the tail."

She cried harder. He drew her to him and settled her head against his shoulder, a totally satisfactory reaction to her.

His next, solemn words were much more than satisfactory.

"I love you, Hannah."

"I love you, too, Dax. I don't think there was any chance I wouldn't from that first walk by the stream."

He kissed her, gently at first, then with a fierceness that told her that his past weeks had been filled with as much loneliness and longing as hers. And then gently again, before he pressed her head back to his shoulder.

After a minute or two, he asked, "You know what you said about Wyoming, about it being wide-open, nothing getting in the way?"

She nodded, which turned into mostly rubbing her cheek against his denim jacket.

"That's how I always liked it, you're right about that. All the sky you could want. Nothing to block your view. Always suited me fine, up to now. Strange thing is, it's been feeling kind of empty now. Like something...something's missing."

He paused, and Hannah held her breath.

"Maybe," he finally went on, "what Wyoming needs is one more person, so it won't feel empty. Maybe it just needs you."

She straightened. "Dax—"

"Hannah, will you come back with me? Marry me." He looked right back at her, the lines deep around his tense mouth. "I'm not much of a bargain. I'm set in my ways and I'm not much good with words. And taking me means taking the Circle CR. I can make changes to the house if you want, but ranch life's hard. No two ways around it. Especially for a woman. And not being brought up to it—"

"Dax." She put her fingers to his lips. "It's a good thing you're such a good rancher, because you aren't much of a salesman."

Holding her gaze with his, he kissed her fingers, drawing two in between his lips and sliding his tongue across their tips. Her breath and pulse caught, then doubled.

"On second thought, maybe you are a very good salesman."

"Will you marry me and come back to Wyoming?"

"Dax, you're making my head spin. That's an awful lot of changes—extreme changes for someone who was so determined not to ever have a woman in his life again."

"You're in my heart—it only seems practical to have you in my life."

It was such a fine example of straightforward Dax logic, she almost laughed.

"Besides, with all the examples we've been setting for Will, he should know when he finds a woman he loves, marrying her seems like the only worthwhile solution."

"Oh, Dax."

"You keep saying that. You're worrying me. How about an answer?"

Instead, she gave him a question. "Are you sure?"

"I'm sure." She studied his face. This was her rock solid Dax. The man she could trust to tell her the truth. "Hannah, this falling in love damned near killed me, but now that I've fallen, I can't imagine not having you in my life. I've changed.''

Hannah stared at him. Of *course!* She couldn't change him, but he had changed himself. "Dax Randall, you are brilliant."

After a startled instant, he grinned and wrapped his arms more tightly around her. "If you say so, Hannah. Does that mean you're saying yes?"

"I most definitely say so. And, yes, I'm saying yes." She cupped his bottom. "You're brilliant and you've also got tight buns. I have it on the best authority."

"Shouldn't say things like that without checking them out personally. A lot can change in three weeks."

A lot had. "You're right. We'll just have to remedy that."

As dark blanketed the Blue Ridge Mountains, though, they discovered a number of things that hadn't changed at all in three weeks, like desire and passion.

When she would have shifted away, Dax held her tight as he settled more comfortably with her as a limp blanket. He tipped his head to kiss the top of her head, drawing the familiar scent of her hair. "You always smell like vanilla. I couldn't put a name to it until the day you made dinner at the house."

"It reminds me of my mother, from baking cookies with her as a kid."

Her voice told him she was smiling. He looked down, and let the sight of it wash over him, warm and sweet.

"So I use moisturizer and shampoo with vanilla scent," Hannah added.

"Shampoo?"

"Yes. Why'd you say it like that?"

"I could've saved myself some embarrassment."

"Embarrassment? I don't understand."

"I'll tell you—later."

Much later, he kissed her damp shoulder before dropping

back to stare at the ceiling with a cat-in-the-cream smile. "Can't wait to tell June. Specially that she was wrong."

"Wrong?"

"Yep. Five weeks ago June told me about you. Said you were nice, attractive, unattached—the perfect stranger for me to flirt with to show Will it was okay, then go back to staying away from women. But she had that wrong. You weren't ever the perfect stranger for that, but you're perfect for me."

Epilogue

The Thanksgiving Day dinner table was packed with delicious food. The Randall family china, silver and glasses were put to full use and Sally's wedding tablecloth was barely visible. But what Hannah liked best was the full house of smiling faces.

After several years of Irene, Ted and Pete Weston going to North Carolina to be with Cambria and Boone's growing brood—which so far included Colin and Caroline—they were all here this year, along with Jessa, Cully and Travis. There'd been no official announcement yet, but Hannah and Cambria had exchanged a look with Irene when Jessa turned green at the smell of cranberry sauce, so the three of them wouldn't be surprised if one came before the day ended.

Hannah thanked the heavens she'd passed that stage with this second pregnancy. She intended to feed the two of them plenty of holiday fare.

"I can't believe you made strudel again in addition to all the pies, Hannah."

"Making strudel's sort of a family tradition, June." Hannah smiled down the length of the table at her husband. His hot look was a sure sign he was thinking of their personal tradition *after* the strudel-making. Including one she'd made in August. This baby's due date came nine months later.

"Sarah, that's a great hairdo," Will said with dignity, as befitted a sophomore in college, "but mashed potatoes are food, not hair gel."

"Will. Tato, peez," responded his one and a half-year-old half sister. She turned her brown eyes on him and smiled, and he immediately gave her more potatoes off his plate.

Besotted. Just like his father. If Sarah had smiled while asking Dax to move the Big Horns, Hannah was certain the view from their family room would have changed within a day.

Mandy and Ethan, who'd come to stay for the full five-week break in their masters' programs, were not far behind. And Sally and June treated Sarah like royalty.

Dax tapped a silver fork his great-great-grandmother had once sold to keep the Circle CR going against a wineglass his great-grandfather had presented to his bride and stood.

"I'd like to thank you all for being with us this Thanksgiving—coming long distances and short. It wouldn't be Thanksgiving without you."

Over the clinks of toasting glasses, June said, "It wouldn't be anything without me, Dax, because without me you two never would have gotten together."

"Hey, if it hadn't been for me—" Will's protest faded out under a surge of laughing claims from Mandy, Boone, Cambria, Ethan, Pete and more.

"Hey, I'm the one who chased her down to North Carolina," Dax said with a laugh.

"In *my* car," Cambria reminded him. And they were off again.

This, too, was a sort of family tradition, with each and every one of them claiming a part in the others' happiness. And they were all right.

Hannah looked around at her family and friends and knew that one day a year was nowhere near enough for all the thanks she had to give. Especially for the man at the end of the table. He'd changed in many ways since two weeks in September four years ago. But his honesty and his love remained constant.

Their eyes met and held, and he lifted his glass to her. Over the hubbub of voices, she couldn't hear his words, but she knew what he said.

"No clouds on the horizon. I love you."

* * * * *

THE BABY OF THE MONTH CLUB

RITA -Award- Winning Author

MARIE FERRARELLA's

*miniseries continues with her
brand-new Silhouette single title*

In The Family Way

Dr. Rafe Saldana was Bedford's most popular pediatrician. And though the handsome doctor had a whole lot of love for his tiny patients, his heart wasn't open for business with women. At least, not until single mother Dana Morrow walked into his life. But Dana was about to become the newest member of the Baby of the Month Club. Was the dashing doctor ready to play daddy to her baby-to-be?

Available June 1998.

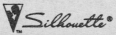

Silhouette®

Find this new title by Marie Ferrarella
at your favorite retail outlet.

Look us up on-line at: http://www.romance.net   PSMFIFWAY

Take 4 bestselling love stories FREE

Plus get a FREE surprise gift!

Special Limited-time Offer

Mail to Silhouette Reader Service™

3010 Walden Avenue
P.O. Box 1867
Buffalo, N.Y. 14240-1867

YES! Please send me 4 free Silhouette Special Edition® novels and my free surprise gift. Then send me 6 brand-new novels every month, which I will receive months before they appear in bookstores. Bill me at the low price of $3.57 each plus 25¢ delivery and applicable sales tax, if any.* That's the complete price and a savings of over 10% off the cover prices—quite a bargain! I understand that accepting the books and gift places me under no obligation ever to buy any books. I can always return a shipment and cancel at any time. Even if I never buy another book from Silhouette, the 4 free books and the surprise gift are mine to keep forever.

235 SEN CF2T

Name	(PLEASE PRINT)
Address	Apt. No.
City	State	Zip

This offer is limited to one order per household and not valid to present Silhouette Special Edition® subscribers. *Terms and prices are subject to change without notice. Sales tax applicable in N.Y.

USPED-696

©1990 Harlequin Enterprises Limited

ALICIA SCOTT

Continues the twelve-book series— 36 Hours—in March 1998 with Book Nine

PARTNERS IN CRIME

The storm was over, and Detective Jack Stryker finally had a prime suspect in Grand Springs' high-profile murder case. But beautiful Josie Reynolds wasn't about to admit to the crime— nor did Jack want her to. He believed in her innocence, and he teamed up with the alluring suspect to prove it. But was he playing it by the book—or merely blinded by love?

For Jack and Josie and *all* the residents of Grand Springs, Colorado, the storm-induced blackout was just the beginning of 36 Hours that changed *everything!* You won't want to miss a single book.

Available at your favorite retail outlet.

Look us up on-line at: http://www.romance.net   SC36HRS9

BESTSELLING AUTHORS
IN THE SPOTLIGHT

.WE'RE SHINING THE SPOTLIGHT
ON SIX OF OUR STARS!

**Harlequin and Silhouette have selected stories
from several of their bestselling authors to give
you six sensational reads. These star-powered
romances are bound to please!**

THERE'S A PRICE TO PAY FOR STARDOM....
AND IT'S LOW

$1.99 U.S.
$2.50 CAN.
Special
Offer

As a special offer, these six outstanding
books are available from Harlequin and
Silhouette for only $1.99 in the U.S. and
$2.50 in Canada. Watch for these titles:

At the Midnight Hour—Alicia Scott
Joshua and the Cowgirl—Sherryl Woods
Another Whirlwind Courtship—Barbara Boswell
Madeleine's Cowboy—Kristine Rolofson
Her Sister's Baby—Janice Kay Johnson
One and One Makes Three—Muriel Jensen

Available in March 1998
at your favorite retail outlet.

PBAIS

Catch more great

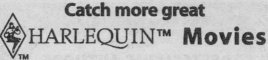
HARLEQUIN™ **Movies**

featured on the movie channel.

Premiering March 14th
Treacherous Beauties
starring Emma Samms and
Bruce Greenwood based on the
novel by Cheryl Emerson

Don't miss next month's movie!
Hard to Forget
based on the novel by bestselling
Harlequin Superromance® author
Evelyn A. Crowe, premiering
April 11th!

If you are not currently a subscriber to
The Movie Channel, simply call your
local cable or satellite provider for more
details. Call today, and don't miss out
on the romance!

the movie channel.

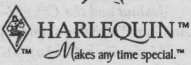
HARLEQUIN™
Makes any time special.™

100% pure movies.
100% pure fun.

Harlequin, Joey Device, Makes any time special and Superromance are trademarks of
Harlequin Enterprises Limited. The Movie Channel is a service mark of Showtime Networks, Inc.,
a Viacom Company.

An Alliance Television Production

HMBPA398

Silhouette Romance is proud to unveil
its newest, star-studded promotion:

Virgin Brides

Celebrate first love in Virgin Brides by
Silhouette Romance®. Look for a new
Virgin Brides title from Romance's
most beloved authors....

Diana Palmer
March 1998: THE PRINCESS BRIDE

Debutante Tiffany Blair was determined to wed gorgeous
rancher Kingman Marshall. But this gruff cowboy would
sooner eat his Stetson than take a wife—until he
imagined Tiffany in another man's marriage bed....

Elizabeth August
April 1998: THE BRIDE'S SECOND THOUGHT

After her fiancé's betrayal, Ellen Reese didn't think her
day could get any worse—until she wound up stranded
in a blizzard with a rugged stranger who was giving her
second thoughts about a lot of things....

Annette Broadrick
May 1998: UNFORGETTABLE BRIDE

Four years ago bull rider Bobby Metcalf had agreed to be
sweet Casey Carmichael's in-name-only groom. But now
that fate had returned his unforgettable bride to him,
could he make their marriage a love match?

Silhouette ROMANCE™

Available at your favorite retail outlet.

Look us up on-line at: http://www.romance.net   SRVBM-M

Return to the Towers!

In March
New York Times bestselling author

NORA ROBERTS

brings us to the Calhouns' fabulous
Maine coast mansion and reveals the
tragic secrets hidden there for generations.

For all his degrees, Professor Max Quartermain has a
lot to learn about love—and luscious Lilah Calhoun is
just the woman to teach him. Ex-cop Holt Bradford is
as prickly as a thornbush—until Suzanna Calhoun's
special touch makes love blossom in his heart.
And all of them are caught in the race to solve
the generations-old mystery of a priceless
lost necklace…and a timeless love.

Lilah and Suzanna
THE
Calhoun Women

**A special 2-in-1 edition containing
FOR THE LOVE OF LILAH and
SUZANNA'S SURRENDER**

Available at your favorite retail outlet.

Look us up on-line at: http://www.romance.net   CWVOL2